ON THE OREGON TRAIL

ROBERT VAUGHAN

On the Oregon Trail
Paperback Edition
Copyright © 2021 Robert Vaughan

Wolfpack Publishing
5130 S. Fort Apache Rd. 215-120
Las Vegas, NV 89148

wolfpackpublishing.com

Paperback ISBN 978-1-639-77415-5
eBook ISBN 978-1-639-77414-8
LCCN 2021950920

WOLFPACK
PUBLISHING
— EST 2013 —

On the Oregon Trail
Paperback Edition
© Copyright 2021 Robert Vaughan

Wolfpack Publishing
5130 S. Fort Apache Rd. 215-380
Las Vegas, NV 89148

wolfpackpublishing.com

Paperback ISBN 978-1-63977-410-4
eBook ISBN 978-1-63977-409-8
LCCN 2021950020

ON THE OREGON TRAIL

DRAMATIS PERSONAE

Members of the Matt Logan Train
Cody McNair
Jared McNair
Ellen McNair
Lon Baker and Norma Baker
Precious Baker (daughter)
John and Ethyl Joyce
Emma Joyce (daughter)
Tim and Anita Murray
David and Nellie Sullivan
Rosie Sullivan(daughter)
Peter Laycock
Raymond Pugh
Howard Raines
Reverend and Susanne Owen
Joe and Cindy Atwood
Phil and Brenda Puckett
Craig and Millie Patterson
Luke and Alice Taylor
Harm and Gretchen Schultz

Dale and Jane Guthrie
Drew Guthrie (son)
Clay and Edna Ditmore

Cowboys with Matt Logan Train
Frank Wiley
Gus Wiley
Deacon Cox
Chub Collins
Sid Beltrain

Members of the Mel Pollard Train
Ian Clinton
Pearl Clinton
Darcy Clinton
Sean Clinton
Connor Clinton
Jimmy Morgan
Edna Piercy

Members of the Elmer Matthews Train
Elmer Matthews
Ed Drury
Sam Woodward
Maurice Cain
Gertrude Cain
Frank Edmonston
Ken Jones

Member of the Arnie Boyd Train
Marvin Long

Members of the Larry Dooley Train
Jim Ledbetter

Gordon Parker
Fred Parker
Nonnie Hughes
Seth and Eunice Michaels
Their three children (unnamed)
Roy Carter
Jennie Lou Culpepper
Agnes Burns
Marilou Simmons
Jennie Mathers

Members of the Hood Riders
Dudley Dace
Emile Potter
Andy Bates
Lenny Richards
Clem Lewis

SACRED HEART ORPHANAGE, CHICAGO –
APRIL 23RD, 1836

SISTER MARY KATHERINE THOUGHT SHE HEARD A CAT ON the front stoop, but when she opened the door, she saw that it wasn't a cat. It was a baby.

The baby was wrapped in a blanket, and she picked him up.

"Oh my," she said. "I'd better take you to the Mother Superior."

A moment later, Sister Naomi Louise was holding the baby in her arms. "There was no letter?"

"No, Mother Superior, just the baby. It's a boy."

"We'll have to have a name for him," Sister Naomi Louise said. "And since you found him, I think you should name him."

"How about Matthew, after St. Matthew?"

"An excellent choice. He'll need a last name, as well."

"What about Logan?" Sister Mary Katherine

suggested. "Logan was my family name before I took the vows."

"Then Logan it will be. Matthew Logan," the Mother Superior said.

1844

"Matt, the Mother Superior wants to see you," Ely Gibbons said.

"What for?"

"She didn't say what for, she just told me to find you, and tell her she wanted to see you," Ely said in an authoritative tone. Ely was twelve, so when he spoke to an eight-year-old, he didn't expect to be questioned.

When Matt went to the Mother Superior's office, he saw a boy there about his same size.

"Matthew," Sister Naomi said. "This is Daniel Dugan. He has just come to live with us, and I want him to be your brother."

"My brother?"

"Yes, your brother. You will introduce him to all the other children . . . as your brother, and you will help him get adjusted. His mother and father have both passed, and he has no one now but you, just as you have no one but him."

From that point on, Matt and Danny formed a relationship as close as blood brothers. Their bunks were next to each other in the dormitory, they sat beside one another in class, the dining hall, and when they were in the chapel for mass. Also, in any game that required partners, they were always a team.

Their togetherness was never better illustrated than it was two years after Danny arrived at the orphanage, when four other boys began bullying Danny.

Matt saw what was happening and flew to his "brother's" defense. Matt and Danny, though but ten years old, stood back-to-back and fought off the bullies, three of them twelve and the fourth one thirteen years old. Although they were getting the worst of it due to the age differences and the numbers, they managed to inflict a little damage of their own, leaving one of the bullies with a bloody nose and another with a cut lip.

The fight drew a crowd on the orphanage playground, as well as one of the nuns who broke up the fight and escorted the six young boys to the office of the Mother Superior.

All the boys stood in front of the Mother Superior's desk with their heads bowed in contrition.

"This may be an orphanage, but it is also the Lord's House, and you were fighting in the Lord's House," Mother Superior said. "I intend to see that you are sufficiently punished."

"Mother Superior, don't punish them two," Grover Burke, the thirteen-year-old said. "We was the ones that started it."

"Nevertheless, they, like you, were fighting, so the punishment shall be equal."

"Thank you, Grover," Matt said quietly, as the six boys were taken into the outer office, where two nuns stood waiting with a paddle.

AT SEA ON BOARD THE SEA SPRITE –
SEPTEMBER 5TH, 1851

CAPTAIN CODY MCNAIR STOOD ON THE QUARTER-DECK of the *Sea Sprite*. She was a clipper ship measuring five-hundred-twelve tons, with a sharply-raked stem, elevated stern, and three masts with many yards of square rig sails.

The *Sea Sprite* had left Newport News, Virginia, one hundred-thirty-seven days earlier, and was now, by Cody's calculation, three days out of home port.

"Cap'n, folks are goin' to be just real pleased with this trip," Alonzo Baker said. "We didn't lose one pound of tea."

"I think they will be. You 'n' the rest of the crew did a good job keeping the cargo dry."

"It'll be good, gettin' back home again," Baker said.

"I plan to stay this time."

"You've decided for sure, that's what you're goin' to do?"

"What about you, Lon?"

Although Cody was a captain, and Alonzo Baker, a crewman, they enjoyed a special relationship that led to a captain calling a seaman by his preferred name, Lon.

"Cap'n, wind's gettin' ahead, sir!" the bo'sun shouted.

"Baker, trim the foresails," Cody ordered.

"Aye, aye, sir," Baker replied.

THREE DAYS LATER, the *Sea Sprite* was being pushed across Hampton Roads toward the mouth of the James River, where the ship would dock at its home port.

At the moment, all her sails were furled, and her forward progress was the result of a steam-powered tugboat pushing her toward the pier. The ship's hold was filled with tea which, as Lon Baker had pointed out, had experienced no loss of value due to the rigors of their days at sea. That meant that the voyage would be quite profitable.

The voyage had also been long and arduous, causing Cody to decide that it would be his last voyage. He was married to Lucinda, who was a wonderful woman. He had two children—fifteen-year- old Jared and twelve-year-old Ellen.

He thought he had not been fair to his family. For the last one hundred-twenty months, he had been at sea for over a hundred of them. He had shared his plans to give up sailing with but one member of the crew, not the first officer, not even the bo'sun, but with Alonzo Baker.

Lon Baker was the only black member of the crew. Lon had, at one time, been a slave on Towson Hall, the Missouri farm that had once belonged to Cody's father. When Cody's father died, Cody sold the farm and granted Lon his freedom.

Cody left Missouri following a life-long dream to go to sea. Because Lon was a free man, he could have gone anywhere he wanted, but he chose to go with Cody. The two had been together ever since, and Cody could truly say that Lon was his closest friend.

"What about you, Lon? Will you be making another voyage?"

"No, sir. If you're leavin' the sea, Cap'n, then so am I," Lon said.

"I thought you might," Cody said, with a smile. "How would you like to go back to Missouri?"

"Do you think a free colored man can get a job there?"

"I plan to buy a farm there, and if you have to, you can come work for me. But Lon, you're the most skilled repairman I've ever met. I know you'll be able to find a job using that skill."

As the ship slipped into position alongside the dock, the bo'sun shouted out orders to the men of the deck crew who were standing by the cleats, waiting for the ropes to be tossed up from the dock.

"Make fast fore 'n' aft lines," he called.

The ropes were tossed up and the sailors and the front and back of the ship quickly wrapped them around the metal cleats and tied them off.

"Fore hawser secure, Bo'sun," the sailor at the bow called.

"After hawser secure, Bo'sun," the sailor at the stern repeated.

"Cap'n, ship is secure, sir," the bo'sun reported to Cody.

"Very good, Bo'sun, shore detail may take leave of the ship."

"Aye, aye, sir."

With shouts of glee, the crewmen who had been granted first shore leave, lowered the gangplank then hurried off the ship.

Cody went into the captain's cabin. His sea bag was already packed and lying on his berth. He took a long look around the place that had been his home for the greater part of the last ten years. Part of him regretted giving it up, but an even larger part of him welcomed the idea of being able to spend more time with his wife and children.

When Cody stepped out of the cabin, Alonzo was standing on deck, waiting for him. Like Cody, Alonzo had his packed sea bag with him.

"You ready, Lon?"

"Yes, sir, I'm mighty ready," Alonzo replied with a smile.

"Good luck to you, Captain," Jed Marcy said. Marcy was the First Mate, and Cody had shared with him his intention to leave the sea. "Good luck to you too, Baker."

"Thank you, sir," Lon replied.

"The ship is yours, Jed," Cody said.

"Aye, aye, sir."

3

AFTER CODY LEFT THE SHIP, HE HAILED AN OPEN CARRIAGE that was driven by a liveried black driver.

"To the Dickerson Shipping Company building, please, driver."

"Yes, sir," the driver said. He looked surprised to see Lon get into the carriage as well.

Dickerson Shipping was less than two blocks from the pier where the *Sea Sprite* was docked.

"Driver, wait for me," Cody said. "After I complete my business here, I'm going to want you to take us to Denbigh."

"Yes, sir."

Cody left the carriage and started toward the shipping company office.

"You the cap'n's man?" the driver asked.

"I'm a free man," Alonzo said, "but I've been with Cap'n McNair for a long time. He's a good man."

The driver didn't reply.

. . .

"Captain McNair," Jacob Dickerson said when Cody stepped into his office. "It's good to see you're back. Any trouble?"

"No trouble at all, seas were calm, holds are full of tea, and none of it lost in transit."

"You're the best captain I have," Dickerson said. "I've got a new ship—a clipper, and I've been holding it for you. It's the fastest thing on the water."

"Mr. Dickerson, I appreciate that, I really do. But I'm going to have to turn it down."

"Why? If it's your crew you're worried about, you can have your pick of as many of your old men as you want."

Cody shook his head. "No, sir, it isn't that. I'm leaving the sea."

"You're leaving the sea? Why in the world would you want to do that?"

"Because my children are growing up without me. I have a beautiful wife that I love and I rarely see. I'm sorry, Mr. Dickerson, you're as good a man as I've ever gone to sea for, but I'm coming ashore for good."

Dickerson stroked his chin, then let out a sigh. "I understand, Cody. And I don't blame you."

"Here are the bills of lading for the cargo," Cody said, handing Dickerson an envelope.

"Here's your pay, less the monthly stipend we paid your wife during your time at sea."

"Thank you," Cody said, taking the envelope from Dickerson. "One of my crewmen, Alonzo Baker, is coming with me. I'd like for you to send the pay due him, by mail."

"I'll do it. Cody, I wish you luck," Dickerson said, extending his hand. Cody took it.

"Thank you, Mr. Dickerson, and the same to you."

. . .

"How did Mr. Dickerson take it, you leaving like you did?" Alonzo asked when Cody got back into the carriage.

"Better than I thought he would. I arranged to have your pay mailed to you."

"Thank you, sir."

"Driver, take us to Denbigh, please."

"Yes, sir," the driver said, snapping the whip over the horse's head.

"Home is the sailor, home from the sea. Is anyone here happy to see me?" Cody shouted in a sing-song voice when he stepped into their house on Warwick Boulevard.

"Cody!" Lucinda called happily, rushing into his arms.

In addition to the warm welcome from Lucinda, his children, Jared and Ellen also greeted him. Jared's greeting was more reserved shaking hands with his father, while Ellen embraced him.

That evening, over supper, Cody shared his plans with Lucinda.

"Lucinda, I was gone four months on this voyage, and I had only a month home between this voyage and the previous one. These two are growing up without me." He took Ellen's hand in his.

"That they are," Lucinda said, but sensing there was more to Cody's thoughts, she continued. "Just what are you trying to say, Cody?"

"What would you say, if I told you that I was leaving the sea?"

"Oh, Cody!" Lucinda said, happily. Jumping up from

her chair, she ran around the table and threw her arms around him and kissed him deeply.

Cody chuckled when they separated. "I think that means you think it's a pretty good idea."

"It's the best thing I've heard you say since you asked me to marry you. Oh, but what will we do?"

"What would you think about us moving to Missouri?"

"Missouri?" Jared questioned.

"Yes, I was raised there."

"I know that," Lucinda said, "but I thought you said you'd never go back."

"I was young, with itchy feet and a thirst for adventure. At the time, the sea seemed to me to be the best way to satisfy that adventure. But now that I've quit sailing, I want to be as far from the sea as I can get." Cody smiled. "And you can't get any farther away from the sea than Missouri."

"You don't regret coming to Virginia, do you?"

"How could I possibly regret that? I was not only able to satisfy that thirst for adventure, it's also where I found the woman I love."

"You don't think you would have found someone to love in Missouri?"

"Were you ever in Missouri?"

Lucinda laughed. "You know I wasn't, silly."

"Then, no, I couldn't have found someone to love as much as I love you."

"This isn't just a spur of the moment thing, is it? You're sure you want to do this."

"For the last four months, it's almost all I have thought about. Yes, I've given it a great deal of thought."

"What about Lon? What's going to happen to him?

The next captain may not appreciate him as much as you do."

Cody smiled. "I've spoken to Lon, and he's decided to leave the ship as well."

"That will make Norma happy. But what will Lon do?"

"Lon will be moving back to Missouri, too. He's as good a repairman as anyone I've ever known, and when he was younger, he was a mighty fine blacksmith, so don't you worry any about him. He'll do fine."

Norma had been a slave on Lucinda's parents' farm. Lucinda Monroe and Norma had grown up together and had played together as little girls. As soon as Lucinda had inherited the farm, she had given Norma her freedom, and they had remained friends. Norma and Lon had met through their friendship with Lucinda and Cody.

ONE MONTH after leaving the *Sea Sprite*, Cody, Lucinda, Jared and Ellen boarded the train in Baltimore, for St. Louis. Lon and Norma were on the same train, but not the same car.

4

SACRED HEART ORPHANAGE, CHICAGO, ILLINOIS – APRIL 23, 1852

TODAY WAS MATT LOGAN'S SIXTEENTH BIRTHDAY. THE day wasn't his real birthday; it was the day he celebrated, because it was the day he was abandoned on the stoop of the Sacred Heart Orphanage.

The sisters were strict on him, but no more than they were with any of the other orphans. There were thirty-seven children in the house, ranging in age from less than a year to seventeen years old. They were turned out on their eighteenth birthday at which time they were expected to earn their own way.

Danny Dugan was the only other orphan who was Matt's same age. Unlike Matt, Danny had once had actual parents, but his father had died when Danny was six, and his mother died when he was eight. Danny's only surviving relative was an uncle, who, declaring himself unable to take care of the child, brought him to the orphanage. Matt and Danny had been "brothers" ever since.

Matt wasn't sure when he decided he wanted to leave. He would be turned out on his own in another two years, but he didn't want to wait two more years. Every minute, of every hour, of every day, of every year was regimented. In all the time he had been here the only times he had been off the orphanage grounds was when he was working at some job the orphanage had secured for him. By arrangement, the money he earned in those jobs went directly to the orphanage.

He wasn't exactly sure what jail was like, but from what he had read, he couldn't imagine jail to be much different from where he was now. And though he knew that people who were in jail had done something to get themselves put there, Matt had done nothing but be born.

He knew that sometimes women had children without benefit of matrimony. He felt certain that must have been the case with his mother. When he was younger, he had hated his unknown mother for abandoning him as she had. But with age, he began to realize that she must have been terribly frightened and would have had no way to support a baby. When he looked at it that way, he knew that she had done the best she could for him, and he held no animosity for the mother he had never known.

But now the time had come for him to go, and he approached Danny with his idea, hoping to persuade Danny to leave with him.

His hope wasn't in vain.

"When are you wantin' to leave?" Danny asked.

"Tonight," Matt said. "The cooks baked bread today. I figure that if we took a loaf of bread and some sliced ham, we could eat on that for two or three days, and by then we'll be long gone from here."

"What about when the food runs out?"

"We'll find work to do that'll keep us alive until we can move on."

"Are you serious about goin' out West?"

"Yes, I'm very serious. I've never known anything in my life but this orphanage. I've read about the West, 'n' I plan to go see what it's all about."

Danny smiled. "Well, then I'll be goin' West with you."

"You're a good friend, Danny. I knew you'd go with me, or I wouldn't have asked."

"We've got two more pair of pants and two more shirts. I'm going to take them with me," Matt said.

"How are we goin' to carry 'em?" Danny asked.

"We can put both pair of pants and one shirt in the remaining shirt, then bundle it up and tie it off with the shirt sleeves. I've tried it, and it works."

Danny smiled. "I'm glad the sisters picked you as my brother. You're one smart fella."

"Not too smart, or I wouldn't be taking you with me," Matt teased.

LANTERNS WERE EXTINGUISHED at ten o'clock that night. By eleven o'clock, everyone in the bay that Matt and Danny shared, was snoring. Matt got up then walked over to Danny's bunk.

"You awake?"

"Yeah."

"Let's go but be quiet."

"Wait," Danny said.

"What?"

"Let's take the money out of the office."

"No, why would we do that?"

"It's not like we're really stealin'. They'd probably spend that much on us in the next two years anyway. Besides we've earned it. We've been workin' at outside jobs for two years now, 'n' givin' ever'thing we make to the orphanage."

"That's true, but they've got a lot of people to take care of," Matt said. "And I don't think it would be right to take it."

"All right," Danny said, "but I still think we should take it."

The two boys with their makeshift knapsack carrying their extra clothes and the stash of food, slipped out through a raised window, then hurried down the back alley until they were several blocks away from the institution.

FOR THE NEXT FEW WEEKS, Matt and Danny headed toward the Mississippi River where they would be able to make better connections to go west.

It had not been Matt's intention to ever steal anything, but Danny pointed out that it was a point of stealing to survive. Danny was much better at it than Matt. He could pick the pocket of an unsuspecting bystander or sneak a coin or two from an open market.

Matt told himself that it wasn't he who was actually stealing, but he gladly ate the food that was bought from Danny's pilfering. With that realization, he came to accept that if he was benefiting from Danny's petit larceny, then in truth, he was as guilty of thievery as Danny.

They didn't engage in full time larceny; they worked when they could find part-time work to do. As a result, it took them more than a month to reach Davenport, Iowa.

"Wow, look at this," Danny said.

"This is the Mighty Mississippi River," Matt explained.

"It's a lot bigger than the Chicago River."

"It's the biggest river in America," Matt said, having read all about it at the orphanage. "Come on, we need to find a way to get a ride on a boat."

"Does this river go out west?" Danny asked.

"No, but it goes to St. Louis and that's where the Missouri River is, and the Missouri goes out west."

"How are we going to get on a boat?"

"This way," Matt said with a smile as he pointed to a sign.

There was a paddle-wheeler riverboat tied up there, and the sign Matt had pointed to read:

Deckhands wanted
for the steamboat
New Madrid.

The two boys walked over to the gang plank and started up.

"Hold on there! Where do you two think you're goin'?" someone on the boat called down to them.

"The sign said deckhands wanted," Matt answered. "That's what we want to do."

"You ever worked on a boat before?"

"I won't lie to you," Matt said. "We haven't either one of us ever been on a boat before, but we're both hard workers."

"Where have you worked?"

"In the orphanage," Matt said.

"And we're hungry," Danny added.

The man on the deck stood there for a moment, his hands on the railing. He made a nodding motion with his head.

"Come with me," he said.

ONE WEEK LATER, the *New Madrid* put into dock at St. Louis.

"You boys make pretty good deckhands," the mate said.

"Where will this boat go next?" Matt asked.

"Why we'll be goin' all the way down to New Orleans," the mate, whose name was Richards, said with a wide grin. "Wait 'til you see New Orleans. 'Couple of young yahoos like you two ain't goin' to know what to do next."

"Are there any boats that go out West?"

"Yeah, the Missouri River boats go west. But you cain't hardly call them things boats. I mean look over there at the *Ben Maxwell*. Why, that thing ain't near half as big as this'n."

"Do you think we could get on that boat as deckhands?" Matt asked.

"Why 'n hell would you want to do that?" Richards, asked. "I just told you what a great place New Orleans is. 'N' I ought to know, seein' as I was borned 'n' raised there."

"Because we want to go out West," Matt said.

"Well, hell, you ain't earned but ten dollars apiece so far. Iffen you was to stay on this boat, you'd get forty dollars whenever we got to New Orleans."

"That would be nice, but like Matt said, we want to go out West," Danny replied.

"All right, if that's what you want. Wait here, I'll get your pay, then take you over and introduce you to Quince. He's the mate there."

Fifteen minutes later, Richards took the two over to the *Ben Maxwell*.

"Hey, Quince!" Richards called.

A man with a full beard came over to the rail. "Richards, what are you doing here? You get fired already?"

"Ha, real funny. I've got two boys here want to get on with you, though why they'd want to work on this mud barge you call a boat, I don't know."

"You know the two?"

"Yeah, they're pretty good deckhands, if you can use them."

"Sure, bring 'em on board."

5

ST. LOUIS COUNTY, MISSOURI – MARCH 5, 1853

JARED MCNAIR WAS WALKING BEHIND A PLOW ON THE FIVE acres nearest the Meramec River. When he reached the end of the row he saw his sister, Ellen, coming toward him, carrying a water jug.

"Whoa, Rhoda," he called to the mule. He used the hem of his shirt to wipe the sweat from his face.

"Is that the straightest row you can plough?" Ellen asked.

"What?" Jared turned to look back at his row, which was straight as a ruler. "What are you . . ."

Before Jared could finish his protest, Ellen began laughing.

"You sure are a sensitive soul, big brother," she teased.

"Yeah, well, I started to say if you could do any better, have at it," Jared said, laughing along with Ellen. "Thanks for the water." He reached for the jug.

"You're going to be one happy person come supper time," Ellen said.

"Oh, no, don't tell me you're cooking supper."

"I am, because mama is sewing. But, if you don't want the apricot pie I've made, I'm sure papa will be happy to eat your share."

"No, no, there's no sense in you doing something crazy like giving away my pie. I'll be happy to eat it."

Ellen laughed. "I thought you might be."

"Did you take water to Pa, yet?"

"Not yet. He's all the way down to the south field."

"Yeah, he's putting out the tobacco plants," Jared said. "I offered to help, but he wants me to plant corn, in case the tobacco fails."

"It's not going to fail. The tobacco is going to make us rich," Ellen said, with a big smile.

"You don't want to get rich," Jared said.

"Why not?"

"Because then, you wouldn't know if the men are coming around you because you're rich, or if they really like you."

"I'd know," Ellen said.

"Well, I don't think you'll have to worry about it, anyway. There won't be any men coming around you whether you're rich or not," Jared teased.

"Jared!" Ellen said, as she picked up a dirt clod and, laughing, threw it at him.

"You better get that water to Pa, he'll be waiting for it."

"I'm going," Ellen said as she began walking away. "And you can just forget about that pie, the way you've acted this morning."

"Wait, what if I said I'm sorry?"

"That might help," Ellen said.

21

"I'm sorry I said no man would ever come around you. You're beautiful, and you could have any man in the state."

"You don't have to go that far, you'll still just get one piece of pie," Ellen called back, as she walked away.

BY MID-SUMMER the tobacco crop had failed.

"Horn worms," Cody said, disgustedly. "Horn worms have destroyed the entire crop."

"Well, then weren't you smart to diversify?" Lucinda replied.

"I'm afraid this is going to be a very bad year," Cody said. "I'm sorry, Lucinda, I thought planting tobacco would be a good idea."

"There was nothing wrong with the idea," Lucinda said. "The horn worms weren't your fault."

"Yeah, well, it was my idea to put so many acres into tobacco."

Lucinda smiled, reached over to put her hand on his. "And it was also your idea to plant some corn as a hedge. And, Cody…"

"Yes."

"I would rather you be here with your family and the horn worms, than be somewhere on the other side of the world."

"I'm glad you don't go to sea anymore, Pa," Jared said.

"Me too," Ellen said.

Cody looked at his wife, son, and daughter, then nodded. "Me too."

MATT LOGAN and Danny Dugan spent two years working on the Missouri River. It was during one of these trips that they met Jim Bridger. For the next year they worked with Jim Bridger as a trapper and wilderness guide. And though the time of the mountain man rendezvous were over, they did meet other mountain men such as Kit Carson and Jim Beckwourth.

The cost of beaver had fallen to two dollars a pound, and with beaver over-trapped, a hundred fifty, to two hundred pounds was the most they could hope for in a year.

Even that was threatened when they caught another trapper stealing from their trap lines. The thief was named Billy Bell Edwards, and Matt and Danny knew him fairly well.

"Edwards, what the hell are you doing here?" Matt challenged.

"I, uh, thought this was my line," Edwards said, mumbling.

"You know damn well it's not your line," Danny said. "Now, drop all the plews off your mule 'n' get on out of here."

"Now wait a minute!" Edwards said angrily. "There didn't a damn one o' them pelts come from this line. These is all my pelts."

"Drop 'em 'n' leave," Danny ordered.

"They hell I will!" Edwards shouted, and he swung his rifle around toward Matt and Danny. But Danny already had his rifle pointing toward Edwards, and he pulled the trigger. With a surprised grunt of pain, Edwards fell from his horse.

Matt hurried over to look at him. Edwards' eyes were open, but it was obvious he wasn't seeing anything.

"You killed him," Matt said.

"Yeah, well, the son of a bitch had no right to take our pelts," Danny said.

Matt shook his head. "But he was right, all those pelts on his mule couldn't have come from this trap line. We've never gotten that many."

"Then we're goin' to have a good year, this year, aren't we?" Danny asked with a smile. "Besides," he added, "you saw him swing his gun around. If I hadn't killed him, he would have killed one of us."

"Yeah," Matt agreed, reluctantly. "I guess you're right."

MATT AND DANNY were twenty-one years old when Beckwourth suggested that they could do better.

"You fellas can stay out here wanderin' around 'n trappin' beaver if you want, but if you want my opinion, there's a better way of makin' a livin', 'n you two would be real good at it. And you could still see as much country as you would want."

"What would that be?" Matt asked.

"Guidin' wagon trains."

"Wagon trains? You mean all those Easterners that's comin' out here, fillin' up the place?" Danny asked.

"Boys, they ain't a' goin' to stop comin'," Bridger said. "So, if they're goin' to come anyway, you may as well make some money out of it."

"How would you get on to doing something like that?" Matt asked.

"Most of 'em's startin' in St. Louis. I'll take you there 'n get you on with one of 'em."

"What do we have to do?" Danny asked.

"Nothin' the two of you ain't already done, 'n that's just find your way around out here. They'll more 'n likely either be goin' to Oregon or California, 'n there's already been enough wagon trains that all you got to do is follow the ruts."

"What would something like that pay?" Matt asked.

"A thousand dollars. If the two of you went in together, it would be five hundred dollars apiece. Oh, 'n' you'll be expected to kill some game for 'em, but for the most part, your food will be furnished."

"Dayum, five hundred dollars?" Danny asked. "We ain't never made that much money with the plews."

"All right, we'll do it," Matt agreed.

THE GUIDE JOB took six months to lead a wagon train from St. Louis to Sacramento, California. Coming back on horseback was much quicker, and they reached St. Louis in two months, ready to take out another train the next spring.

After the second trip together, they decided they could make more money if they split up and each take a train by themselves. Once they put that plan into effect, they often found themselves separated from one another by several hundred miles. They went for well over a year, without seeing each other again.

6

BALLWIN, MISSOURI – NOVEMBER 5TH, 1858

WHAT HAD STARTED AS A COLD RAIN EARLY IN THE morning had turned to snow by the time of the funeral. Cody had asked the Reverend Festus Elwood to come to his house to conduct the funeral. He held the funeral at home for two reasons. He wanted Lon, Norma, and Precious, their six-year-old daughter, to attend the funeral. Norma was especially saddened by the death of someone she had known for her entire life, and he knew there would be some difficulty with having colored people come to an all-white church. He also wanted to bury Lucinda right here on the farm, where they had been the happiest.

Lucinda lay in an open casket in front of the living-room fireplace. Whatever malady it was that had killed her ... and Dr. Urban admitted that he had no idea what it could have been, struck her down in the prime of life. Because there was no prolonged illness, her face was free of any of the ravages of sickness. She was as beautiful lying in the coffin now, as she had been while lying in their bed one week earlier.

Norma, who was a very pretty woman, stood alone beside the casket, looking down at her friend. Tears streamed down her light-toned cheeks.

The Kinders and the Underhills, families who flanked the McNair farm, were the only mourners besides Lon, Norma, and Precious.

While Reverend Elwood preached the funeral, his words faded into the background as Cody watched the snowflakes swirling around just outside the window.

"Oh, I love the snow," Lucinda told him shortly after they met.

Virginia Kinder had commented on how unfortunate it was to be snowing on the day of Lucinda's funeral, but Cody didn't see it that way at all. Cody looked at the snow as Lucinda's way of telling him goodbye.

Cody stared at the snowflakes falling against the window that was on the same side of the house as the grave that had already been opened. He made no effort to stop the tears.

Reverend Elwood was just concluding the service.

"Dear Lord, thank you for Lucinda's life, and the years Cody, Jared, and Ellen were able to share with her."

"Please give us the strength to leave this beautiful soul in Your care, in the certain knowledge of her eternal rest in glory. Amen."

INDEPENDENCE, MISSOURI – FEBRUARY 15TH, 1859

Matt Logan was now twenty-three years old and stood six feet tall. His time on the river, in the mountains, and leading wagon trains, had given him a body that was both muscular and agile. He was a good horseman, an excellent shot, and a fearless guide.

He had taken to coming to Independence to pick up a wagon train to guide, rather than going all the way to St. Louis. That was because the wagon trains could get to Independence on their own—it was only after they left Independence that they would need a guide.

About as many wagon trains left from St. Joseph, as left from Independence, and Danny had chosen to make his connections in St. Joseph. The two friends had talked about it and decided this would be the best way to handle it, because this way they would not be in competition for the same job.

Although they were guiding separate wagon trains, and often as much as five hundred miles apart, they were able to keep up with each other by leaving messages at the various forts and trading posts along the route.

Matt knew that there would be no wagon trains starting before April, so he took a room in a boarding house, and relaxed until his next job. The three months of relaxation would be most welcome.

ASH HOLLOW CREEK – APRIL 2ND, 1859

Danny Dugan had left St. Joseph a month earlier, guiding a train led by Mel Pollard. At the moment the train was stopped in an established campground on the banks of Ash Hollow Creek.

"Some of our people are complaining of it being too cold," Pollard said. "They're thinking we should have waited a month before we left."

Danny shook his head. "No, no sense in doin' that. This way we're sure to be into the mountains before the passes are closed by snow. That's somethin' you defi-nitely don't want to have to deal with."

"Yeah, I guess I can see that," Pollard said. "I told ever'one you know your business, 'n' if you think we should'a left in early March, then I think that's the way it should be."

Danny chuckled. "When we get into the desert and it's so hot everyone's tongue is hangin' out, let's remind them that they were cold back in March and April."

Pollard laughed as well. "Yeah, that's a good idea."

"We can stay here for the rest of the day and tonight, but we'll need to get started, first thing in the mornin'. I'm goin'y to ride on ahead and make sure there aren't any unpleasant surprises waitin' for us."

"You're a good man, Dugan," Pollard said.

"Yeah, that's what all the ladies say," Danny replied.

Pollard laughed. "All the ladies say, huh? You're a windbag, Dugan. You're a good man, but a windbag."

BALLWIN, MISSOURI – MONDAY, APRIL 4, 1859

Cody McNair was reading through the letter for a second time, not sure he understood it. The letter was from Boatman's Bancshares in St. Louis.

> *Having acquired all assets and obligations of the Farmer's Bank of Ballwin, we are calling in all loans. You have an outstanding loan for $3,500 dollars, secured by an eighty-acre farm located two miles west of Ballwin, Missouri. You have thirty days to retire this loan or forfeit the property by which the loan is secured.*

"Oh, Lucinda, I'm glad you never had to deal with this," Cody said, quietly.

Cody, who had been devastated by Lucinda's death, was able to maintain his composure, only because of Jared and Ellen. He shared the letter with them.

"What are we going to do, Pa?" Jared asked.

"I'll have a talk with Cecil to find out what this is all about," Cody said.

THE FOLLOWING MONDAY, Cody went into Ballwin to meet with Cecil Barnes, who had owned the Farmer's Bank of Ballwin, and from whom, Cody had secured the initial loan.

"Can they do this, Cecil? Can they foreclose on my farm?"

"I'm afraid they can," Cecil said.

"But how? I've made every payment on time, and I'm not a day behind on the loan."

"The country is caught up in an economic panic, Cody. Businesses and banks are being forced to close; I had no choice. The Farmer's Bank had made too many loans and while, in normal times, that would be an asset, in these troubled times it is considered a liability. I was forced into bankruptcy, and Boatman's Bancshares took over. Now, they are calling in all the loans."

"I don't have thirty-five hundred dollars," Cody said.

"I have a possible solution for you. I mean, it's not an ideal solution, it won't save your farm, but it would keep you from losing everything."

"What would that be?"

"Phil Grant is buying up some of the farms that have been put in distress. He would pay you for what equity you have in your land. Your loan is so heavy that you don't have much there, but at least you would get away without losing everything."

"Phil Grant, you say?"

"Yes, do you know him?"

"I know him, he owns a few riverboats."

"Yes, half-a-dozen in fact. You might go into St. Louis to meet with him."

WHEN CODY RETURNED HOME, Ellen was fixing supper, and Jared was tending the fireplace.

Ellen was an exceptionally pretty young woman, high-bosomed and dark hair with the bright blue eyes of her mother. Jared was somewhat taller than his father, slender, but muscular from his work on the farm. His hair was dark, and his blue eyes were laced with a thin golden matrix.

"What did Mr. Barnes say, Pa?" Jared asked.

"There's no way we can stop the foreclosure," Cody said.

"Oh, Papa, what will we do?" Ellen asked.

"There may be a way out, not to save the farm, but at least to get us some money, enough to go somewhere else and start over."

"Start over where, and in what?" Jared asked.

"Start over," Cody replied without being any more specific.

7

As Cecil had suggested, Cody left the next morning to go to St. Louis to meet with Phil Grant. The team of mules, Harry and Rhoda, stepped out quickly on this brisk day so that he reached the Mississippi River front in less than three hours. There were at least two dozen riverboats tied up on the bank, and he drove past several of them until he reached a building that had a sign advertising:

GRANT MISSISSIPPI RIVERBOAT COMPANY

As it turned out Cody knew Phil Grant, because Grant, calling upon Cody's experience as a sea captain, had once tried to recruit him to captain one of his riverboats.

"Hello, Cody, Cecil told me you might be coming to see me," Grant greeted.

"Hello, Phil. Yes, I'm here to see if you actually will buy the equity in my farm."

"Yes, I'm prepared to do just that."

"What about the loan with Boatman's Bancshares? What will you do about it?"

"I've already spoken with them. They'll let me pay the loan off, rather than foreclose on you, and that will leave you with some equity to sell."

"Do you know how much equity there is?"

"Yes, Boatman's appraised it for me. It's two thousand dollars for your farm and livestock."

"I'd like to keep my milk-cow, my two horses, and my two mules. That would leave fifty-five head of cattle that would be part of the sale."

"I think we can do that," Grant said. "If you can meet me at Boatman's Bancshares at one o'clock next Monday, we'll close the deal."

"I'll be there," Cody promised.

"Now let me ask you a question, Cody. Would you want to stay on the farm and operate it on shares?"

"No, I don't think I'd want to do that."

"Would you like to work for me? I can't hire you on as a captain because all of my boats currently have a captain. But I could hire you on as a senior member of the crew until a captaincy opens up."

Cody shook his head. "No, I don't really think I'd like to do that, either."

"Then, what will you do?"

Cody shook his head. "Frankly, Phil, I don't have the slightest idea."

"Would you be interested in something like this?" Grant asked, handing Cody a copy of the *St. Louis Democrat* newspaper.

Wagon Train Being Formed

A wagon train, to consist of no less than forty wagons, is being formed for a mid-April departure from this city, and participants are now being solicited. The destination of the wagon train will be the Willamette Valley in the newly admitted state of Oregon. The valley, being well watered by the Willamette River and of temperate climate is said to be ideal for farming. Those who choose to make the journey will have the opportunity to purchase land from the state of Oregon for $1.25 per acre.

Interested parties are advised to call upon Tom Murchison, attorney at law, 512 Lindell, in this city.

DUTCHTOWN DISTRICT OF ST. LOUIS

Harm Schultz had migrated to St. Louis, coming from Eschwege, Germany, in 1849. He had initially started his life in the new country as a grocer. What set him apart from other grocers was his ability to supply an item that wasn't sold by any of his competitors – lager beer.

Schultz had learned the art of brewing from his father, so in 1852 he gave up the grocery business entirely and built a modest brewery on South Second Street. By 1854, there were twenty-four breweries in St. Louis, and though Harm was able to make enough of a living to take on a bride, there was too much competition for him to expand beyond the small brewery he was operating.

Then, the larger breweries began putting pressure on the smaller breweries, undercutting their prices, preempting the supply of hops, until finally Harm was forced to sell his brewery to Aldolphus Busch.

Harm had received a little over two thousand dollars for his brewery, which gave him the luxury of studied contemplation over his next venture. He was trying to decide what it would be, as he was reading the *St. Louis Democrat*. That was when he came across the article about a wagon train going west.

"*Ja, das ist es!*" he said, resolutely, slapping his hand on the table.

"What is it?" his wife asked.

"Gretchen," he called. "*Kommen sie auf diese.*"

Gretchen had been born in America to German parents, so though English was her first language, she spoke fluent German.

"Harm, you are in America now so you must speak English," she said with a slight laugh. "Now what is it you want me to see?"

"*Dieser zeitungsartikel*, uh, this newspaper article," he said, correcting himself.

Gretchen read it quickly, then returned the paper to her husband.

"Why did you want me to read about a wagon train going west?"

A broad smile spread across Harm's face. "Because we are going to be on it," he said.

"Oh, Harm, you don't mean that," Gretchen said, the tone of her voice suggesting her apprehension over such a venture. "You would give up our home and travel so far?"

"Liebchen, I gave up my home in Germany and travelled halfway around the world. I can do it again."

"But I was born here in St. Louis. This is the only home I've ever known."

"Your *Mutter* und *Vater* were not born here. They left their home in *Deutshland* and came here where they had no family but each other. Can you not do that?"

"I . . . ." Gretchen paused before she continued her sentence. "I will go where you go, my husband."

"Das ist gut, mein Liebchen."

Gretchen laughed. "You are impossible."

8

WHEN CODY MCNAIR CALLED UPON TOM MURCHISON, he saw a man about his own age, a little shorter, with blue eyes, light brown hair, and a shadow of freckles. "You're here to inquire about the wagon train?" Murchison asked.

"Yes. What will I have to do to join, and when will it leave?"

"In order to join, you must furnish your own wagon and team, and agree to the contractual arrangements which means you must follow the laws of the train as adopted by a majority vote of all members of the company."

"How much will it cost?"

"It will cost you fifty dollars to join the train." Murchison smiled. "That's my fee. And, once you reach Independence, a guide should be hired, someone who has taken trains before. His salary will be one thousand dollars, and that cost will be equally divided among all the members of the party."

"If the forty-wagon goal is reached, the cost per

wagon will be twenty-five dollars, so your total cost to be a part of the train will be seventy-five dollars. As to how much it will cost above that seventy-five dollars, it will be up to you, depending on how much you spend for your wagon, team, and provisions."

"How many have signed up?"

"I'm not sure how many people it will be, but as of now, we have thirty-five wagons committed. We would like to have forty wagons to participate, but even if we don't get that many, we already have enough to ensure that the train will depart. Many of the participants are from Illinois, so the train will form here in St. Louis at LeClede's Landing as that is a central location."

"When will this be?"

"Monday, April twenty-second. That's only two weeks from now, so if you are going to do this, you need to get all your affairs in order."

"All right, I'll be there. I may be able to talk someone else into making the trip," Cody said. "Will he have to declare before we leave?"

"No, all he will have to do is show up," Murchison said. "He'll be expected to pay the fifty dollars at the formation of the train."

"Oh, there's another thing you should know about him."

"What? He isn't a wanted criminal, is he?"

"No, nothing like that. He's a colored man—a free man, with a wife and child. I've known him for all my life, and he's as good a man as you would ever want to meet. He's also a very good blacksmith, all-around repairman, and he's good with animals. I think he would be a great asset for the company."

Murchison grinned. "There may be some who might object, but from what you say, I think most would welcome him. And anyone who doesn't like it, can join up with another company."

"Well then, I thank you for all the information, Mr. Murchison. I guess now I had better start making all the arrangements I'll need to be able to go."

"I wish I could go as well," Murchison said. "But I'm afraid my skills are limited to being a lawyer, and it will probably be a while before there's need enough for legal representation to support a lawyer. Have a good, safe trip."

KNOWING he would need a wagon and team, Cody stopped by the Mitchell-Sharp Wagon yard on Olive Boulevard. Here, he saw at least two dozen wagons, from Prairie Schooners to the much larger and heavier Conestoga wagons.

He set the brake on the buckboard, then climbed down to examine the wagons. He was approached by a heavy-set, bald-headed man. "I'm Henry Mitchell," he said. "Are you interested in a wagon?"

"Yes, but I don't know what kind I'll need."

"What will you be using it for? To haul freight? Farm produce?"

Cody shook his head. "I'm joining a wagon train, heading west."

"Oh, yes, I know of the train, I've sold five wagons for it, so far. This is a Conestoga, and much as I would like to sell it to you because I make more money from them, the Conestoga is too big and too heavy a wagon for what you'll need."

Mitchell led Cody to another, smaller wagon. "This is what they call a Prairie Schooner. It will do a much better job for you, and it's cheaper. Do you have a team?"

Cody pointed to Harry and Rhoda.

"You'll need at least four more mules, and even then, it's going to be hard on them. What would be better, would be six oxen. Mules will take you faster on flat road, but you aren't going to always have flat roads, and there will be times when you don't even have roads. And when you're going across rough land, oxen are stronger and can pull heavier loads."

"Where would I get oxen?"

Mitchell smiled. "Well, as it so happens, I've got mules and oxen here. And if you decide to go with oxen, and you want to, I'll buy your mules from you."

"I think I should keep my mules. I'll be wanting to start a farm once I get there, and I'll need the mules."

"Perhaps but consider this. So many of the wagons are pulled by mules, that there will be an excess of mules, once you get there, so you won't have any trouble buying a pair. And, if you sell the mules to me, you won't have to feed, water, and tend to them during your trip out."

"Yes, I suppose that's right, isn't it?"

"I'll give you a hundred and fifty dollars apiece for the two mules, and thirty dollars for your buckboard."

Cody nodded. "Mr. Mitchell, it looks like we're going to do business."

"Will you be buying your wagon and team today?"

"No, I'll be selling my farm next Monday. I won't have the money until then."

Mitchell stuck out his hand. "All right, I'll see you next Monday."

"Oh, there's a possibility I might need two wagons and two sets of oxen. I'll know by the time I return."

"That will be all right, sir, if you need an extra wagon and team, I'll be able to supply them for you."

"Thank you," Cody said.

9

BALLWIN, MISSOURI – APRIL 7TH, 1859

CODY WAS OF CONFLICTING EMOTIONS AS HE DROVE BACK
home from the wagon dealer. On the one hand, he was
excited at the prospect of a new adventure, but he was
also ashamed that he had failed, even though he knew
the failure wasn't his fault. Also, he was worried as to
whether or not he would be able to convince Jared and
Ellen to go with him. They were adults, and certainly
able to make up their own minds, but he hoped they
would want to come with him. He also couldn't help but
feel a sense of sadness at leaving what had been his home
with Lucinda, but this had not been his first major life
change. That had occurred when he left the sea.

Now that he was about to make another move, he
was filled with a tumult of emotion, but of all the
emotions, what he felt most, was determination.

"I will make this work," he said aloud.

He had left Virginia to go to Missouri with the
same degree of determination, but it was different this

time. Cody had been born and raised in Missouri. By the time he was eighteen, he had done every job there was to do on a farm, so that when he returned, it wasn't as a big a transition as it might seem at first glance.

But now he was going to Oregon, and that was a major move, especially for Jared and Ellen.

Before leaving Virginia for Missouri, Cody had discussed the move with Lucinda. He felt the need to discuss this one with her as well.

LUCINDA'S GRAVE was under a big river birch tree, a tree that Lucinda had once told Cody was her favorite.

"Of all the trees on the farm, why is this one your favorite?" Cody had asked.

"Do you remember the time that Ellen got sick and almost died?"

"Yes, of course."

"I was sitting in the parlor, looking out the window, praying that Ellen would recover. That's when I noticed that every leaf on this tree was glowing as if covered in gold. I don't mean they were yellow; I mean the way the sun was hitting them; they were a glistening gold. I knew then that God was telling me He would answer my prayer."

Lucinda had been dead for four months now, and the grief was still right there, just on the other side of memory.

"Lucy, 1859 hasn't been a good year. This financial panic is spreading all over the country," Cody said, speaking to the grave. "Businesses are going bankrupt, and folks are losing their jobs. It doesn't look like it's going to ease up anytime soon. There was nothing I could do but sell the farm and I see no way out of this but to leave."

Cody reached out to pull a couple of weeds from the grave mound.

"I've asked Jared and Ellen to go with me. They're both full grown now, and can do whatever they want, but I'm glad to tell you that both of them have said they will be going.

"I have to tell you; I don't know what I would have done if they had told me they didn't want to go. Losing you has put a hurt on me that I can never recover from. I honestly don't know if I could go on, if I didn't have them.

"Of course, that means I'll be leaving you here. But not really." Cody patted his hand over his heart. "You've been right here with me all along, and you'll be right here in my heart, until I take my last breath on this earth."

ELLEN WAS STANDING at the window looking out toward the river birch tree.

"Is Pa still squatting beside Mom's grave?" Jared asked.

"Yes," Ellen said. "Oh, Jared, will he ever get over losing her?"

"I don't think he wants to," Jared said. "But that hasn't slowed him down any. He's the hardest working man I've ever met, and I'm not saying that just because he's our Pa."

"He's telling Mama goodbye," Ellen said.

"I asked him if it would bother him to leave her, and he said the strangest thing," Jared said. "He said he wouldn't be leaving her. When I asked if that meant he had changed his mind about going, he said, no, he was going, but he wouldn't be leaving her. I have no idea what he was talking about."

"I know what he's talking about," Ellen said.

"Yeah, well, you 'n' Pa always were able to understand each other better 'n anyone else could."

"How do you feel about going, Jared?"

"I'm looking forward to it. I think it will be exciting. Besides, there sure isn't anything left around here for me to do. How do you feel about it?"

"It doesn't make any difference how I feel about it. Papa needs me to help him through the grief, and there's no way I'm going to abandon him now. I will be going."

"I won't argue with you there, Sis," Jared said.

"He's coming back," Ellen said, stepping away from the window.

"I've kept breakfast warm for you," Ellen said when Cody stepped into the house.

"You're a good girl, Ellen."

Ellen chuckled. "I'm not a girl. I'm a full-grown woman, Papa."

Cody smiled and reached out to put his hand on her head. "That's true, darlin', but you'll always be my little girl."

The three went into the kitchen where Ellen served biscuits, bacon, and bacon gravy.

"You know, darlin'," Cody said as he took his first bite. "When I eat your biscuits and gravy, I could swear that your mama just dished up the plate."

"WHISKEY," Peter Laycock said. "We'll fill up our three wagons with whiskey, join that wagon train that's makin' up now, 'n go out to Oregon 'n' open us up a saloon. We'll get rich."

"What about women?" Raymond Pugh asked. "I ain't never seen me no saloon what didn't have women in it."

"Let's get the saloon set up first, then we'll worry 'bout the women," Laycock said. "Hell, we can send back for 'em."

"Yeah, I'm all for it," Raines said. "Only problem I can see is whether or not we can get whiskey out there before Pugh drinks it all up." Raines laughed at his comment.

"Hell, it ain't me we got to worry about," Pugh said. "It's Laycock."

For the next few minutes, the three men teased each other about who was the biggest drinker.

"See, this is just what I'm talkin' about," Laycock said. "There ain't no man, that's a real man, but what don't like whiskey. 'N' if we got the whiskey to sell 'im, we're goin' to do real fine. Let all them others work their fool heads off, ploughin' up half of Oregon. We'll sit back without breakin' a sweat and make a ton o' money sellin' 'em whiskey."

"FIFTEEN HUNDRED HEAD, YOU SAY?" Frank Wiley said. "Yeah, me 'n' my brother Gus can take 'em."

"That's over two thousand miles," Joe Atwood said. "I don't know if just the two of you can drive fifteen hundred head of cattle two thousand miles, all by yourself."

"It won't be just the two of us," Frank said. "There's three more of us that drove twenty-five hundred head of cattle up here to St. Louis from San Antonio, and that was near a thousand miles."

"Yes, well, from here to Oregon is twice as far, and you'll have to keep up with the wagon train."

"We'll get the job done," Frank promised.

"Be honest with me now. Of the fifteen hundred we'll be startin' out with, how many cows do you think we'll lose?"

"I don't think we'll lose over maybe a hundred to a hundred and fifty head," Frank said. "Less'en we don't lose none to the Indians."

Atwood smiled, then stuck out his hand. "Well at two dollars a head for every cow you get there, it's to your advantage to keep as many of them alive as you can."

"We'll do our best, Mr. Atwood," Frank said, sealing the deal with a handshake.

10

CHIMNEY ROCK – OREGON TRAIL – APRIL
12, 1859

EVEN AS THE WAGON TRAIN WAS FORMING UP IN ST. Louis, there were already several wagon trains on the Oregon Trail. One such train was the Mel Pollard train. This wagon train was considerably west of St. Louis, very near a landmark known as Chimney Rock. One of the members of the wagon train, Darcy Clinton, set a bucket of water down next to the wagon in which she, her mother, father, and two younger brothers, were traveling. Darcy's father, Ian, had been a shoe cobbler in Decatur, Illinois, when he read about how cheaply land could be bought in Oregon.

"But, Ian, you've never been a farmer. You know nothing about farming," his wife, pointed out.

"Oh, I won't be farming, Pearl," Ian said. "Folks will always need shoes, and I'll do the same thing there as I'm doing here. But with the land that cheap, it can't help but go up in value as more people come in. I'll buy the land and hold it for an investment."

Darcy, who had just graduated from McKendree College in Lebanon, Illinois, planned to be a school-teacher when they got to Oregon.

"Sean, how about gathering some firewood?" Darcy asked her youngest brother who was nine years old.

"Why do I always have to gather firewood?" Sean asked.

"Because we all have to work," Pearl said.

"Besides, you do want to eat, don't you?" sixteen-year-old Connor asked. "How are we goin' to eat if mom and Darcy don't cook, and how are they goin' to cook, if they don't have a fire?"

"Why don't you gather the firewood?" Sean asked.

"All right. As soon as I get back with the water, I'll get the wood. But that means I get your share of the food tonight. And mom is goin' to be makin' a cobbler from the dried peaches."

"No, that's all right," Sean said. "I'll do it."

Darcy laughed, then reached out to rub her hand through her little brother's hair. "I thought you might."

BALLWIN, MISSOURI – APRIL 12, 1859

"Jared I'm going into St. Louis today to pick up the wagon. I may be getting one for Lon too, if I can talk him into going with us, and I'll need someone to drive it back. Would you like to come along with me?"

"All right, Pa," Jared said.

"Papa, I need to come along as well. I need to buy a few things before we leave and I'm more likely to find them in St. Louis than I am in Ballwin. . . that is, if we have enough money."

"We should have enough. Phil Grant is meeting me at Boatman's Bancshares. He's giving us two thousand dollars for what we've got in the farm. The wagon's going to cost us eighty-five dollars, and a team of six oxen will cost us a hundred and eighty. I'll be getting the wagon and oxen team from Henry Mitchell, and he's going to give us thirty dollars for the buckboard, and a hundred and fifty dollars for the two mules. Plus, we already had a little over three hundred dollars in savings."

"I'm going to miss Rhoda and Harry," Ellen said.

"They're good mules, but it isn't practical to take them with us, and the money Mitchell is paying for them means that after our wagon and team and Lon's wagon and team are bought and paid for, we'll still have plenty to buy the provisions we need, and whatever you have in mind to buy."

"What about the fifty-five head of cattle, Pa?" Jared asked. "Will we be taking them with us?"

"Those that weren't taken by the bank in foreclosing on the loan, are included in what I sold to Grant."

"You didn't say anything about our two horses," Jared said.

"We'll be keeping them," Cody said with a smile.

"Will we be spending the night in St. Louis?" Ellen asked.

"Yes, by the time we get all of our business taken care of, it'll be too late to come back home." Cody smiled. "So, I'm going to spend the money to get us a hotel room."

"Oh, that will be fun!" Ellen said. "I've never stayed in a hotel room before."

. . .

49

THE McNAIR FARM was six miles west of Ballwin, and when they got to town, they stopped at the Heckemeyer stables. Bill Heckemeyer came out to meet them.

"Have you got 'ny idea how big that wagon train is you're goin' to be joinin' up with?" Heckemeyer asked.

"When I left, they had thirty-eight wagons committed, counting me, and I'm told by the time they leave, there might be at least forty or more. Is Lon here today?"

"Yes, sir, he's out back. I'll get him for you."

LON HAD a wide smile on his face as he approached.

"Yes, sir, Cap'n," Lon said. "Mr. Heckemeyer said you wanted to see me."

Cody chuckled. "I've been telling you for several years now, Lon, you don't have to call me captain anymore. We aren't at sea."

"Yes, sir, Cap'n, 'n' you can keep on tellin' me that from now on, but far as I'm concerned, you still are, 'n' always will be Cap'n."

Cody laughed again. "If you say so. Lon, how much money do you have?"

"You need to borrow some money, Cap'n? I got some, not a whole lot, but I got some 'n' I'll lend you as much as I can."

"Thanks, Lon, I know you would. But I don't need a loan. I'm asking you for another reason. How much do you have?"

"I got a hundred 'n' forty-seven dollars."

"That's not enough to get you outfitted, but I think it'll be enough to give you a start, once we get there."

"Once we get where?"

"Oregon," Cody said with a broad grin. "There's a wagon train forming up for the trip out to the new state of Oregon and we're going. I'd like for you to come as well. You're a good blacksmith, and good at making repairs, and that would make you an asset for the trip."

"Lord, Cap'n, I don't have enough money for a wagon and team."

"I'll loan you enough money to buy a wagon, team, and provisions. When we get to where we're going, land is cheap. Why, for a dollar and a quarter, you can buy enough land to build a house and a blacksmith and repair shop. And between here and Oregon, you'll be earning money as a wheelwright, because we're going to need one for sure. Then, when you can afford it, you can pay me back."

"Where is this, Oregon?"

"It's a long way from here." Cody smiled. "But it isn't as far as some of the places we went to when we were at sea."

Lon returned the smile. "No, sir, I don't reckon it is."

"I'm going into St. Louis to take care of some business today. That's where I'll buy a wagon and a team of oxen for me, and if you're willing to join the train, I'll buy a wagon and team for you as well. I'll get your provisions put together, too."

"Cap'n, I . . . there ain't nobody never done nothin' like that for me before. But what about the other folks in the train? How do you think they'll take to havin' a colored man travelin' with them?"

"Don't you be worrying about that. On a trip as long as this one is going to be, there's going to be a need to repair wheels, axles, double-trees, and the like. I expect it won't be long before folks will be thinking you're the most valuable man in the whole train. And, you'll probably make enough money by doing such things, as to allow you to get your own business set up once we get there."

"My own business?" Lon said with a broad, proud, smile.

"Your own business," Cody seconded.

Lon reached out to shake Cody's hand. "Cap'n, I'll tell Norma 'bout it soon's I get home today. How long you think before we get goin'?"

"Just a few more days," Cody said. "We'll be leaving from St. Louis, so we'll need to be there a day or two before the train gets underway."

"I hope Mr. Heckemeyer don't get too upset, what with me leavin' 'im 'n' all."

"You needn't worry about Bill Heckemeyer, I've already spoken to him, he knows I was planning on asking you to come with me. Do you think Norma will be all right with it?"

"I 'spects she will be. She'll be worryin' some about our little girl. Precious is only seven years old, but I 'specs she'll make the trip just fine."

"Oh, I'm sure she will. I'm going to St. Louis now to buy our wagons and provisions. I'll be back tomorrow or the next day, and I'll leave your wagon with you so you can get it loaded for the trip. Be careful that you don't try to take too much."

11

Cody, Jared, and Ellen arrived in St. Louis at three o'clock in the afternoon, and the first thing they did was go to Boatman's Bancshares bank on Market Street. There, Jared and Ellen remained with the buckboard while Cody went inside.

Phil Grant was already there, and he smiled and greeted Cody with a handshake.

"Phil, I can't tell you how much I appreciate you doing this for me," Cody said.

"You've been a good neighbor, Cody. I hate to see you go, but I'm glad I can help you keep the bank from taking everything you have."

"Mr. Grant, Mr. McNair, Mr. Hamilton will see you now," a very thin man with a protruding Adam's apple and a pencil-thin mustache said.

Frank Hamilton had a very round face with heavy eyebrows and multiple chins. He had a protruding stomach, and he wheezed as he breathed.

"Mr. Grant, as I understand it, you are willing to pay off what Mr. McNair owes the bank."

"Yes."

"Mr. McNair, that seems like a pretty good deal for you. It will keep us from foreclosing on you," Hamilton said.

"I don't know why you were going to foreclose in the first place," Cody said. "I was not behind on my loan with Farmers' Bank."

"Yes, well Farmers' Bank has closed, and we have assumed all their assets and encumbrances, and we established guidelines by which to judge certain loans. We have seen fit to foreclose on those loans that we deemed uncertain, and your loan fell under those guidelines. I hope you have no hard feelings toward us."

"I have no feelings for you one way or another," Cody replied. "As soon as my business is conducted here, I am making preparations to move my family to Oregon."

"Oh, my, that will be quite an undertaking, won't it? Are you sure you want to do such a thing?"

"If you don't mind, Mr. Hamilton, I would like to get this business completed. I have several more things I have to take care of."

"Yes, uh, of course," Hamilton replied, knowing that he had just been dismissed.

After finishing his business with the bank and Phil Grant, Cody returned to the buckboard where Jared and Ellen were waiting with anxious expressions on their faces.

"Papa, did everything go well?" Ellen asked.

Cody flashed a broad smile. "Yes, everything went well," he said.

FROM THE BANK they went to the Planters' Hotel at Fourth and Vine.

"There are three of us. Do you have a room with two beds?" Cody asked.

"Yes, sir, we do," Kelsey, one of the proprietors responded. "The cost will be four dollars and twenty-five cents, but that will include all meals."

"Boarding for my mules?"

"Boarding is free for our guests, sir."

"Well worth the price," Cody said, as he signed the guest register book.

"Jared, take Harry and Rhoda to the livery around back, you can board them there, and leave the buck-board. Ellen and I will be in room four twelve, on the fourth floor."

To Ellen's delight, after Jared came back to join them, they went back downstairs to the hotel dining room. It had many Doric columns and was decorated in tones of green and silver.

"Everything is so elegant," Ellen said after they were seated by the maître d'. The menu offered an imposing array of foods, including filet de boeuf, fried oysters, broiled grouse, saddle of antelope, and wild duck. Desserts included custard pudding and apple, plum, and pumpkin pies.

"Oh, Papa, look at this," Ellen said, excitedly as she perused the menu. "I've never seen so many wonderful things."

"You two enjoy it. We're going to have a long trip with limited fare in front of us."

NONNIE GENOA HUGHES WAS AN ATTRACTIVE FORTY-ONE-year-old woman. She was also a widow, having lost her husband a year earlier. Andrew had been a doctor partnered with Dr. Gordon Parker who was Nonnie's brother. Gordon was a widower as well, with a fourteen-year-old son, Fred.

It had been Gordon's idea to go to Oregon, and when he came to tell Nonnie goodbye, she surprised him by suggesting that she could come with him.

"There is nothing to keep me here, Gordon. My husband is dead, our parents are dead, and if you leave, I'll be here all alone."

"It's going to be a long, hard trip, especially for a woman," Gordon cautioned.

"Are you suggesting that I would be the only woman?" Nonnie asked.

"No, of course not. There will be other women with the train."

"Then perhaps you are suggesting that I don't have the intestinal fortitude of the other women. Look

Gordon, if you would rather I not come."

"No, no!" Gordon said quickly. "I would love for you to come. I just wanted you to know what you would be letting yourself in for, is all."

That conversation had taken place in Dyersburg, Tennessee, over a month earlier. Now Gordon Parker, his son Fred, and his sister, Nonnie, were in St. Joseph, Missouri, part of a wagon train being led by Larry Dooley. A few moments earlier, Dooley had come riding down along the line of wagons.

"All right, folks, this is it!" Dooley said. "We'll be leaving right after breakfast tomorrow morning. I advise you all to get a good night's sleep."

"Pa, how 'm I goin' to get a good night's sleep with you snorin' the way you do?" Fred teased.

"You could sleep with your fingers stuck in your ears," Gordon said with a laugh.

"THERE ARE ONLY SEVENTEEN WAGONS," Jim Ledbetter said, after Dooley announced that they would be leaving the next morning. "Are you sure that's enough?"

"I've taken trains with from fifteen to fifty wagons," Dooley replied. "Trust me, when I say that fifteen, or in our case, seventeen wagons, are much easier to handle. You will find that your trip will be quicker than that of some of the larger trains. The more wagons you have, the more problems there are that seem to pop up. Seventeen wagons are just about right."

"Well, you're the one we hired to take us there, so since we're payin' you, we may as well listen to you."

"There's nothing to worry about, Mr. Ledbetter. We'll get underway first thing in the morning."

"You DRIVE, Fred, and I will walk," Gordon told Nonnie, as all the wagons were lined up ready for departure.

"That's going to be a long way for you two to walk," Nonnie said.

"We'll trade off. Sometimes you'll walk and either Fred or I will drive. But most of the time, it'll be you driving."

ST. LOUIS

The first thing Cody did after he, Jared, and Ellen had breakfast in the hotel the next morning, was to hitch up the team to the buckboard and drive to the Mitchell-Sharp wagon shop.

"Ah, Mr. McNair, you've come for your wagon," Asa Sharp said.

"As I told Harry, the last time I was here, I'm actually going to buy two wagons."

"Well, if you're going to buy two of them, I think we can give you a better price, say five dollars off each wagon."

Cody smiled. "Why, thank you, Asa. It's good doing business with you. I told Harry I would also need two teams."

"All right, we can take care of that. Oxen, or mules?" Asa asked.

"I've been giving this a lot of thought, and I've decided on oxen."

"Very well, twelve oxen and two wagons, minus the trade in of a buckboard and two mules, comes to a total of three hundred and thirty dollars."

After leaving the Mitchell-Sharp wagon dealer, they drove to Rafferty's General Store to buy the provisions they and the Bakers would need for the journey. Ellen was riding with Cody, and Jared was driving the second wagon.

"Papa, how do we know what kind of stuff to buy?" Ellen asked.

"Darlin', I can't see as it would be that much different from what we had to take on the ship when I was at sea. There, we could augment our food with fish. For this trip, I've no doubt but that we'll have game along the way, deer, antelope, buffalo, birds, even squirrels and rabbits. Also, I've been told that there are a few trading posts where we'll be able to replenish some of our larder."

At Rafferty's, Cody bought flour, cornmeal, bacon, butter, potatoes, rice, beans, yeast, dried fruit, crackers, dried meat, dried vegetables, sugar, coffee, baking soda and baking powder.

STOPPING in Ballwin on the way back, they left a wagon, oxen, and the food supplies with Lon so he could prepare for the trip. Then they went back to the farm to make their own final preparations.

"We must be very careful in choosing what to take," Cody said. "If the wagon weighs more than two thousand pounds, it will put too much of a strain on the oxen."

"Papa the three of us weigh over four hundred pounds," Jared pointed out.

"Precisely, that's why we'll never have more than one person in the wagon at a time. You and I will ride the horses most of the time. Ellen, I'm afraid you're going to be the one driving the wagon. Do you think you can do that?"

"Papa, I know I can do it."

"I know you can, too, sweetheart, or I wouldn't ask you."

"Let's begin by choosing what we must have, as well as what we can take with us. We have to have farming equipment—a plow, an auger, a rake, and a scythe. We'll need a saw and an axe, and of course, cooking utensils and clothes."

"What about furniture?"

"We can bring three of the kitchen chairs, but not the table. Two lanterns."

"Mama's armoire?" Ellen asked.

Cody shook his head. "I'm afraid not."

"But Mama loved it so," Ellen said.

"I know she did, sweetheart, and I would give anything if we could take it. It would be like having a little of your mother with us, but we just can't. It weighs too much."

"What about Mama's Bible? We can take that, can't we?"

"Absolutely we can take it. And when we read it, Lucinda will be with us."

13

BACK IN BALLWIN, ALONZO BAKER WAS GOING THROUGH the same thing with Norma, telling his wife the limitations of what they would be able to take with them.

"Lon, what do you mean we can't take our bed?" Norma asked.

"The bed's too heavy. We can take the blankets, but not the bed. I'll make us another one when we get there."

"Do you think we're doin' the right thing?"

"Cap'n McNair explained it all to me," Lon said. "Land is no more than a dollar and a quarter an acre, Norma. I can build us a house, and because I'm a good mechanic, I can find jobs to do, that will help us until we can get our own business started."

"But we'll more 'n likely be the only colored people there, Lon. You know there ain't no colored folks in Oregon."

"Then maybe we'll just be people."

"But if we're not just people, if we're just colored people, what will happen to us?"

"Norma, I sailed around the world with Cap'n

McNair, 'n' I was the only colored man on his ship. He didn't treat me no different from how he treated all the other sailors. He's a good man, 'n' I trust him. Besides, he was married to Miss Lucinda, 'n' you know'd her for her whole life. She was the one what give you your freedom when her mama 'n' papa died 'n' you came to her."

"You're right, Miss Lucinda 'n' I played together when we was little girls. 'N' if she was still alive 'n' makin' this long trip, I wouldn' have no question 'bout it at all. But she ain't still alive."

"No, she ain't. But Cap'n McNair is, 'n' I know he will treat us good, 'cause he always has treated us good. I mean, look at that wagon 'n the oxen he's done bought for us. He wouldn' do somethin' like that if he didn't really want us to go with him. 'N' he wouldn't be wantin' us to go with 'im if he warn't goin' to treat us good."

Norma was quiet for a moment.

"Norma, if you don't want to go, I won't make you go. I love you 'n' I love our baby girl, 'n' I want you 'n' Precious to be happy all the time. You tell me you want to stay here, 'n' that's what we'll do."

"You really want to go, don't you?"

"Yes, but what I want more is for you to be happy."

Norma smiled at her husband. "Big man, all it takes to make me happy is for you to be happy."

Lon returned her smile. "Then I'm a happy man."

WHEN CODY ARRIVED in front of Lon's house, Lon's wagon was already loaded. By prior arrangement, Cody, Jared, and Ellen were going to have breakfast with Lon and Norma. Lon and Precious, came out to meet them.

"Norma's made us a big breakfast," Lon said. "Come

on in 'n' eat, it's prob'ly goin' to be the last one we'll eat around a table for a good while."

"Hello, Precious, sweetheart," Ellen said with a warm smile. "Are you ready to make this trip?"

"Mama said this will be a long, long trip," Precious said.

"Yes, it will be, but I think it will be exciting too, don't you?"

"Uh, huh," Precious replied. "Daddy, will there be any little girls for me to play with?"

Lon was quiet for a moment. He was certain there would be other children on the wagon train, but he was equally certain they would all be white children, and he didn't know whether any of them would want to play with his daughter or not.

"I don't know, sweetheart, I guess we'll just have to see."

Ellen was aware of the uncomfortable pause and response.

"I'm a girl, Precious, and if you can't find anyone else, I'll play with you."

Precious laughed. "You aren't a girl, you're a lady."

"But aren't ladies, girls?"

"Yes. All right, if I can't find any girls to play with, I'll play with you, even if you are a big girl."

Norma had fixed flapjacks, eggs, bacon, grits, and coffee.

"Well now, this is a feast fit for a king," Jared said with a broad grin as he surveyed the table.

THE McNAIR and Baker families weren't the only ones preparing to leave St. Louis by wagon. In the Hyde Park Neighborhood of the city, sometimes called Dutchtown,

Harm and Gretchen Schultz were preparing to leave as well. By the time Harm had loaded his pot, brewing kettle and air-lock, and two crates of hops rootstock, which he hoped would produce a hundred acres of hops, there was room for little else. Gretchen took the news that she would be able to take very little, with the stoicism that was indicative of her.

"Liebchen, when our brewery is going, I will buy you anything you want," Harm said. "Come, I wish to show you something."

Harm led Gretchen to the front of the wagon, then showed her a board in the floor.

"Beneath this board is our money. If you must get money, do not let anyone else see."

"I will be most careful, my husband."

WITH THE WES POLLARD COMPANY AT CASTLE ROCK

"Why do they call it Castle Rock?" Sean asked.

"Because it looks like a castle," Darcy said.

"You mean King Arthur lived in something like that?"

Darcy chuckled. "Well, not quite like that."

"Darcy, you'd better get used to young people asking a lot of questions," Pearl said. "When you start teaching school, children will be asking you all sorts of questions."

"I don't mind, Mama. I'm looking forward to it," Darcy said. "That's why I went to school to be a teacher."

The wagons were stopped and in a circle at the Castle Rock camping ground. They weren't really at Castle Rock, because that formation was at least five miles away from where they were parked.

"I just hope there is a school for you when we get there," Pearl said. "I know how badly you want to teach."

"There'll be one, there has to be," Ian said. "There are too many kids making this trip now, not only on this train, but on all the others. And if there isn't one yet, you can just bet that a school will be one of the first things built. That, and a church."

"Until then, I'll teach Sean and Connor," Darcy said with a big smile.

"Ha!" Connor said. "I'd like to see you teach me somethin'."

"You're right, you might be too dumb to teach," Darcy teased.

Mel Pollard was walking around the circle of wagons, checking in with all the travelers.

"And how are the Clintons doing?" he asked, as he approached their wagon.

"We're doing fine, thank you, Mr. Pollard," Pearl said.

"Mr. Pollard, is there a schoolhouse where we're goin'?" Sean asked.

"Well, to be honest with you, young man, I don't know whether there is or not," Pollard replied.

"I hope there ain't."

"You mean you hope there *isn't*," Darcy corrected. "And right there is the perfect reason why there should be a school."

Pollard laughed. "You'd better listen to your big sister, Sean."

"How long will we be staying here?" Ian asked.

"We'll be getting underway first thing after we have a bite to eat and get the teams hitched up," Pollard said.

14

LITCHFIELD, ILLINOIS

IN LITCHFIELD, ILLINOIS, JOHN AND ETHYL JOYCE WERE sitting on the front porch of their house. Actually, it wasn't their house anymore, as they had recently sold it to raise money to go west.

"I just wish that I could be as sure as you are that we're doing the right thing," Ethyl said.

"Darlin', we can buy cheap land out there," John said. "Neither one of us has any family here, so what is there to keep us from going?"

"But Emma is only eight years old. I just can't imagine how hard this trip is going to be on her."

John laughed. "Ethyl, she'll make the trip easier than we will. She's young, healthy, and a ball of energy. Why, I expect it will be quite an adventure for her."

"I do hope you're right."

"I know I'm right. I've already spoken to her about it, and she's excited about going."

"The wagon train is forming up in St. Louis?" Ethyl asked.

"Yes."

"How long will it take us to get to St. Louis?"

"About three days. There we'll join up with the others who are going, and we'll camp until the train is formed up and we're ready to move out."

"Daddy, will there be any little girls my age?" Emma asked, having come out onto the porch then.

"I'm sure there will be, sweetheart, as they want as many as forty wagons to go together. There's bound to be a girl close to your age."

"I hope so," Emma said. "It would be nice to have a friend."

ST. LOUIS

Tim and Anita Murray were already in St. Louis. Just married, they had made the decision together to join a wagon train, going to the new state of Oregon.

"Green beans, carrots, and corn are what we'll grow to market," Tim said. "But we'll also be able to grow everything we'll need for our own use. We'll plant a big garden."

"That'll be my job, and I'm going to grow potatoes, onions, and sweet peas in the garden," Anita said. "Oh, and some blackberries and blueberries too."

"Then you can make a black and blue pie," Tim said.

Anita smiled. "I plan to. That is, if I can find someone who'll eat it."

"Oh, I think I can help you there."

Anita laughed. "I thought you might."

"Anita, thank you for agreeing to do this," Tim said.

"You are my husband. Wherever you go, I go," Anita

replied with a smile. "Besides, I think it will be an exciting adventure."

FENTON, MISSOURI

"You're twenty-one years old," David Sullivan said to his daughter, Rosie. "You are old enough to make your own decision, you can go with us, or you can stay."

"But we hope you choose to go with us," Nellie added.

"I choose to go," Rosie said. "All of the men I know are spineless and dull. Any man I might meet in Oregon is bound to have some gumption, or he wouldn't be there in the first place. Besides," she added, "I would miss you terribly."

Nellie pulled her daughter to her in an embrace. "Oh, darling, I am so glad you'll be going with us. I don't know what I would do without you."

ST. LOUIS – APRIL 20, 1859

There were thirty-nine wagons already assembled when Cody and Lon arrived at LeClede's Landing. For the moment, the wagons were lined up in three parallel lines. The people were gathered in several conversation groups, getting to know each other. Cody and Jared dismounted, and Ellen climbed down from their wagon. Lon was just behind Cody, and he and Norma climbed down as well. Lon lifted Precious down from the wagon, and as soon as he did, Precious ran over to take Ellen's hand.

"Precious, you get back here and don't be botherin' Miss Ellen," Norma called out to her.

"Oh, she's fine, Norma," Ellen said.

"And you said you would play with me if there aren't any little girls for me to play with."

"I did indeed," Ellen said with a big smile. "Because we're real good friends, aren't we, Precious?"

"Yes."

"What did you say?" Norma asked.

"I said we're real good friends."

"No, you said yes. Is that how you speak to an adult? What are you supposed to say?"

"Yes, ma'am," Precious corrected.

"That's better."

"Hey, what are them colored folks doin' here?" a man asked in a loud, and obnoxious voice. "We ain't got no room in this train for no coloreds."

The man who spoke had a beak nose and dark, shining eyes. His face had a dry and scaly look.

"Who are you?" Cody asked.

"The name is Laycock, Peter Laycock," the man answered.

"Well, Laycock, *Mister* Baker and I have been friends for a very long time, and I've invited him to come with me. Do you have a problem with that?"

Cody spoke with authority, as someone who was used to command. Laycock inherently knew that he didn't want to push this issue any further.

"No, I reckon as long as you can keep 'im out of trouble, it'll be all right."

"Oh? And just what sort of trouble do you expect?"

"I don't have no idea what kind of trouble, I just know that colored folks seems to always be gettin' into one kind of trouble 'n' then another."

By now, several who had been standing nearby, stopped what they were doing so they could follow the conversation between Cody and Laycock.

"Laycock, Mister Baker is minding his own business, and I suggest that you do the same. Right now, you seem to be the only one who is causing any trouble," Cody said.

Laycock glared at Cody for a moment longer, then walked away. Another man came over to Cody then.

"I like the way you handled that." He extended his hand. "The name is Atwood, Joe Atwood. My wife, Cindy and I will be makin' this journey as well."

"It's good meeting you, Mr. Atwood."

"You may have noticed the cattle we have gathered," Atwood said.

Cody chuckled. "It's hard not to see them."

"Six hunnert of 'em. Three hunnert of 'em belong to me, three hunnert of 'em belong to Phil Puckett. We've gone together, that is, Puckett, 'n' me, 'n' we've hired us five cowboys who'll be lookin' after the cattle."

"That's probably a pretty good idea, having men to watch over the cattle," Cody said.

"Yes, sir, I figured we'd have enough to do, just lookin' after our wagon 'n' team."

Over the next hour, Cody walked among the gathered wagons, meeting people and introducing himself.

He met the young recently married couple, Tim and Anita Murray. They were going west for the adventure of it. Craig and Millie Patterson hoped to start a restaurant. Luke and Alice Taylor were about Cody's age. Luke was a cabinet maker.

As Cody approached the next wagon, the man and woman appeared to be in their thirties. She was a very attractive woman he noticed. They were speaking in German.

Cody spoke to them.

"*Guten Morgen. Mein name ist Cody McNair. Es sieht so aus, als würden wir diese Reise gemeinsam machen.*"

"*Bist du Deutscher?*" the woman asked.

"No, I'm not German, but I was a sea captain and I have been to Germany many times."

"Ah, I see. And to answer your question, *Ja*, we will be making this trip together," the man said. "I am Harm Schultz, this is my *frau*, Gretchen."

"What do you plan on doing in the new country?" Cody asked.

Harm smiled. "I will make beer."

Cody returned the smile. "Well now, I think I can say without fear of contradiction, that everyone in this train will be glad that you are making this trip with us."

As Cody continued on down the line of wagons, he met Phil Puckett, who was traveling alone, John and Ethyl Joyce and their eight-year-old daughter Emma, David, and Nellie Sullivan, and their twenty-one-year-old daughter, Rosie, Dale and Jane Guthrie, and their sixteen-year-old son, Drew.

A short while later, as the travelers continued to visit with each other, Tom Murchison approached Cody.

"Ah, Captain McNair," Murchison said.

"Mr. Murchison, I thought you weren't going with us."

"I won't be going," Murchison said. "I'm just here to help you get organized. The first thing you'll need to do is elect someone who will act as a captain for your trip. And as I have processed most of you, I feel qualified to make a suggestion."

"And just who would that be?" Laycock asked, standing close enough by to have overheard the comment.

"My suggestion would be Cody McNair."

"McNair? Yes, I heard you call him captain. What gives you the right to select the captain for us?"

"You misunderstand, sir. I called him captain, because he was a sea-captain for some time. And it is for that reason, that he has experience in command and leadership, that I would recommend him. But of course, it is up to you to elect your own leader."

"I sailed under Cap'n McNair," Lon Baker said. "I think he would make a very good cap'n for us."

"Thank you, Lon," Cody said

"You're a colored man," Laycock said. "What makes you think you even have a voice in this matter?"

"Tell me, Laycock, just what makes you think that he doesn't have a voice in this matter?" Murchison asked.

"Coloreds can't vote in any elections. That's the law."

"This isn't just any election, and that law doesn't apply here," Murchison said. "And I am speaking as a lawyer, Mr. Laycock."

"Ah, well, he's only one vote anyway, so it won't make that much of a difference. But just so you know, I will be standin' for election as well, and I think I'll win."

"Just so *you* know, Mr. Laycock, I intend to vote for Captain McNair," Puckett said. Puckett had been standing close enough to overhear the conversation, too.

"If McNair is good enough for Mr. Murchison to suggest him, then I vote for him too," Tim Murray said.

"Me too," David Sullivan added.

Harm had come to join the conversation, and he also voiced his support for Cody.

When the final vote was taken, Peter Laycock voted for himself, and was supported by Raymond Pugh. Everyone else voted for Cody.

"We'll leave at first light in the morning," Cody said, giving his first order. "So, I recommend that we have breakfast before sunrise. We should reach Independence within two weeks and once there, we'll hire a guide."

"Shouldn't we hire a guide before we leave?" someone asked.

Cody shook his head. "Because Independence is the jumping off place there will be several guides there for hiring. And as far as getting from here to Independence, I have a map that will take us there, and if there's one thing I can do well, it's read a map."

There were a few more questions, and introductions as the men, women, and children, continued to visit.

"Captain McNair?" the address came from a tall, slender, bald-headed man.

"Yes?"

"My name is Owen, sir. Reverend E.D. Owen, and I would like your permission to conduct church services ever' Sunday for our long trip."

"That would be fine, Reverend. We have an arduous journey ahead of us. I think we could use a little help from the Lord."

"GRETCHEN, I think Captain McNair will be a good man," Harm said.

"*Ja*, I think so as well."

"It is good to have such a man as our leader."

"I fear Mr. Laycock might give us some trouble," Gretchen said.

"I have known such men as Laycock and such men as Captain McNair. If Laycock becomes too difficult, Captain McNair will strike him down *wie ein käfer*."

Gretchen laughed. "Like a bug, *Ja*, I think so too."

For the next few hours people came to enter their

names in Cody's journal. There were sounds of conversation, and the squeals of children at play.

Ellen McNair and Rosie Sullivan, the two single women who were closest in age, formed a quick friendship, sharing stories and laughter. As the sun set, the wagon park was permeated with the aroma of suppers being cooked. Then, finally it grew quiet as people took to their beds. Somewhere one of those who had signed up, Craig Patterson, began playing a guitar and singing, *Home Sweet Home*.

Cody wondered how many nights they would have that were as peaceful as this one.

15

ON THE OREGON TRAIL, SEVERAL HUNDRED MILES WEST of where the McNair wagon train was being formed, the wagon train led by Elmer Matthews, was camped for the night.

"I'm tellin' you, there's someone in this train that's a damn thief," Ed Drury said. "They was a hunnert dollars that was took from my wagon."

"Yeah," Sam Woodward said. "I've lost fifty dollars my ownself."

"You two is lucky. I had two hunnert dollars took from me," Frank Edmonston said.

Matthews turned to their trail guide.

"What about it? This ain't the first train you've took across the country," Matthews said. "Does this happen often?"

"That's pretty common. There's been some stealin' on just about ever' train I been with."

"I don't doubt it," Maurice Cain said. "Especially if you was there."

"What are you sayin'?" their guide replied, defensively.

"Yes, Maurice, what are you saying?" Matthews asked.

"I'm sayin' that I seen this son of a bitch comin' out of Edmonston's wagon. I thought it was some strange 'n' was goin' to ask Edmonston about it. Now I know what it was. Our guide is stealin' from 'im, 'n' there ain't no doubt in my mind but what he's the one what stole'd from Drury 'n' Woodward too."

"You son of a bitch!" the guide shouted, reaching for his pistol.

"He's got a gun!"

The man they had hired to guide and protect them, fired twice, and as Cain collapsed, he ran to his horse, which was saddled, mounted, then galloped off into the night.

Edmonston knelt beside Cain, then looked up with a pained expression on his face.

"Maurice is dead."

"What'll we do now without a guide, Elmer?"

"A guide like him, we don't need," Matthews replied. "Ken, I know you ain't no actual preacher, but you been doing the praying for us. Would you mind coming with me while I go tell Gertrude what happened to her husband?"

"What's going to happen to her now?" someone asked. "Here she is, half-way to Oregon, and nobody to look after her?"

"Wrong," Edmonston said. "We'll all look after her."

INDEPENDENCE, MISSOURI

When Matt Logan was in Independence, he always stayed in a boarding house owned by the widow, Della

Hines. Mrs. Hines was in her sixties, and because her late husband had been a trail guide, those trail guides who were in Independence waiting for their next trip west, made up the bulk of her guests.

"And how is the most handsome guide on the plains this morning?" Della teased Matt who was having breakfast.

"Ah, now, Mrs. Hines, you're going to make all the other guides jealous. Unless," Matt stopped in mid-sentence, and laughed. "Wait a minute, you say that to all the guides, don't you?"

"Well, as you know, my own sweet, late husband was a trail guide, so you might say I just have a soft spot in my heart for all of you."

"Then to answer your question, this, uh, *handsome* guide is doing very well, thanks to the great breakfast you provided this morning. Flapjacks, ham and over-easy eggs."

"Nothing's too good for my boys," Della said, beaming under the praise.

"Logan? Matt Logan?" someone called from the door of the dining room.

"I'm Matt Logan," Matt said, raising his hand.

"I have a telegram for you, sir." The telegram messenger was a boy in his mid-teens. He was wearing a high-crowned, billed cap upon which were the words "Western Union".

Matt took the telegram, then gave the boy a quarter.

"Thank you, sir," the boy said with a happy smile.

Matt took the telegram from the envelope.

CAPTAIN MCNAIR TRAIN FORTY ONE WAGONS
REACH INDEPENDENCE THREE WEEKS STOP
WILL BE GOOD FOR YOU STOP MURCHISON

Matt smiled, then folded the telegram over and put it in his pocket.

"Another job?" Della asked.

"Possibly. It's a lead on a job from Mr. Murchison."

16

ST. LOUIS – APRIL 20, 1859

FORTY-ONE WAGONS WERE GATHERED AT LECLEDE'S Landing ready to get underway. Cody's journal indicated ninety-one adults, of which thirty-one were women, and fifty-three were men. In addition, there were twenty-nine children, ranging in ages from two to fourteen. There were more between fourteen and eighteen, but as they would be doing the jobs of adults, Cody didn't really consider them children.

There were several relatives who wouldn't be making the journey, and they were at the landing for the tearful goodbyes. As Cody watched them, he couldn't help but think of his own poignant leave-taking of Lucinda, though it wasn't the same thing since he had said goodbye, not to her, but to her grave.

He hated to pull the wagon people away from their loved ones, but he had no choice—it was time to get underway.

"Heah!" Cody shouted, popping the whip over the

heads of his team of oxen. As they started forward, Cody, who was mounted, put the bull whip back in its holder as Ellen handled the reins. Cody then rode back along the long line of wagons watching as gradually all slack was taken up and the entire train got underway.

As the forty-one wagons and the six hundred head of cattle moved down Delmar Avenue, they stretched out for a little over a quarter of a mile. More than five thousand of St. Louis's 160,000 residents were turned out to watch the grand spectacle of wagons, cattle, and horsemen. Cody rode up and down the line making certain that all were proceeding at pace. There were five men, Frank and Gus Wiley, Chub Collins, Deacon Cox, and Sid Beltrain, riding alongside the cattle, having been specifically hired to tend to the herd.

On his return to the front of the train, when Cody rode by Lon Baker's wagon his daughter, Precious, stood on the seat by her mother and, waving, flashed a smile at him.

"Hello, Capman M'nare," she called.

"Hello, Precious. Are you helping your mama drive?"

"Yes, sir, I'm helping," Precious said proudly.

THE WAGON FOLLOWING the one being driven by Lon belonged to John and Ethyl Joyce. Before the end of the first day, their daughter, Emma, had become friends with Precious, who was the closest child to her same age. They would sometimes walk together alongside the wagons, while at other times they would ride together, either on the Baker wagon or the Joyce wagon.

When they stopped for lunch, Peter Laycock complained to Cody about it.

"It ain't right, havin' a little white girl ridin' with coloreds like that," he said.

"I see nothing wrong with it," Cody said.

"You was elected captain of this train, if you can't see nothin' wrong with it, you got no business bein' the captain."

"It looks to me like Precious and Emma have become friends," Cody said. "It's going to be a long, hard trip, especially for children. I think it's a good thing when they can make new friends."

"Well, it ain't fittin', I can tell you that right now," Laycock said with a grunt of disapproval. He walked back along the line of wagons, passing Precious and Emma who were laughing and playing some game together in Lon's wagon, totally unaware that they had been the subject of a complaint.

Over the first few days, travel was easy as they had good roads. Also, as they passed through farmland, they were able to buy fresh eggs and freshly churned butter. Most of the travelers had been strangers when they met, but gradually, friendships began to develop.

On the first Sunday morning, the Reverend Owen conducted a church service that was attended by most of the travelers. Because Lon Baker and his family were in attendance, Peter Laycock, and a couple of others, refused to participate.

On the sixth day out, one of the men came hurrying up to Cody. "Captain McNair, Captain McNair," he called.

Cody, who was riding alongside his wagon stopped and turned to see who was calling him.

"Ditmore, isn't it?" Cody asked.

"Yes, Clay Ditmore. I've got a big problem."

"What's wrong?"

"My wagon's broke down. The team can't pull it, 'cause my doubletree has come apart."

"Are you going to be able to repair it?"

"I don't know. I'm not handy with things like that. I'm a store clerk, and I'm planning on opening my own store when we get to where we're going. That is, if I'm able to get there."

"I've got the answer to your problem," Cody said.

Cody called up to Lon, whose wagon was second in line, and just behind his own.

"Lon, Mr. Ditmore needs your service."

"You're asking the colored man?" Ditmore asked, in surprise.

"Do you want your wagon fixed or not?"

"Yes, of course I do."

"Lon Baker is the best all-around repairman I know. If he can fix your wagon, does it really matter whether or not he's colored?"

Ditmore chuckled. "No, I don't guess it does."

"What's the problem, Cap'n?" Lon asked as he came up to join them.

"Mr. Ditmore has a problem with his doubletree."

"That I do, Mr. Baker," Ditmore said. "Captain McNair says he thinks you can repair it, and if you can, I'd be much obliged."

"I'll do what I can, sir."

Cody, Lon, and Clay Ditmore headed back down the line of slowly moving wagons until they saw that one of the wagons was sitting off to the side of the road while the other wagons slowly passed it by.

"Can he help us, Clay?" an anxious looking woman asked. An equally anxious looking young boy was sitting beside her.

"Ma'am, I'm goin' to have to unhitch the team," Lon said.

"Oh, Clay, what's happening?"

"Hand me the reins, Edna," Ditmore said. "Let Mr. Baker unhitch the team so he can get a good look at the problem."

The team was disconnected, and Lon began to examine it as the other wagons in the train continued to roll by. The people in the wagons, or those riding or walking alongside, looked over in concerned curiosity.

"Can you fix it, Lon?" Cody asked.

"I can splice it. That'll hold it until we get to where he can get a new one."

"All right, Lon, do that," Cody said. "Mr. Ditmore, we'll be in Independence in a few more days. Do you have enough money to buy a new doubletree and to pay Mr. Baker to replace it for you?"

"Yes, I do."

"It's about time for dinner, so I'm going to stop the train for an early noon break, so the others don't get too far ahead. Come on up and join us as soon as you can."

"Thanks, Captain," Ditmore said.

"I'm not the one to thank."

"Let me amend that. Thanks, Captain, for connecting me with Mr. Baker, the man I *do* have to thank."

17

Just under three weeks after leaving St. Louis, the McNair Company reached Independence. There, Ditmore bought a new doubletree and paid Lon to put it on for him.

"Pa, you know what might be a good idea," Jared said.

"What's that?"

"What if we were to buy about ten doubletrees, half a dozen wheels, a couple of axles, some grease, and anything else Mr. Baker thinks we could use? That way, when someone needed it, they could buy it from us, and Mr. Baker could do the work. We could make some money from selling the parts, and Mr. Baker could make some money from doing the work."

Cody smiled broadly. "That's a good idea. You know what, you'd make a good hand even if you weren't my son."

When they told Lon what they planned to do, Lon thought it was an excellent idea, but had a few suggestions of his own. "Lot of times, all the wheels need is a new tire. You might get some iron bands about two feet long, two inches wide, and an eighth of an inch thick. Also, some bolts and nuts. I've got a drill and some bits that I can use."

MATT LOGAN WAS PLAYING cards in the Trail Head Saloon when a friend came in to see him.

"Matt, they's a new wagon train just come into town. Could be the one you're lookin' for."

"Thanks, Sam," Matt replied. "Boys, deal me out. I've got work to do."

"Which is also a good excuse for you to quit a winner," one of the players said.

"Damn, Carl, let 'im go," one of the other players said with a good-natured chuckle. "The longer he plays the more of our money he's gonna take."

After Matt left the saloon, he saw a long line of wagons parked along Necessary Road. When he walked up to the first wagon, he saw an exceptionally pretty young woman standing by the oxen team, as if she were talking to them. He stopped for just a moment to take in the beautiful sight, then he drew a deep breath and approached her.

"Excuse me, Miss, but would this be the Captain McNair train?"

The woman turned around quickly, caught unaware of his presence.

"Uh, yes, that would be my father," she said.

"Could you tell me where I can find him?"

"Yes, he is at the wagon fitters, getting some repair parts."

"Thank you."

Ellen watched him walk away, embarrassed at having been caught talking to oxen.

· · ·

CODY, Jared, and Lon returned to the same wagon outfitter to buy the spare parts they had discussed.

"If you don't mind my asking, how do you plan to take all this along with you?" Ralph Wyatt, the proprietor asked.

"We've got several wagons, so I was planning on spreading the parts out among them," Cody suggested.

"You could do that, I suppose," Wyatt said, "but I've got a hoodlum wagon here. It's actually a two-wheeled cart, but it's big enough to carry what you've just bought, and you won't need a team. It's light enough so you can just hitch it up behind your wagon."

"How much do want for it?"

"Twenty-five dollars."

"You've got a deal, sir," Cody said.

When Cody and Jared stepped outside, they were met by a tall, muscular-looking man with dark hair and dark eyes. He was clean-shaven and looked to be in his mid-twenties.

"Would you be Captain Cody McNair?" the young man asked.

"I am, and who are you?"

"My name's Matt Logan, sir," he said as he extended his hand.

Cody paused for a second, then extended his hand as well.

"What can I do for you, Mr. Logan?"

"You're taking a wagon train to the Oregon Territory?"

"I am. Do you wish to join the train?"

"Yes, in a matter of speaking," Matt answered, a smile crossing his face.

"A matter of speaking? I don't understand."

Matt reached into his pocket. "I have a telegram here from Mr. Tom Murchison. He suggested that I look you up and offer you my services as a guide."

"Mr. Logan, I, uh, am looking for a guide. But you seem a little younger than I thought my guide would be."

"Jim Bridger was seventeen when he came to the mountains as a trapper. I'm twenty-three, and I spent some time with Jim Bridger. And I've already taken more than just a few previous trains to Oregon."

Cody smiled, broadly. "All right, then that's good enough for me."

JARED HOOKED his horse up to the hoodlum wagon and he drove it as Cody, Lon, and Matt rode alongside until they returned to the others.

There were people scattered out along the three rows of parked wagons, many visiting, some making minor adjustments, a few just resting.

"People, people, people!" Cody shouted. "Gather around, we need a meeting."

"What do you want, McNair?" Peter Laycock asked in a derisive voice. "Just 'cause you got yourself elected captain, that don't mean you can call a meetin' anytime you want. Most of us has got somethin' to do."

"I want twenty-three dollars and eighty cents from you, Laycock. Then you can do whatever it is you have to do," Cody said. "In fact, I want twenty-three dollars and eighty cents from every wagon in the train."

"And just why the hell should we give you twenty-three dollars and eighty cents?"

"Mr. Laycock, I do not appreciate anyone swearing in front of my daughter, and I'm quite sure the other

87

gentlemen of this train don't like it in front of their wives and daughters, so I'll have no more of it."

"Why should we give you twenty-three dollars?" Laycock asked. That wasn't exactly an apology, but he did omit the swear-word this time.

"And eighty cents," Cody added. Then he answered Laycock's question. "You were all informed when you joined this train that we would be hiring a guide for one thousand dollars. I have just made that hire and I want to introduce you to him now."

Cody held out his arm toward Matt.

"Folks, meet Matt Logan. Mr. Logan will guide us to our final destination."

"Him?" Laycock replied, the word little more than a scoff. "Shouldn't he be in grade school?"

Peter Laycock, who had been very negative about everything from the moment Cody had been elected train captain over him, laughed at his own mocking comment. Howard Raines, one of the few friends Laycock had made, laughed as well.

"What do you know about the Lolo Pass, Mr. Laycock?" Matt asked. "Devil's Gate, the Dalles? What's the only way through the Blue Mountains?"

"Well, I... uh don't know."

"Well, I do know, Mr. Laycock, and as I told Captain McNair, I've taken previous trains through."

"That's good enough for me," Ditmore said.

"Me too," Joe Atwood added.

"Yes, I say we hire him," Tim Murray said.

"I know I'd feel better having Mr. Logan guiding us," John Joyce said.

There was universal agreement from all the others.

"And I say we're crazy for hirin' someone this young," Laycock insisted.

"If you feel that way, Mr. Laycock, you may want to withdraw from this train and find another more to your liking," Cody suggested. "In fact, I would prefer it if you did leave. I've no wish to be fighting with you for the entire trip to Oregon."

"I'll stay," Laycock said as he kicked at a clod of dirt.

"Then we'll have no more complaints coming from you—not about Mr. Baker and not about Mr. Logan. Mr. Logan, would you like to address the company?"

"Yes, thank you, Captain McNair. First of all, I want to thank you folks for hiring me. From here, it's about nine miles to Kansas City and that's where we'll cross the Missouri River. If we leave now, we'll be there in time for supper and we can cross first thing in the morning."

"Mama, will we have to swim across the river?" Emma asked.

"Oh, I don't think it'll come to that," Ethyl Joyce said.

"Can Precious eat supper with us? I ate dinner with them."

"Yes, of course she can if her parents don't mind."

"They won't mind," Emma said. "They like me," she added with a big smile.

89

18

CASPER TRADING POST

THOUGH THERE WERE VERY FEW TOWNS ALONG THE Oregon Trail, there were trading posts and settlements. One such settlement was Casper, which took its name from Fort Casper, which was located on the North Platte River. Casper survived by providing ferry service across the river, as well as needed supplies to the wagon trains.

One service, the need of which could be argued, was the Wagon Trail Saloon. One of the customers of the saloon was the trail guide, Dudley Dace.

After the incident with the Matthews Company, Dace had escaped to the east, knowing full well that the train would not turn around to pursue him.

He hadn't intended to kill Cain. The Matthews wagon train wasn't the first wagon train he had pilfered from. He had always been careful not to take everything his victim had. He took enough to augment his fee, but not enough to arouse suspicion. But it had been his intention for this to be his last train to guide and he wanted enough money to let him start a freighting business.

But he dipped too deeply, and he got caught. And as a result of that, he had killed a man.

His plan of starting a freighting company to serve the western settlers would no longer work, because he was a wanted man. But if he could put together enough money, he could go back East somewhere, to perhaps Chicago or New York, where no one would have heard of Dudley Dace.

To do that, however, would take a lot more money, so he had come up with a plan. It had been recommended in all the guidebooks and articles, that those traveling west should have at least two hundred-fifty dollars in cash. This, the guidebooks said, was the minimum amount of money necessary to get established in a new location.

That would be an average of about eight thousand dollars per train, and possibly more. It was because of this that he conceived a plan to rob the wagon trains as they came over the trail.

In order to do this, though, he would need to recruit some men to ride with him. There were enough failed trappers and gold prospectors, men who had come West with a wagon train but quit in disillusionment, and deserters from the army, to make up a gang with sufficient strength to deal with any wagon train. They would have the advantage that the people with the wagon trains would not be expecting an attack by white men.

Shortly after he arrived in Casper, Dace saw someone who might be useful to him. He invited Emile Potter to have a drink with him.

"Whiskey," Potter told the bartender.

"I'll pay for it," Dace said.

"You're buyin'?" Potter asked.

"I am."

"Hah. Who do you want me to kill?" Potter joked.

"Funny you would bring that up."

"Funny I would bring it up? What do you mean? Wait, are you sayin' you do have someone you want me . . ."

Dace held up his hand to stop Potter in mid-sentence. "Let me tell you what I have in mind."

"Is there money in it?" Potter asked.

Dace smiled. "Oh, yes, a great deal of money."

"Then I'm listenin'."

THE MEL POLLARD TRAIN – TWIN MOUNDS, MAY 2ND 1859

The wagon train led by Mel Pollard, had already been underway for more than two months.

One morning, just as the members of the train were awakening from their night's sleep, the encampment was rent by a woman's scream.

"Pearl, what is it? What's wrong?" Edna Piercy, from the neighboring wagon, yelled.

"It's Sean!" Pearl Clinton cried. "He's . . . he's dead!"

News of the death of the nine-year-old boy spread quickly throughout the train.

"We'll need to bury him, fast," Mel Pollard said. "There is no doubt but that he died of cholera."

"No, it was pneumonia," Ian Clinton said.

"Man, get your son buried as fast as you can," Pollard said. "Once cholera gets established, it could wipe out an entire train in a matter of days."

. . . .

IAN AND CONNOR dug the grave. When others in the wagon train offered to help dig the grave, Pollard forbade it. He also prevented anyone except the Clinton family from taking part in the burial. Only Ian, Pearl, Darcy, and Connor were able to pray over the young boy's grave.

But the worst was yet to come. As the wagon train made up to leave, Pollard came to see Ian.

"You will keep your wagon here for twenty-four hours," Pollard said.

"What? What do you mean?"

"I will not take the chance on your family infecting the rest of this train."

"What are you talking about? None of us are ill."

"If you are still not sick tomorrow morning, you can try and catch up with us. But I'll not let you near the train until then."

Later that morning Ian Clinton watched the wagon train depart without his family.

"Oh, Ian, what are we going to do?" Pearl asked.

"We're going to stay here until tomorrow morning, then we're going to rejoin the train," Ian said, resolutely.

93

19

THE NEXT MORNING THE CLINTON FAMILY BROKE CAMP early in an attempt to rejoin the Pollard Company. They moved along as quickly as the oxen would allow them to proceed, but they didn't catch up with the wagon train. That night, they sat around a campfire eating a supper of bacon, potatoes, and biscuits.

"It seems so quiet and lonely without the others," Darcy said.

"Ian, are we doing the right thing?" Pearl asked.

"Pearl, m' darlin', we talked about this before we left Paducah, and we agreed that going to Oregon and starting our own farm was the thing to do. They tell us land is only a dollar twenty-five an acre."

"Yes, but that was when we were with other wagons. We're by ourselves now. I wonder if it wouldn't be better to go back."

"Ma, no," Connor said. "We've got to go on, now. Besides, it's just as far back as it is goin' ahead, and this way, if we get a good start every mornin' and go until after sunset, we'll catch up with the others within a week. Right, Pop?"

"What if they won't take us back? They kicked us out once," Pearl said.

"When they see that we don't have the sickness, they'll let us stay," Ian insisted.

"All right, if you say so," Pearl said, putting her hand on her husband's arm.

"I'm certain of it," Ian replied.

"You know what, Ian? We have made a wonderful family," Pearl said. "I miss Sean, terribly, but somehow I feel he will always be a part of us."

Ian squeezed her hand. "Of course, he will be, Pearlie. We'll always remember our little boy."

A gas bubble trapped in one of the logs in the fire popped almost as loudly as a gunshot and it startled everyone. Then, realizing what it was, they all laughed.

"It's time to get to bed," Ian said, stretching. "I want to . . ."

The entire family finished what he was going to say.

"Get started before sunup," they said in unison.

That night, as Darcy lay on her pallet in the wagon, she listened to a chorus of howling coyotes, chirping crickets, and hooting owls. The oxen could be heard chomping grass. This had become her regular nighttime symphony and, as it did every night, it lulled her to sleep.

"DARCY, why don't you and Connor get the breakfast fire going?" Pearl asked the next morning.

Darcy started gathering wood as Connor began building the fire. Pearl was rolling out biscuits, while Ian walked down to the Platte River to get a bucket of water.

When Ian came back, he sat the pail of water down,

then looked at Connor with a smile. "I know I said I wanted to get started early, but I just saw a deer. Get the rifles out of the wagon and let's go get 'im. We can eat off him for two weeks."

"All right!" Connor replied, the expression in his voice reflecting his enthusiasm.

"Ian, shouldn't you stay and have breakfast first?" Pearl asked.

"Ah, we'll be back before you and Darcy even have it cooked."

Connor climbed down from the wagon with the two rifles and, with a big smile spread across his face, handed one of them to his father.

"Let's go, son," Ian said.

"Yes, sir."

NEARBY, and for the moment unseen by any of the Clinton family, ten Indians were watching the morning tasks being performed. Hunting Bear, the leader of the group, held up his hand.

"Men gone," Hunting Bear said. "We will take women first, then when men come back, we kill them."

"Do we kill the women?" Mean to His Horses asked.

"We kill old woman, we keep young woman," Hunting Bear said.

"BE REAL QUIET NOW, we don't want to scare him off," Ian said as he and Connor approached the deer.

"Pa, I've hunted before," Connor said, miffed at being patronized.

Ian chuckled. "You've hunted them, but so far you haven't taken any of them."

"Yeah, well, it ain't been my fault," Connor said.

The two moved as quietly as they could, sneaking up on the deer.

"Shh, we're almost there," Ian said.

"MA, LOOK! INDIANS!" Darcy said as she saw several Indians coming toward them.

One of the Indians drew back his bow and loosed an arrow. It flew silently through the air, then buried itself almost half-shaft deep into Pearl's chest.

Darcy screamed.

"PA!" Connor shouted.

"That was Darcy, I heard it! We must get back to the wagon! Hurry!"

The two ran as fast as they could through the sage-brush and prickly pear.

"Pearl, Darcy, we're coming!" Ian shouted.

DARCY SAW her father lift his rifle to fire, but before he could pull the trigger, she heard a gunshot from one of the Indians, and her father dropped the rifle as he fell face down. Connor was next, and with a sickening heart, Darcy realized that she was all alone.

DARCY STOOD in shock as she looked down at the bodies of her mother, father, and brother. She was aware of the approaching Indians, but she made no effort to run. At this moment she would have welcomed the opportunity to join the souls of her family as they departed this life.

Two of the Indians came to her, and she closed her eyes waiting for death's final blow. But it didn't happen.

"Come," one of the Indians said.

That wasn't what she was expecting, and when she opened her eyes, she saw the two Indians beside her, and a third just in front of her.

"Come," the Indian said again.

The Indians to each side of her grabbed her arms, then lifted her up onto a horse, behind a rider. There was a blanket thrown over the horse's back, but no saddle.

As she sat astride a horse behind one of the Indian warriors, she turned to look back toward the wagon. There, she saw some of the warriors gathered around the bodies of her family, but she closed her eyes so she couldn't see what they were doing to their bodies.

With a loud yell that was more like a scream, the Indians mounted their horses and galloped away. Darcy had no choice but to wrap her arms around the waist of the Indian in front of her. As they galloped away from the scene, Darcy realized that she was going faster than she had ever gone in her entire life. She found the ride to be as frightening as the thought of what may lie before her.

Shortly thereafter, the sky was split with jagged streaks of lightning. Each flash of lightning was followed by a roar of thunder. Oddly enough, Darcy found the sudden thunderstorm to be consoling. In the lightning and thunder, she could believe that her family was speaking to her—telling her not to have fear, that they would keep watch over her.

The rain began coming down in thick, heavy drops. As the rain continued, the Indians slowed from a gallop to a trot and then to a walk. Her dress was soaked through, and the wind, blowing against her wet dress, made her quite cold. Involuntarily, she pulled herself closer to the Indian in front of her, seeking some warmth from his body.

The rain lasted for what Darcy judged to be about fifteen minutes, and within another fifteen minutes, they reached a small village, though Darcy thought that the gathering of tipis was more like an encampment, than an actual village.

There were some women here though, and some of them came out to stare at her. The expressions on the faces of the younger women were hostile, though the expression on the face of the oldest of the women seemed to be more compassionate than hostile.

The compassionate woman wrapped Darcy's now-shivering body, in a buffalo robe.

"Thank you," Darcy said, welcoming the warmth.

"I am Spirit Woman," the woman with the buffalo robe said.

"Oh, Spirit Woman, what is going to happen to me?"

"You come," Spirit Woman said, and she led Darcy into one of the tipis.

As Darcy sat huddled in the robe inside the tipi, Spirit Woman lit a fire, and soon the inside of the tipi was warmed.

"I was to be a schoolteacher," Darcy said. "Oh, dear Lord, what is to become of me now?"

WITH THE MCNAIR COMPANY

After breakfast, Cody, Matt, Lon, John Joyce, Clay Ditmore, Craig Patterson, and Luke Taylor, met to make plans as to how they would cross the Missouri River.

There were five cowboys with the train, and they were unattached to any wagon, as their job was to herd the six hundred head of cattle accompanying the train. Two of them were brothers, Frank and Gus Wiley, and they were standing on the bank of the river with the others.

"Mr. Logan, can we take the cattle across here?" Frank asked.

"Not here, but there is a good fording place about four miles upriver. It's marked with a couple of signs, so you should be able to find it easy enough. Our route will take us right by where you will be coming ashore on the Kansas side. Let us have one of your men to go with us, if we've passed by before you've crossed, we'll leave him there to tell you. If you don't see him, it means we haven't gotten there yet, so you can just hold up until we rejoin."

"All right," Frank said. "I'll get 'em started now."

The wagons could be ferried across the river on the steam ferry boat *Chippewa*. The *Chippewa* could carry twelve wagons and teams, per crossing, ten dollars for the wagon and two yokes of oxen, two more dollars per yoke beyond that. All of the wagons had six oxen, which meant it would cost them twelve dollars each.

There was also available for those who didn't want to pay twelve dollars, a flat boat that could carry one wagon and three yokes of oxen for four dollars. It was propelled by two men using long poles to pole the boat across.

"Cap'n, if you don't mind, I think I'm going to use the flat boat," Tim Murray said. "It's cheaper 'n' I would rather not spend the extra money."

"All right, I've got no problem with that," Cody said. "Since they can do that while the steam ferry is operating, I can't see as it would hold up the train, any."

Although Cody's wagon was normally first in the train, he held back, choosing to go on the last crossing so that he would be in position in case there was a problem. Lon Baker, Harm Schultz, and John Joyce would also remain on the Missouri side until the last trip across.

"Mama, can I go down with Precious and watch the ferry?" Emma asked.

"I don't know, I'm a little afraid to let you go."

"I'll watch over both of them," Norma offered.

"All right, in that case you can go. But you listen to what Miz Baker says, and you do what she tells you to do."

"Yes, ma'am," Emma said, then with a broad smile she reached out to take Precious' hand, and hand in hand, the two little girls started running down toward the landing.

"You two girls just stop right there," Norma called. "Wait on me."

Precious and Emma waited until Norma joined them.

ELLEN McNAIR WAS SITTING on the seat of the McNair wagon, watching as the other wagons drove out onto the flat deck of the *Chippewa*. Or at least, that was the illusion she was giving. Actually, she was watching Matt Logan as he was providing assistance to the wagons while they were loading. She wished she knew more about him. Would he stay with them when they reached Oregon, or would he find another train to guide? She found herself hoping that he would stay, but she realized that might be a false hope. This wasn't the first train he had guided, so the chances were, this wouldn't be his last.

What in the world has gotten into you? She asked herself. *You just met him.*

She may have just met him recently, but it could take

them as long as six months to get to the Willamette Valley in Oregon, so she would have plenty of time to get to know him better. And him, her.

She smiled at the thought.

She saw Matt raise his hand to stop a wagon that was about to drive onto the boat.

"Hold it up there!" Matt called.

"What do you mean stop? I've paid my fee," Peter Laycock said.

"Yes, sir, I know you have, but the boat's got all it can carry for this trip. You'll be first in line for the next one."

"You're gettin' a little high and mighty there, aren't you, Logan?"

"I'm just doing what I'm being paid to do," Matt said. He cupped his hands around his mouth and called out to the ferry pilot. "You're all loaded, Mr. Tate, take her away!"

The engine clattered and clanked, and the steam relief valve boomed like cannon fire as the sternwheel began slapping at the water. The boat backed away from the bank, then turned around and started toward the far shore, where at least two dozen wagons had already crossed, and were waiting.

Ellen had made some friends that she didn't particularly want to leave behind, but the one thing that had made her leaving somewhat easier, was that she had no particular man friend that she would be abandoning.

And with no man to have claim to her heart, she was left free to admire Matt Logan. And admire him she did. He was, she thought, a good-looking man, but it was more than looks that attracted her to him. She liked the way he handled himself. There was a confidence to his assumption of the role of guide.

Ellen particularly liked the way he handled Laycock.

Laycock was such an asshole. She laughed. Asshole was a word that she would never say aloud, but she could certainly think it, and it was a word that fit Mr. Laycock perfectly.

Laycock was first in line for the next trip over, and as he drove his wagon onto the boat, he was still complaining because he had not been on the first crossing.

As Tim Murray had said, he didn't intend to use the
steam ferry, and now the flatboat was ready to take him
across. The flatboat was propelled by two men, using
long poles.

"All right, Mr. Murray, we're ready for you now,"
Matt directed, then Matt took the harness of the lead
oxen and led the team onto the boat. With the wagon
loaded, Matt stepped ashore, and the boat pulled away.

The raft, which was barely large enough to accom-
modate the wagon and three yokes of oxen, began to
bounce in the choppy waves of the wake from the large
steamboat ferry.

"Oh, Tim," Anita said, reaching out to put her hand
on his arm. "I don't like this."

"Hold on, the steamboat's going a lot faster than we
are, so we'll be out of its wake, soon."

True to Tim's reassurance, the larger boat moved on,
and the wake waves stopped.

There would have been no further problem after that,
until the sternwheeler's relief valve made another

cannon-like boom, and that startled the oxen. The team moved toward the edge of the flatboat, throwing it out of balance so that it tipped up on its side. When it did so, the team slid off the boat into the water, pulling the wagon with it.

"Oh, Tim!" Anita screamed in panic.

ELLEN WAS WATCHING both the steamboat and the flatboat crossing. Both boats seemed to be making the transit without incident until the flatboat reached the middle of the river. Then, to her horror, she saw the boat tip to one side, far enough over that the oxen and wagon were tossed overboard. The boat righted itself, but Tim and Anita were still in the wagon, and it bobbed up and down as it was swept downriver.

"Matt!" Ellen shouted as loud as she could and Matt, who was lining up the boats for the next crossing looked up at her, curious as to her shout. She pointed to the middle of the river, but that wasn't needed, because by now many of the women still ashore were screaming, and the men were shouting, and all were pointing.

"Oh, Precious, look!" Emma called.

IN THE WAGON, Anita clung to Tim as the wagon bobbed along through the river. Fortunately, the wagon was buoyant enough, that it didn't sink, but water was coming in. Anita was terrified that they were going to drown, and she continued to cling to Tim. Then, suddenly, and unexpectedly, the wagon stopped.

"Oh, we've stopped!" Anita said.

"I think we must have hit a sandbar. We have to get out of here, now," Tim said. He helped Anita first, then started to crawl out, but before he exited the wagon, he grabbed the gutta percha bag that hung from a nail just inside. He just managed to escape before the wagon was swept free from the sandbar to resume its way down river.

BACK AT THE LANDING, more than half the people of the wagon train were watching the Murray wagon as it tumbled downstream.

"Oh, Papa, they're going to drown, aren't they?" Ellen asked, grabbing her father's arm.

"No, look," Cody said.

As the wagon worked itself off the sandbar and again began to tumble down river, Tim and Anita were left standing waist deep in the water.

"Jared, get a couple of lines and tie them together," Cody ordered.

"Pa, it's going to take more than two ropes," Jared said.

"I have two more," Lon offered.

"*Ja, ich habe ein Seil,*" Harm said. Then, realizing that in his excitement he had spoken in German, he translated. "Yes, I have a rope."

"Good, good," Cody said. "Jared, get them tied together."

When the five ropes were tied together, they made a line two-hundred-fifty feet long.

"How are we going to get this to them? It's too far to throw it," Ditmar said.

"Tie the rope around me, I'll swim it out to them," Matt said.

Jared tied the rope around Matt's waist, then Matt

waded out into the water until it got so deep that he had to swim.

"Oh, Matt, be careful," Ellen said, though she said the words so quietly that nobody could hear them.

Dozens of people were gathered at the edge of the river, watching as Matt swam toward the sand bar. When he reached it, and stood up again, there were cheers from those who were watching.

"Let's get you folks back," Matt said.

"Take Anita first," Tim said.

Matt smiled. "No need to. We can all go at the same time."

"How are we going to do that?"

Matt loosened the rope that was tied around his waist, made one loop around Anita, another around Tim, then one around himself, tying it off.

"All right!" Matt shouted to Jared who, by now had Lon and Harm helping him. "Pull us back!"

The three men managed to pull all three ashore. When they climbed out of the water, there was a universal cheer of joy.

Tim and Anita thanked Matt and the others for saving them. Then, reality hit Anita.

"Oh, Tim, what are we going to do now?" She asked. "Our wagon, our team, all our clothes, everything is gone."

"Papa, can they use our second wagon?" Ellen asked.

"Yes, of course they can."

"We're about the same size," Ellen said to Anita. "I can let you have one of my dresses."

A thankful Anita wept with appreciation.

Jared, taking the cue from his sister, provided Tim with a change of clothes.

Because of all the excitement, the steamboat ferry

was delayed for its next crossing. Cody, Tim, Lon, Harm, John Joyce, Craig Ditmore, and Matt were on the last boat. Most of the children had already gone across so that, besides Emma and Precious, there were only six more. As the other six were considerably older, Precious and Emma stood apart from them.

"My daddy used to do this on a really big boat," Precious said, proudly. "He was a sailor on the ocean, and he went everywhere in the world."

"Oh, that sounds like it would really be fun," Emma said.

"Cap'n M'nare was cap'n of the boat my daddy was on, too."

WHEN THEY REACHED the other side, Cody was met by an impatient Peter Laycock.

"It took you long enough, McNair," Laycock said, irritably.

"You may have noticed that we had a little trouble," Cody replied.

"You're talkin' about that fool that tried to save money by takin' the flatboat instead of the ferry. I guess he learned his lesson all right. Tryin' to save hisself eight dollars, he wound up losin' ever'thin'. What are they goin' to do now? They lost their wagon, 'n ever'thin' else."

"They are going to continue the trip with us."

"How?"

"They'll be using my smaller wagon."

"What are they goin' to eat?"

"Our train is large enough, that everyone can share a little without being hurt until we can get somewhere, where Mr. Murray can resupply his larder."

"Ha! Don't plan on them gettin' nothin' from me," Laycock said.

Cody smiled. "That's exactly what I do plan for. What they'll be getting from you, Laycock, is nothing."

When all the wagons were gathered, Matt came over to speak with Cody.

"We're about eight days from Cottonwood Station. If anyone needs anything, there's a general store, a wagon repair, and a blacksmith shop there. Oh, and there's also a restaurant and a saloon."

"Do you know the place well?" Cody asked.

"Pretty well, yes."

"The reason I ask is, as you know, we've got some single men traveling with us, and I'm wondering if the saloon might cause us any trouble."

"The fella that runs the saloon, Nate Jones, is a good enough man, but I won't lie to you, Cap'n. I've had problems with a few in the other trains I've taken through."

"Yes, well, from time to time you're going to get that with any saloon, I guess," Cody answered.

The train got underway with Anita riding in the McNair pup wagon that was being towed by the main wagon, and Tim walking alongside.

21

WITH MEL POLLARD – HAYSTACK BUTTE

MEL POLLARD HALTED THE TRAIN FOR THE NIGHT, AND AS several cooking fires were built, he saw a familiar figure coming toward the encampment.

"Dudley Dace," he said. "I thought you were leading a train. It's too soon for you to have gone to Oregon and back. What are you doing here?"

"Ah, we had a difference of opinion, and Matthews fired me, the son of a bitch."

Pollard nodded his head. "Some of the folks on this train got all out of sorts because I said we had to leave a wagon behind. But they got the cholera, 'n' we didn't have no choice."

"Yeah, I know what you mean. If you would've kept the wagon with you, ever'one on this train would have come down with the cholera. Tell me, Mel, is there much money on this train?"

"Yes, quite a bit, actually. But you've led enough trains,

you know how it is. Before they leave where they were, they sell everything so they've got enough money to get started all over when they get to where they're going."

Dace turned and shouted. "Come on in, boys!"

At his shout, nine more men, all of them wearing hoods, came riding out of the trees.

"What's this all about?" Pollard asked. He was actually more curious than he was worried. When he looked back toward Dace, he saw that Dace was wearing a red hood.

"These are the men who are going to help me rob this wagon train," Dace said, and pulling his pistol, he shot Pollard in the stomach.

With that, the group of hooded men moved around the wagon circle, killing every man they saw.

With the dead and dying lying on the ground, they went through every wagon, taking all the money they could find. Then, laughing at their success, they rode away.

JIMMY MORGAN WAS sixteen years old, and when the shooting started, he managed to hide. Not until the hooded men rode away, did he come out of hiding, to be greeted by dead and dying men, as well as crying women and children. As he looked around, he realized that he was the oldest male still on his feet.

"How will we get to Ft. Laramie? All the men are dead or close to death," one of the women wondered aloud.

"I'll get us there," Jimmy said.

"How can you say that? Have you been there before? How will you know where to go?"

"It shouldn't be that hard. All we have to do is follow the wheel ruts," Jimmy said.

WITH THE TRAIN LED BY MATT LOGAN

On the day after the McNair wagon train crossed the river, they advanced twenty-two miles, stopping at a place that Matt knew would have a source of water. After they stopped, Matt approached Cody.

"Cap'n, if you don't mind, I'd like to put the wagons in a circle tonight. It's actually the best way to spend the night. For one thing it keeps everyone together, and it provides a place for the oxen inside the circle. And if we ever encounter Indians, it makes a secure fortress."

"All right, Matt, give the order."

"Folks!" Matt called. "If you would, please, I'd like for you to put all the wagons in a circle."

"Why?" someone asked.

"It maintains the integrity of our encampment. Besides, it's the best defense against an Indian attack."

"Ha! You mean they got hostile Indians in this part of Kansas?" Laycock challenged.

"No, Mr. Laycock, but we will be going through areas where we might encounter hostiles, so it's best to learn how to do this now, rather than when we are under attack."

"Yeah, well you folks just go ahead 'n' play your game, but I ain't 'a plannin' on doin' nothin' like that."

For a moment after the order was given, there was no reaction because it was obvious that nobody knew what to do. Matt took the harness of the lead yoke of oxen on Cody's wagon, then with a signal to the others to follow, began leading it around in a circle. When the circle was formed, the oxen were unharnessed, and led into the center of the circle, the front left wheel of the trailing wagon was put even with the right, rear wheel of the wagon in front. In that way, a closed fortress of wagons was formed.

Pointedly, there were three wagons that did not join with the others. Those were the wagons belonging to Peter Laycock, Howard Raines, and Raymond Pugh. All were single men.

By ARRANGEMENT, Matt was taking all his meals with the McNair family.

But tonight, on this first evening after crossing the river, and because Tim and Anita Murry had lost everything in the accident, Matt invited them to take supper with them as well.

"Tim, Matt tells me that there is a general store at Cottonwood Station, where you can resupply yourself. I can lend you money if you . . ."

Tim held up his hand. "I won't need to borrow any money. I was keeping all my money in a gutta percha bag, and I was able to save it before we lost our wagon. I have five hundred and sixty-four dollars."

"That's very good," Cody said. "If they don't gouge the travelers at the store, you should be able to re-equip yourself without too much trouble."

"Ernest and Thelma Dunnigan run the store," Matt said. "They're good people. They charge a little more than what you'd pay if you bought supplies in St. Louis, but that's because they have to pay freight to get it to them. But they're honest people, and they don't cheat their customers."

After supper, Lon came over to the little group.

"Hello, Lon," Cody greeted.

"Cap'n, Norma made three apple pies. She wants to know if you'd like me to bring two of 'em over, so's you 'n' your guests could have some dessert."

"No," Cody said. He smiled. "Don't bring two of them over, bring all three of them over and you, Norma, and Precious join us."

"The little Joyce girl is with us," Lon said. He smiled. "Emma came to have some pie. Is it all right if she comes too?"

"Of course, it is."

Lon smiled. "We'll be right back."

"How long has your man been with you?" Tim asked, after Lon walked away.

"He's not my man, he's his own man," Cody said. "But we grew up together and Lon sailed with me, when I was a sea captain. Also, Norma, and my late wife, Lucinda, were friends since childhood."

"Really. I never heard of any colored sailors before."

Cody chuckled. "We wouldn't even be here, if it weren't for colored sailors. Many of Christopher Columbus's crew were colored, including a man named Nino, who was navigator of the *Santa Maria*."

"Lon must be a pretty good man to have been with you this long," Tim said.

"He once stopped an attempted mutiny on my ship."

"Now, that's a story I'd like to hear," Matt said.

"It happened when a few of the crew decided they wanted to return to Fiji and let us say revisit, the welcoming women there. It was led by a man named Vernon Stone who planned to take over the ship. Lon stepped up behind Stone, grabbed him by the seat of his pants and the scruff of his neck, and threw him overboard. After that, the others who were thinking about mutinying changed their minds."

"What happened to Stone? Did he drown?" Matt asked.

Cody chuckled. "No, I put a boat overboard and brought him back. He spent a week in the brig, then apologized to me and the rest of the crew, and never gave me any more trouble."

"I can see why you and Mr. Baker are still together," Matt said. "He seems like a good man."

"One of the finest men I've ever known," Cody said.

22

IN THE MONTH FOLLOWING THE ATTACK ON THE WAGON train led by Mel Pollard, two more wagon trains were attacked, not by Indians, but by white men wearing hoods and led by someone wearing a red hood. And in every case, nearly all the men were killed.

There were enough survivors, however, that up and down the trail at every fort and trading post, there were warnings of a group of white men, now called the Hood Raiders led by an unknown, identified only because the hood he wore was red.

A wagon train of seventeen wagons was being led by the guide, Larry Dooley. It had been at Alcove Spring for two weeks, much longer than a normal encampment would be.

They had come a little over a hundred miles since leaving St. Joseph, Missouri, three weeks earlier. Halfway between St. Joseph and Alcove Spring in South-east Nebraska, they had been hit with an outbreak of cholera. Fifteen people had died, and their six wagons had been burned.

Now the train was down to eleven wagons, and the remaining people were debating what they should do.

"Well, you folks can go on if you want to, but I'm headin' back to St. Joseph. I shouldn't 'a never left in the first place," Jim Ledbetter said.

"Why are you doing that?" Dooley asked.

"'Cause, as far as I'm concerned, eleven wagons ain't enough," Ledbetter said. "Why, iffen we was to get attacked by Indians, with no more 'n eleven wagons, 'n' only thirteen men, we'd be sittin' ducks. No, sir, I ain't a' goin' no farther 'til I can hook up with a train that's got more people in it."

"Jim, can't you see that what you're doing is just weakening it for the rest of us?" Gordon Parker asked.

"I ain't tellin' none of the rest of you, you shouldn't go on," Ledbetter said. "All I'm sayin' is, I ain't goin' on. I'm goin' back to Missouri."

A few others suggested they might go back as well.

"All I'm asking is that you all should think it over," Dooley said. "Give it one more night. Then tomorrow, whatever happens, happens."

"All right," Ledbetter agreed. "One more night."

"It's up to you, Nonnie, whether or not we go on," Gordon Parker said to his sister as they huddled around a fire.

"Since Andrew died, what do I have back in Tennessee?" Nonnie Hughes, a forty-one-year-old widow replied. "Besides, since Abby died, you need help with Fred. You can't raise him yourself."

Gordon put his hand on Nonnie's shoulder. "You've been good for Fred. You're a good sister, Nonnie." He smiled. "You were a good wife to Andrew, and I've no doubt but that you'll meet someone out here and be a good wife again."

117

"Gordon, I'm not in any hurry to get married again, so you can just forget about being a match maker."

Gordon laughed. "I don't think there'll be any match making needed. Some good man is going to come along and sweep you off your feet."

"You seem awfully anxious to get rid of your sister," Nonnie said.

"I won't be getting rid of my sister—I'll be getting a brother-in-law."

THE NEXT MORNING the wagon team members met again, and when the meeting was over, Ledbetter, and five of the wagons started back, leaving only six.

"Folks, you can do what you want," Dooley said to the remaining six. "If you want to go back, I'll take you. If you want to go on, I'll do that, too."

"What about Indians?" someone asked.

"This will be my fourth trip, and the only Indians I've encountered so far, have been friendly. I don't anticipate any trouble."

"I say we go," Gordon said.

WITH THE TRAIN LED BY MATT LOGAN

They had been on the trail for two weeks since crossing the Missouri River when Matt approached Cody with a suggestion.

"There's something else that we should do," Matt said.

"What's that?"

"Well, if you think about it, we've got as many people in this train as a small town. And like any small town we need a . . ."

118

"Sheriff," Cody said, completing the sentence.

"Yes, well, a sheriff, and about five deputies who can police the train."

Cody nodded. "Jared," he called.

Jared rode over to join them. "Yes, Pa?"

"I've just appointed you sheriff."

"Sheriff of what?"

"Sheriff of the wagon train," Matt put in. "You probably won't have to do anything, but on a couple of the previous trains, we've needed a sheriff. We had a murder on the first train and some thievery on the last one."

"And with people like Laycock, Raines, and Pugh, you never can tell," Cody added.

"You might want to get yourself three or four deputies," Matt added.

"It could be a problem finding that many who would want to leave their wagon to take on the job. I can do it because you can stay with our wagon," Jared said, addressing his father.

"They won't have to leave their wagon," Matt said shaking his head. "You'll just have them available to back you up if the need arises."

"All right," Jared said. "I've got a few ideas as to who I might ask."

The wagons formed another circle that night, doing so much easier than they had the first time. When everyone was in place, Cody called for a meeting, and the entire company gathered, including all the children.

"Folks, the reason I've called you all here, is to tell you that we have a sheriff now, to sort of keep an eye on things. And he's selected some deputies, so I'm going to let him say a few words to you. Jared?"

"Wait a minute!" Laycock shouted, angrily. "I don't recall havin' any election for sheriff."

"We didn't have an election. I appointed him."

"And you appointed your own son?"

"Who in this company do I know better?" Cody challenged.

"Yeah, well that ain't right. We should vote for the sheriff."

Matt spoke up then. "It's the tradition for the wagon master to make all appointments during the trip out. Captain McNair has appointed Jared McNair, and anyone who doesn't like that, is free to leave the train."

Jared spoke up then.

"Folks, first of all, let me introduce my deputies, Gus Wiley and Chub Collins. I'm sure you all know that they're a couple of the men hired to watch the cattle."

The two cowboys nodded at the company.

"Clay Ditmore, Joe Atwood, and Luke Taylor will sort of be my backup deputies. Gus, Chub, and I aren't married, so we don't have a family to be concerned with, so most of any actual sheriff work that has to be done, we'll do it. If the job gets bigger, then Mr. Ditmore, Mr. Atwood, and Mr. Taylor have agreed to help us out."

"What kind of things will you be doing?" John Joyce asked.

"Hopefully, it'll just be small things like settling disputes and the like. But if it gets any more serious than that, well then we may have to throw someone in jail."

"In jail? What are you talking about? We don't have a jail," someone said.

Matt smiled, broadly. "Let's just say that we have the kind of jail that you don't want to be thrown into."

Several laughed.

"I don't intend to be payin' no attention to a sheriff that wasn't elected," Laycock said.

"That will be fine, Mr. Laycock," Jared said. "It doesn't

matter whether you pay any attention to me or not. What you don't want to happen, is for me to start paying particular attention to you."

Again, there was laughter, even louder this time, and Laycock, fuming with anger, hurried away from the gathering.

23

ROSIE, WHO WAS THE TWENTY-ONE-YEAR-OLD DAUGHTER of David and Nellie Sullivan, had become Ellen's friend since the wagon train had left St. Louis. They hadn't known one another before starting on the trek, but of all the single women, they were the two closest in age so they naturally gravitated together. And, like Ellen, Rosie was a particularly attractive woman.

"I know he's noticed you," Rosie said.

"Who has noticed me?" Ellen asked.

"Who has noticed you?" Rosie laughed. "Matt Logan, of course."

"I doubt it. He's too busy being the guide. Besides, he's gone most of the time, riding way out in front of everyone."

"But doesn't he eat all his meals with you?"

"Well, not with me alone, don't forget Jared and Papa. And that's because it's part of the deal we signed for him to be the guide. It says he'll eat with the wagon master."

"He is very good looking, don't you think?"

Ellen's face flushed. "I suppose you could say that."

"He's almost as good looking as Frank Wiley."

"Ah ha! So, I'm not the only one with a new beau," Ellen said.

"That would be true," Rosie agreed. She laughed. "Except that neither one of us actually has a beau now."

WHEN THE TRAIN arrived at Cottonwood Station, Ellen and Rosie went with Anita Murray to Dunnigan's general store where she began the expensive operation of replacing the items she and Tim had lost in the Missouri River.

Cody wanted a meal where he could actually eat from a table,7 so he and Jared joined Matt for dinner at a place called the Oregon Trail Café.

"If it isn't Jake Bray," Matt greeted when he saw the proprietor. Jake was a one-time trail guide who had left the trail to start the café.

"Hello, Matt. Someone told me you were bringing another train through."

"I am. This is the wagon master, Cody McNair and his son, Jared," Matt said.

Jake extended his hand. "You're in good hands. Matt's one of the best. By the way, have you heard of the Hood Raiders?"

"No, I can't say that I have," Matt said. "Who, or what, are the Hood Raiders?"

"They're a group of white men who've been attacking and robbing wagon trains, but worse than that, they kill all the men. They all wear black hoods so nobody knows who they are, except the one who seems to be in charge wears a red hood."

"That's terrible," Matt said. "How many are there?"

"As near as we can tell, seven or eight, but it could be

more, 'cause nobody's really sure. Generally, it's only some of the women who are left alive, 'n' they're all so nervous 'n' scared that they don't ever give the same number or even tell the same story."

"And nobody knows who the leader is?"

"It might be someone named Dudley Dace, but it's only a couple of people who heard the name Dace called."

"Dudley Dace?"

"Word is he used to be a wagon guide. Do you know him?"

Matt shook his head. "No, I don't think I've ever run into a Dudley Dace."

WHILE MATT, Jared, and Cody were enjoying their meal, Laycock, Raines, and Pugh, as well as Cox and Beltrain, had taken the opportunity to stop at the Watering Hole Saloon.

After the meal, Cody, Jared, and Matt returned to the parked wagons and were headed toward Tim Murray to see if they could help him bring back some of his supplies.

"Sheriff McNair?" Drew Guthrie yelled as he came running toward the three men.

For just a moment, Jared hesitated, then he realized that Drew was speaking to him.

"Yes, Drew?"

"We need you down to the saloon."

"What is it? What's wrong?"

"It's Mr. Raines."

"What about Mr. Raines?"

"What he done was, he just kilt Sid Beltrain."

"Oh, damn." Jared took a deep breath, then let it out

with an audible sigh. "I'd better go," he told Matt and his father as he headed to the wagon to get his pistol.

"Matt and I are coming with you," Cody offered.

"Thanks."

TENSION WAS high when the three men reached the saloon. At least two dozen men were on one side of the saloon, many of whom belonged to the wagon company. Raines was on the opposite side of the saloon, holding a pistol and standing over the body of Sid Beltrain, who was one of the cowboys hired to herd the cattle. There was a pistol on the floor beside Beltrain's body.

"What's going on here?" Cody asked.

"I'll tell you what's goin' on," Raines said. He pointed to the body lying on the floor. "This son of a bitch drawed a gun on me. I didn' have no choice but to defend myself."

"That ain't right, Raines," Deacon Cox said. "He never drawed agin' you."

"Yeah, well, he was about to. The onliest thing they was, is that I beat 'im to it."

"Put your gun away, Raines," Jared ordered. "Put your gun away and we'll decide whether or not you're telling the truth."

"What do you mean, you'll decide? Just how the hell are you goin' to do that?"

"We'll have a trial."

"Ha! What do you mean we'll have a trial? There ain't no judge here, 'n I don't reckon you'll be a' takin' me back to Independence."

"We won't need to take you to Independence. The company will hold your trial."

Raines, who was still holding his pistol, turned

toward Jared, Cody, and Matt. "You ain't givin' me up for no trial."

Matt smiled.

"What are you smilin' about?" Raines asked.

"I'm smiling because the bartender is behind you with a double-barrel shotgun," Matt said.

"Ha! You think I'm goin' to fall for that old trick?" Raines asked.

"Let 'im know it isn't a trick, Nate," Matt said.

Nate Jones poked Raines in the back with his shotgun. "Mister, if you don't drop that pistol now, I'm goin' to put a hole in you big enough to drive one o' them wagons through."

With a look of fear on his face, Raines dropped the gun and as it hit the wooden floor with a loud clatter, he put his hands up.

24

MATT HAD SEEN THREE WAGON-TRAIN TRIALS, SO HE TOLD Cody and Jared how the trial should be conducted.

"We'll need a judge," Matt said. "Jared is the sheriff so he can act as the bailiff. Select two people to act as the defense counsel and the prosecutor."

"I've held Captain's mast a few times," Cody said. "I suppose that can qualify me as a judge. But, what about the jury?"

"That's easy," Matt said. "We'll put two dozen sticks in a hat, twelve long and twelve short. Whoever draws the short sticks will be the jury."

As it turned out, Luke Taylor had once worked for a judge, so he was selected as the prosecutor. Peter Laycock volunteered to defend Raines.

"Now, all we need is some place to hold the trial," Taylor said.

"Why, we'll hold it right here in the Watering Hole," Jones suggested. "It won't be the first court that was in session right here."

By midafternoon, the saloon had been turned into a

courtroom, and many folks from the wagon train company, as well as several residents of the little community of Cottonwood Station, were in attendance.

Taylor opened the trial by calling Deacon Cox as his first witness.

"Mr. Cox, would you tell us in your own words, what happened?" Taylor asked.

"Yeah, well, what happened was, me 'n' Sid was just drinkin', 'n' talkin' like old friends, which is what we was, 'n we was visitin' with the young lady there," Cox said, pointing at one of the two bargirls who worked the saloon.

"And what Raines done was, he come up 'n' grabbed Julie 'n' pulled her away, just like that. 'N' he didn't do it none too gentle neither, 'n' where he grabbed her was by her . . ." Cox halted in mid-testimony, then noticed that several of the women from the company were present. "Well, sir, he just grabbed her."

"And what did Beltrain do?"

Cox smiled. "What he done was, he knocked Raines right on his ass."

The others in the saloon-turned-courtroom laughed, and Cody had to bang on the table he was using as the judge's bench, to restore order.

"Did Raines get up, right away?"

"Yeah, he did, only what he done was, when he come up, he had already drawed his pistol, 'n' he shot Sid right in the chest. 'N' he musta hit Sid in the heart, 'cause he went down, 'n' he didn't get back up. I checked on 'im then, 'n' I seen that he was dead."

Taylor glared at Raines. "Me 'n' Sid was good friends, 'n' you kilt 'im, you son of a bitch."

Cody banged on the table for order. "Here now, Mr.

Taylor, we'll have none of that. Witnesses are not allowed to address the defendant."

"Your witness, Mr. Laycock," Taylor said.

Laycock walked over to stand in front of Deacon Cox. "Do you have a wagon in this train, Cox?"

"You know I ain't got no wagon in this train. I'm one of the cowboys that was hired to bring along the cattle. There was me, Frank and Gus Wiley, Chub Collins, 'n Sid Beltrain, only Sid ain't cowboyin' no more, on account of he's dead."

"Would you say that you 'n Beltrain was friends?" Laycock asked.

"Sid was the best friend I ever had."

"Would you say that you'd do anythin' for him?"

"Hell yes, I would."

"So you would lie, 'n' say that he didn't already have his gun out when Raines come up off the floor?"

"No, that ain't no lie!" Cox insisted. "Sid wasn't holdin' no gun when Raines shot 'im."

"And yet, there was a gun lyin' on the floor beside him."

"He musta tried to draw it when he seen that Raines was fixin' to shoot 'im."

"No more questions," Laycock said.

Luke Taylor called four more witnesses to testify, and all four substantiated Deacon Cox's statement that Sid Beltrain wasn't holding a pistol when Raines shot him.

Laycock called Nate Jones.

"Are you the bartender in the Waterin' Hole Saloon?" Laycock asked.

"I am."

"Did you see Beltrain, viciously knock Mr. Raines down?"

"Yes, I seen it."

129

"Was Beltrain holdin' a pistol in his hand when Raines got up from the floor?"

"I don't know."

"What do you mean you don't know? You were here, weren't you?"

"Yeah, but Raines was standin' between me 'n' Beltrain, so I couldn't tell if Beltrain was holdin' a gun or not."

In Laycock's summation, he pointed out that Beltrain had knocked Raines down without challenge or forewarning.

"That, in itself, is called an attack," Laycock said. "Raines could've broke his neck when he fell. If that had happened it would be Beltrain on trial for murder, rather than Mr. Raines. The bartender was the closest witness to the fight, and yet he can't say if Beltrain was holdin' a gun or not. And, don't forget, we all saw Beltrain's gun layin' on the floor beside 'im."

TAYLOR STOOD to give his summation. "There have been six witnesses testify today. Five of them, under sworn oath, have said Sid Beltrain didn't have a gun in his hand when the shot that killed him was fired. The sixth said that his view was blocked, so he could not say one way or the other, so we must base our assumption upon the testimony of the five who did see it. Three of the witnesses say that he started his draw, but not until Raines already had his gun out and was shooting. That would explain why the pistol was lying on the floor beside Mr. Beltrain. There is only one verdict to be made, and that is that Howard Raines is guilty of the murder of Sid Beltrain."

. . .

THE MEN who had been picked to serve on the jury gathered in the far corner of the room so they could discuss the fate of the accused.

"There's no doubt in my mind, but that the son of a bitch is guilty," Joe Atwood said.

"I don't know, Joe, Beltrain did knock him down," Dale Guthrie said.

"He had ever' reason to do it, Dale," David Sullivan said. "Raines grabbed that young woman by the tittie. He hadn't ought to a' done that, so Beltrain knocked 'em down. But that didn't give Raines no reason to shoot 'im, which was what he done."

After less than fifteen minutes of deliberation, Atwood signaled to Cody, that they had reached a verdict.

No one had left the saloon *cum* courtroom and there were several discussions ongoing as members of the gallery were conducting their own mini-trials. Cody silenced them by banging on the table.

"Court will come to order," he said.

The courtroom grew quiet.

"Who speaks for the jury?" Cody asked.

"I do, Captain – uh, Your Honor," Atwood said.

"Mr. Atwood, has the jury reached a decision?"

"We have."

"What is the verdict?"

"We find the son of a bitch guilty," Atwood said.

At first, there was a burst of laughter, which Cody stopped by once more banging his gun on the table.

"Bailiff, bring the prisoner before the captain's mast . . . uh, the bench, please."

Jared took Raines by the arm and walked him up to stand before the bench.

"Mr. Raines, you have been tried before a jury of your

peers and found guilty of the crime of murder. As the duly appointed captain of this company, it is within my jurisdictional purview to assess the sentence. The prescribed sentence for murder, is death by hanging, and I hereby sentence you to be hanged by the neck until dead."

"The hell you say!" Raines called out. "You ain't got no right to do that!"

ONE HOUR later a makeshift scaffold had been created by raising the tongues of two wagons, the wagons selected by chance. Jared and Frank Wiley walked Raines, with his wrists tied behind him, out to the contrived scaffold. They lifted him up onto a couple of boxes of sufficient height to keep him off the ground.

"Please, Mr. McNair, may I say a prayer for the condemned?" Reverend Owen asked.

"Yes, of course," Cody replied.

"Lord, as Your Son granted entry into heaven to Dismus, the good thief who died on the cross with Him, we ask that you receive into heaven the soul of Howard Raines. Amen."

There was a rope attached to the top box and one to the bottom. At a nod from Cody, the four remaining cowboys, Frank and Gus Wiley, Chub Collins and Deacon Cox, avenged one of their own by jerking the boxes out from under Raines.

Raines died quickly and without a sound.

Not every member of the wagon train was present for the execution, but those who were, watched in silence as the final chapter of Howard Raines' life was playing out before them.

Cottonwood Station already had a cemetery with

more than two dozen graves, mostly from the wagon trains that had passed through. It was decided that both Beltrain and Raines would be buried there.

"I just hate it that we'll be burying Mr. Beltrain and the man who killed him, right beside one another," Brenda Puckett said.

"We won't be burying them together," Cody said. "We'll bury them on opposite sides of the cemetery."

"And not at the same time, I hope," Joe Atwood said.

"We'll bury Mr. Beltrain tomorrow morning, and Raines tomorrow afternoon," Cody said.

ALMOST THE ENTIRE train turned out for Beltrain's burial the next morning. Deacon Cox asked the wagon master if he could say a few words about his friend, and Cody said yes.

Cox took off his hat and held it in front of him as he spoke.

"I know that most of you only know'd Sid as one of the cowboys drivin' your herd. But me 'n' Sid has know'd each other since we was both twelve years old, 'n' come to work together on a farm back in Missouri. He was as good a man as anyone I ever know'd 'n' I'm goin' to miss him, somethin' awful."

Reverend E. D. Owen said a prayer, then Lon Baker sang *Nearer My God to Thee.*

Howard Raines was buried that afternoon, his burial attended only by Laycock, and four more. Reverend Owen offered to give prayer at Raines' interment, but Laycock said it wasn't needed.

"What are we going to do with Raines' wagon and team?" David Sullivan asked.

"I have an idea of what we could do with it," Cody

replied, "but I think it's something we should put to a vote, because I wouldn't want to take it upon myself to do it."

"If you're going to suggest that we give his wagon and team to Tim and Anita Murray, I agree. In fact, that's what I had in mind when I asked you," Sullivan replied.

"I'll call a meeting," Cody said.

"Good, I've already spoken with some of the others," Sullivan said with a smile. "And I'm happy to say that they agree that the outfit should go to the Murrays."

Although Laycock and Raymond Pugh were opposed, the wagon train company voted to give Raines' wagon and team to Tim and Anita Murray.

"That wagon's full o' whiskey, just like mine 'n' Pugh's is. We're fixin' to start us up a saloon when we got to Oregon, 'n' it's not right for you to just give it away, like that," Laycock said.

"How are you planning on getting the whiskey that's in Raines' wagon to Oregon?" Cody asked.

"What do you mean, how are we plannin' on gettin' it there. Why, we'll just . . . uh," Laycock paused in mid-sentence. "I don't know."

"I have a suggestion," Cody said. "Why don't you hire a driver?"

"Hire a driver?"

"Hire Tim Murray. His pay will be that you'll let him use the wagon."

Laycock smiled. "Yeah, yeah, that's what I'll do. I'll hire Murray to drive the wagon for me, 'n' his pay will be that I let him use the wagon to get him 'n' his wife to Oregon."

"I thought you might see it that way," Cody said.

. . .

THE TRAIN LEFT Cottonwood Station the next morning, and two days later, Matt brought a deer that he had shot to Ellen.

"I thought maybe you could fry up some steaks tonight and we could sneak away from the others and have a picnic on the Platte. Just the two of us," he added.

"Picnic on the Platte," Ellen said with a smile. "That sounds like it should be the title to a song."

"It is," Matt teased. "And if you'll have a picnic with me, I'll sing it for you."

Ellen laughed. "No, please no. I'll have a picnic with you if you promise not to sing."

Matt laughed as well. "Trust me, you've just made a good decision. I assure you, I'm no Lon Baker."

"Doesn't he sing beautifully though?" Ellen asked.

"Yes, indeed, he certainly does."

"Papa said that Mr. Baker used to sing for his crew sometimes, and they all loved it."

Jared butchered the deer, then gave some of it to Lon and Norma Baker and their daughter, Precious, to Tim and Anita Murray, to David and Nellie Sullivan and their daughter Rosie, to John and Ethyl Joyce and their daughter Emma, and to Dale and Jane Guthrie, and their son, Drew.

"Oh, that smells good," Cody said, when he saw Ellen cooking their supper.

"It's from the deer that Matt shot."

"You mean he's good for something other than just pointing what direction we're supposed to be going?"

"Papa, he does a lot more than that," Ellen insisted.

"I'm teasing, darlin', I know he does."

"Then why did you say that? It's not funny. By the way, I'm going to have supper with him tonight."

"What do you mean you're going to have supper with him tonight? We have supper with him every night."

"Not we, Papa. Matt and I are going to have a picnic down by the river. That is, if you don't mind."

"I wondered when it would come around to that," Cody said.

"What do you mean?"

"Darlin', he's barely been able to keep his eyes off you from the first day he joined the company."

"Really?"

"Yes, you haven't noticed . . ." Cody paused in mid-sentence. "You know that too, don't you?"

"Sort of."

Cody laughed. "Sort of my hind foot. But he's a good man and I'm glad you're going to have some private time together."

25

FOR THE FIRST HALF OF EACH DAY, EMMA WOULD RIDE IN the wagon with Precious and her mother. All afternoon, and until the train stopped, and circled the wagons, Precious would ride with Emma and her mother. Now, as cooking aromas filled the air, the two little girls ran from wagon to wagon playing hide and seek.

"Look at that," Laycock said to Raymond Pugh. "You'd think that Joyce would have more pride, than to let his girl run around with that colored girl."

"Yeah, you see them two together all the time," Pugh said. "I wouldn't be surprised if they was stealin' stuff, too."

"They prob'ly are. A colored would rather steal somethin' than work for it, 'n' that's the absolute truth."

"Yeah, but the little Joyce girl ain't colored," Pugh said.

"I know she's not, but she might as well be, runnin' around with one like she's doin'."

.   .   .

WHEN MATT SHOWED up at the McNair wagon at supper time, Cody greeted him.

"I hear you're taking my little girl away with you tonight."

"Well, yes, sir, but only down to a little spot by the river. It's not far."

"If you're sure it's safe."

"It's safe, all right. We're not even close to any Indians yet."

"Matt?" Ellen called over to him. "I've got our picnic ready."

Ellen followed Matt down to a flat, grassy area overlooking the Platte River. The circle of wagons was still in view, so she felt no anxiety about being away from them. But even if the wagons weren't within view, she wouldn't have been nervous. She had trust that Matt would not only be a complete gentleman, but that he would also be able to defend her against any danger.

It was a pleasant experience, being together as they were, and they spoke of things that had happened on the trip so far, laughing over the humorous things, and saddened by what had happened to Sid Beltrain.

"Matt, where did you come from?" Ellen asked.

"What?"

"I know nothing about you other than the fact that you have guided other trains before this one. And since you know so much about me, it only seems right that I should know a little about you."

"Well, I'll tell you what I can," Matt said. "I think I was born in Chicago."

Ellen laughed, nervously. "You *think* you were born in Chicago? You mean you don't know?"

"As a newborn baby, I was left in a box on the front

step of Sacred Heart Orphanage in Chicago. There was no note, no name, nothing. Just me in a box."

"So, you mean your name isn't really Matt Logan?"

"Oh, it's my name all right, at least it's the only name I've ever known. One of the sisters at the home gave me my name, and it's worked fine for twenty-three years."

"How did you go from living in an orphanage to being a wagon train guide?"

"A friend and I ran away from the orphanage when we were both sixteen. I had read about the West, and it seemed interesting to me, so we decided to somehow get there. That's when Danny and I met Jim Bridger. We traveled with Mr. Bridger for a bit, then we came back to St. Louis with him. And that's where we heard about wagon trains forming up. Mr. Bridger convinced Danny and me to sign on with one of them as guides, so we did."

"How did you know you could do that?" Ellen asked.

"Because when we were with Jim Bridger, we had been all over the West, trapping and exploring."

"What happened to your friend?"

"Danny and I took a couple of trains together, but then we decided we could make more money if we split up, so we did. And we've been guiding wagon trains ever since. He's been operating out of St. Joseph so we wouldn't be competing for the same jobs. I'm sure he's on the trail now, but whether he's in front of us or behind us, I don't know."

"Do you ever cross paths with him?" Ellen asked.

"Every now and then I run into him, and sometimes we leave notes for one another somewhere on the trail, but it's been over a year since I've heard from him."

"So if you were just left on the doorstep, you never knew your mother or your father did you? Oh, how awful," Ellen said.

"It's worked out all right. At least my mother, whoever she is, left me with an orphanage rather than out on the street somewhere. And in a way, I was better off than the others in the orphanage."

"Danny, for example, didn't have parents either, but he had parents who had died, and he had to deal with the grief. I like to think that I helped him do that."

"You and Danny must be close," Ellen said.

"Yes, we are. Neither one of us had any family, so we became each other's family. Danny Dugan is the brother I never had, and I'm his brother."

"I miss my mother, terribly," Ellen said, "but I think Papa misses her even more. It's awful when two people love each other, then one of them is gone."

"Yes but think how much worse it would have been if they had never found each other. It's better to have someone that you can love, and then lose that person, than it is to have never had anybody at all."

Ellen was surprised by the depth of Matt's comment, and she paused for a moment before she replied. "Alfred Lord Tennyson."

"Who?"

"He's a poet, and in one of his poems he wrote the line, 'Tis better to have loved and lost, than to have never loved before'."

"Yes," Matt said with a nod. "I've never heard that before, but I believe it's true. And it's true for your father."

"It is, isn't it? And I know Papa realizes it, even in the midst of his grief."

"When you left Missouri, did you leave someone behind?" Matt asked.

"You mean a man?"

140

"Yes."

"I left no one. Have you left anyone?"

"No."

Ellen smiled. "Then that adventure is still before us, isn't it?"

Matt smiled as well. "Yes, I believe it is."

IN THE ENCAMPMENT OF HUNTING BEAR

Darcy Clinton had lost track of time. She knew she had been a prisoner of the Shoshone for several weeks. But as there was no calendar, nor any other form of reference, she had no way of knowing.

Since she had been captured, she had been able to communicate through an older woman called Spirit Woman. She could speak rudimentary English and she had befriended her.

Darcy had been a virgin when she was captured, but she was no longer so. She had been passed around from warrior to warrior and she prayed that she would not get pregnant. So far, thanks to Spirit Woman, she hadn't.

"Drink," Spirit woman told her after she had been taken the first time. "Drink and you not have," she formed her arms as if holding a baby.

It was a tea that Spirit Woman called *puccoon*, though Darcy soon learned that the tea came from the roots of what had been identified as the stone seed plant.

Darcy had cried almost continuously in the first few days after her capture. She wanted to go home, though she realized with a feeling of total despair, that she no longer had a family or a home to go to. As far as she knew, she had no living relative anywhere.

Spirit Woman had, for all intent and purposes,

adopted her and she treated Darcy as her daughter. Spirit Woman had helped her find a few other friends as well, but Darcy had to be careful, for many of the young women were jealous of the attention the warriors paid to her.

"Don't they know that I do not want the attention from the warriors?" Darcy asked Spirit Woman.

Spirit Woman put her hand on Darcy's shoulder. "You beautiful woman. Warriors want you. Others are mad."

Darcy prayed the same prayer every night: *"Dear Lord, please show me a way to be free."*

WITH MATT LOGAN'S TRAIN

Several times during the day, first John, and then Ethyl Joyce, would have to halt the wagon, hurry off to find a place of privacy, then return to the wagon.

"Are you having a solid movement?" John asked.

Ethyl shook her head. "No. And it is a strange color, like rice water. Are you?"

"No. I'm having diarrhea, and like you, it is a white water. I've vomited a few times, also."

"Me too, and I'm having pain in my gut."

"I wonder what it is," John questioned. "It has to be something we ate."

"Yes, but what have we eaten that Emma hasn't eaten?"

"Nothing, that I can think of."

"I'm going to have to stop again," Ethyl said, and bringing the team to a halt, she climbed down from the wagon and hurried off the trail to find a secluded spot.

"Daddy, where do you and mama keep going?" Emma asked.

"To use the toilet," John answered.

"So many times?"

John scooped a dipper of water from the water barrel and began drinking, thirstily.

"Maybe if you and mama would stop drinking so much water you wouldn't have to go so many times."

John chuckled, as he returned the dipper. "That's true honey, but I'm awfully thirsty."

"Mama's thirsty too. I've seen her drink a lot of water."

Ethyl returned then, and less than ten minutes later, John had to go again.

When the wagon train stopped for the night, they formed the circle, then several cookfires were made.

Neither Ethyl nor John made any effort to start a fire.

"Mama, aren't you going to make supper?" Emma asked.

"Oh, honey, I'm afraid I just don't feel like it tonight. Why don't you see if Mrs. Baker will feed you?"

"I know she will," Emma said. "She likes to fix supper for me."

"WELL, HELLO, EMMA," Norma said a few minutes later, when Emma walked up to their wagon.

"Mama said she doesn't feel like making supper and said for me to come eat with you. Is that all right?"

"Why of course it's all right, sweetheart."

"Oh, goodie," Precious said.

THE NEXT DAY dawned cool and Emma wrapped up in her blanket, then dozed off again. She awakened a short time later and lay there for a few minutes, wondering why she hadn't been called for breakfast. She could smell the cooking fires of the others, but when she stepped down from the wagon, she was surprised to see that her mother hadn't even started their fire.

"Mama, I'm hungry," Emma said. "Why haven't you fixed our breakfast?"

Emma's parents were lying together under the wagon.

"Mama, Daddy, why are you still asleep? Everyone else is up, I can hear them, and I can smell the bacon. It's time for breakfast."

When Emma still got no reply from her parents, she reached down and gently shook her mother's shoulder.

"Do you want me to go have breakfast with Precious?"

When she got no response, she shook her father's shoulder.

"Daddy, what's wrong with Mama?" Emma asked. "I can't wake her up."

She shook his shoulder. "Daddy, wake up. Mama, Daddy? MAMA, DADDY, WAKE UP!"

When she could wake neither of them, she grew more frightened than curious.

"Mama? Daddy?"

Emma ran to the Baker wagon.

"Precious! Mr. Baker! Precious! Mr. Baker!"

Precious, hearing the call and recognizing something disturbing about it looked up at her mother.

"Mama, something's wrong with Emma."

"Go to her, Precious. See what it is," Norma replied.

Precious, who had been helping her mother cook breakfast, ran back to meet Emma.

"Oh, Precious," Emma said, and Precious could see

tears streaming down her cheeks. "Mama and Daddy won't wake up. I'm scared."

"Let's go get Daddy," Precious said.

WHEN THE TRAIN stopped the night before, Lon had made a slight repair to the wagon belonging to Craig Patterson, and now he was talking with Cody about it.

"It wasn't hard, the tire had come loose, and all I had to do was tighten it."

"Well Craig was mighty pleased, I tell you," Cody said. "You've been a real asset to this train, Lon. That's the fourth wagon you've repaired."

"Daddy! Daddy! Come quick!" Precious said. "Emma can't wake up her mama and daddy."

"What?"

"They won't wake up, Mr. Baker," Emma said with tears streaming down her face.

"I'd better go with you," Cody said.

"Cap'n, maybe we should take Norma with us," Lon suggested.

"Yes, I think we should."

When they reached the Baker wagon, Norma was cleaning up the skillet she had used to fry their breakfast bacon.

"Norma, we need you to come with us," Cody said. "It's the Joyces."

"Oh, Lawd, somethin' bad is wrong, ain't it?"

"I'm afraid it might be."

Cody, Lon and Norma followed the two anxious little girls to the Joyce wagon where they saw John and Ethyl lying on the ground under the wagon. They stopped to stare down at them.

"What's wrong, Mr. Baker? What's wrong Mr.

McNair? Why can't I wake up my Mama and Daddy?" Emma asked.

Cody reached down to put his finger on the pulse of each of their necks, then he looked up at Lon and Norma and shook his head.

"Oh, you sweet child," Norma said, putting her arm around Emma and pulling the little girl to her.

26

"IT WAS THE CHOLERA THAT KILLED THEM," MATT SAID. "I've seen it before."

"But they were just fine yesterday," Tim said.

"No, they were both running off to be by themselves a lot," Dale Guthrie said. "I was wondering what was going on."

"Diarrhea," Matt said. "That's one of the symptoms of cholera. And when it comes on, it will hit you fast. You can be fine one day, and dead the next."

"We'd better get them buried," Cody said.

"Wouldn't it be better to just leave them here?" someone asked. "You'd have to touch them to bury them, and you could catch the cholera from them."

"It wouldn't be good for the little girl to just leave her mama and papa like this," Lon said. "I'll bury them."

"I'll help you," Harm Schultz said.

While the other members of the wagon train kept their distance, Lon and Harm dug the grave. They had thought about digging two graves but decided that if

147

they had been together in life, they could now be together in death.

After they were buried, and as there seemed little chance of anyone contracting the disease from them now, everyone gathered for a grave-side service conducted by the Reverend E.D. Owen.

"We, here, commit the earthly bodies of John and Ethyl Joyce to the ground, their final resting place; earth to earth, ashes to ashes, dust to dust. In the hope of resurrection unto eternal life, through the promise of Our Lord Jesus Christ, we faithfully and victoriously give them over to Your blessed care. What good they have shown us, we will show to others. John and Ethyl, we release you now to the next part of your spiritual journey as you walk hand in hand with your Creator. Amen."

Lon sang *Nearer My God to Thee*, then with the funeral over, several of the women came to embrace Emma.

Afterward, the members of the train went back to their wagons, leaving Emma to stand alone over the mound of dirt, which was all she had left of her parents. Precious, who was standing beside her, reached out to take Emma's hand. Emma had cried until she could cry no more.

"Oh, Precious, what am I going to do?" Emma asked, lost and afraid.

"Daddy will know," Precious said.

"WE'LL HAVE to burn the wagon," Raymond Pugh insisted.

"Why should we burn the wagon?" Cody asked.

"On account of it's got the disease now, 'n' iffen we

don't burn the wagon, why, like as not, someone else will die, then someone else, then maybe all of us."

Cody looked at Matt, and Matt nodded.

"It's happened before," he said. "Folks have gotten cholera and died, and we've had to burn their wagon."

Cody sighed. "All right, let's do it."

"Papa, what about the little girl?" Ellen asked.

"We'll leave her here," Laycock said.

"What?" the word exploded from Cody's lips. "What the hell are you talking about?"

"We're goin' to have to leave the girl here," Laycock insisted. "If the wagon's got the disease, then she's got it too. Seems to me like we ain't got no choice.

"She'll prob'ly die in a day or two anyway, so it won't really matter none," Laycock added. "'N' if she don't die, why they's wagons comin' along the trail ever couple o' days, 'n' one o' them would more 'n likely pick her up."

"If you're willing to abandon her, what makes you think someone else would pick her up?" Cody asked.

"Well, if she ain't died by then, it means that she ain't likely got the cholera. Besides which, they wouldn't know nothin' 'bout her 'n' the cholera anyway."

"So you're willing to expose another train to the disease?"

"Yeah, I mean, well, it'd be better'n all of us a' catchin' it."

"The girl stays with us," Cody said, resolutely. "If you don't like that, you can pull your own wagon out, now."

"No, I ain't goin' to do nothin' like that. If the girl stays, she stays I guess, but when lots more folks start in a' dyin' on account of that girl is spreadin' the cholera around, well you can't say I didn't warn you."

"Who do you think will be willin' to take her?" Pugh asked.

"I'll take her in my wagon," Lon said.

"You can't take her," Laycock said. "She's a white girl, 'n you're colored."

"You are an absolute idiot, Laycock, do you know that?" Matt asked. "A few minutes ago, you were willing to just leave her on the side of the trail, now you're saying that she can't go with Mr. Baker because he's a colored man?"

The fact that Matt had not used the word mister when he addressed Laycock but had used the honorific for Lon Baker was noticed by all the others.

"I know it wouldn't be fittin' for her to stay with us forever," Lon said. "But she and Precious are good friends, and she has spent a lot of time with us. I think it would be easier for her now, especially since she just lost her mama and papa."

"I think so as well," Reverend Owen said.

"And that's prob'ly how come the Joyces up 'n died," Laycock said. "Her bein' around coloreds so much, prob'ly got it from them, 'n she give it to her mama and papa."

"If that was true, why haven't the Bakers gotten it?" Jared asked.

"That's on account of coloreds is different from white people," Laycock said.

"Laycock, the more you talk, the more you make me want to knock you on your ignorant ass," Jared said.

"You think you could handle both of us?" Pugh asked. "'Cause I ain't a' plannin' on just standin' by 'n' watch somebody attack my friend."

"He won't be alone," Matt said.

"I'm goin' back to my wagon," Laycock said. "I can see that I can't talk no sense into you folks. How long before we're goin' to be a' goin' again?"

"We're going to stay here for a day," Cody said.

"What for?" Laycock asked.

"Out of respect for John and Ethyl Joyce, and for Emma," Cody said.

"I reckon, seein' as you're the wagon master you can do purt nigh anythin' you want, but in my mind, it's just a waste of time, stayin' here for the whole day."

As THE WAGONS pulled away the next morning, Emma and Precious sat in the back of the Baker wagon. Emma cried as she saw the still burning wagon she had called home.

"I'll never see my Mama and Daddy again," Emma said between sniffles.

"Yes, you will," Precious said. "You'll see them in heaven."

"Thank you for being my friend," Emma said as she hugged Precious.

"No, I should thank you. You could have any friend you wanted, but you're my only friend."

The two girls watched the wagon until all they could see was a column of smoke, curling into the sky.

Two DAYS after they buried John and Ethyl, Phil and Brenda Puckett died of the cholera, and a week later, Seth Michaels, his wife Eunice, and all three of their children contracted cholera and died. Like Emma's parents, the Pucketts, and later the Michaels were buried alongside the trail, and their wagons and all the contents were burned as well. By then they had passed several other graves, and Matt told them that cholera was the number one killer on every train.

After they buried the Michaels family, Cody suggested it might be good to take the rest of the day off, and the others agreed with him.

"You can't say I didn't warn you," Laycock said, pointedly.

"Warn us about what?" Cody asked.

"You know damn well, what. I warned you about lettin' that Joyce girl travel with us. She 'n' the coloreds is what has started this cholera business in the first place."

"Laycock, I told you if you don't want to travel with us, you're free to go out on your own."

"The hell you say. I've paid just like ever'one else to be a part of this train, 'n' you ain't got no right to kick me out."

"That's certainly true," Cody said, "but I don't want to hear one more complaint about Alonzo Baker's family or Emma Joyce."

"I ain't the only one what feels this way," Laycock said.

Cody addressed the others who had been close enough to overhear the conversation.

"Peter Laycock is of the belief that Mr. Baker and his family are responsible for the cholera outbreak that has hit us. Does anyone else share Laycock's concern?"

"Why no, if it was them don't you think they'd already be dead?" Joe Atwood asked.

"You would think so, wouldn't you?" Cody answered.

"Pugh?" Laycock said, speaking to those who had signed onto the train with him.

"We got to get there, Laycock, 'n' I can't see no other way, other'n to go along with this train," Pugh replied.

Laycock stood there for a moment longer with a sour expression on his face, but he said nothing more.

THERE WERE NO MORE deaths in the following week, and the wagons covered fifteen miles per day. They stopped on Sunday to rest the teams and for a church service conducted by Reverend Owen. The cowboys took the herd out to find a good graze, while the others visited or shared meals.

"Mr. Baker, I wonder if my wife and I might join you for supper," Tim Murray said. He smiled. "We'll bring our own food, but we'd enjoy your company."

"Why, yes, sir, yes, of course," Lon replied with a welcoming grin.

A few minutes later Tim and Anita, carrying their own food, came over to join the Baker family.

"I want to tell you what a good thing we think it is that you have taken in Emma as you have."

"She's a sweet little girl and she and Precious have become good friends, so that seemed like the thing to do. You don't think it's a bad thing, do you?"

"No, not at all. The poor child has been through a lot, and she should get comfort anywhere she can. If that is from your Precious, then so be it."

"Yes, sir, but it can't go on like this," Lon said as he looked away.

"What do you mean?" Tim asked.

"While we're all travelin', it'll be all right, but when we all get to where it is that we're goin', I'm thinkin' it wouldn't be good for a little white girl to be a part of a colored family."

"So you'll be looking for a white family to take her in?"

"Yes, sir, I 'spects I will be."

"You don't have anyone in particular in mind, do you?" Tim asked.

"No, sir, no one that I'm thinkin' of anymore 'n anyone else."

Tim was quiet for a moment, and he glanced over at Emma who, with Precious, was sitting far enough away to hear the conversation between Tim and Lon.

Emma laughed at something Precious said.

"It's good to see her laughing again," Tim said.

"Yes, sir, it sure be."

"Mr. Baker, when you start considering a lifetime family for her, I would like for you to consider my wife and me."

Lon smiled, broadly. "Yes, sir, I'm not sure that will be my decision to make, but I sure will put in a good word for you."

ABOUT TWO HUNDRED miles west of where the wagon train was spending the night, Darcy Clinton was lying on a buffalo robe. Spirit Woman had told her that the ten tipis were not the home village of the Shoshone. It was a small group of about thirty Indians, warriors and women that had separated from the Northwestern Band of Shoshone.

The Shoshone were at peace with the white man and had even traded game with the wagon trains, and in some cases, acted as guides for them.

But Hunting Bear, whose father had been killed by white men a few years earlier, could not align himself with those who wanted peace. He found others who agreed with him, and it was that band of warriors, led by Hunting Bear, that had killed Darcy's family and captured her.

Several times during Darcy's captivity, her mother had come to her in her dreams. When she shared those dream with Spirit Woman, Spirit Woman told her that it was actually the spirit of her mother who had come to offer her comfort.

Darcy had been with the Indians long enough that she was willing to believe Spirit Woman, at least to the degree that she could find comfort in Spirit Woman's words.

Darcy had awakened a few minutes earlier, and now she was lying in the darkness. Through the canvas of the tipi, she could see the glow of a campfire, and she could hear the Indians talking outside, and even though the voices were muted, she recognized Hunting Bear's voice. But as her knowledge of Shoshone was still quite limited, she was unable to follow what they were saying.

Would she spend the rest of her life with the Indians? If so, how long would that be? If this was to be her fate, she couldn't help but hope her life wouldn't be very long.

THE DOOLEY WAGON train had come a little over six hundred miles since five wagons had left the train to return to St. Joseph. When they passed through Ft. Laramie, a few officers commented on how few wagons there were in their train, but the travelers said they weren't concerned. There had been no problems and they would sometimes joke about the five wagons that had left the company.

"You think Ledbetter's tellin' tall tales about fights with the Indians?" Roy Carter asked.

The others laughed and added derisive comments about some of those who had left with Ledbetter.

Dr. Gordon Parker's wagon was the third in the little train of wagons. His sister was riding beside him, and his fourteen-year-old son was walking alongside the wagon.

It had been their routine for Fred and Gordon to change places so that one would walk while the other rode. Sometimes both would walk, and Nonnie would drive.

Gordon had been talking about the practice he intended to open as soon as they got to Oregon.

"I expect we'll make a pretty good living, since we'll likely be the only doctor and nurse there."

"I'm not going to work as a nurse," Nonnie said.

"What? What do you mean you aren't going to work as a nurse?"

"Gordon, you don't actually need a nurse. I know you've been using me as a nurse since Andrew died, just to give me something to do."

"All right, well if you aren't my nurse, what will you do?"

"I'm going to open a boarding house."

"A boarding house? Why would you want to do that?"

"I've been thinking a lot about it," Nonnie said. "As more and more people come out to Oregon, there's going to be a need for a place for them to stay until they can get settled. And after months of sleeping outside, I expect a lot of them would be more than willing to pay to have a warm bath and a bed to sleep in."

"You know what, I was going to suggest that you live with Fred and me but running a boarding house just might be a pretty good thing to do," Gordon said.

"I'm glad you like it," Nonnie said, pleased that she didn't have to sell her brother on the idea.

27

AFTER THEIR CONVERSATION WITH LON, TIM MURRAY GOT Cody's permission to move their wagon up in line so that they were just behind the Baker wagon. Then, over the next few days, Tim and Anita began inviting Emma and Precious to ride in their wagon with them. They said nothing to Emma about having her come live with them, because they thought it would be better to let the little girl come to know them first.

Soon Emma, and Precious as well, became well acquainted with the Murrays. It was as comfortable for Emma to ride with them as it was for her to ride with the Baker family. She and Precious took as many meals with Tim and Anita as they did with Lon and Norma.

"How would you two girls like to sleep in with us tonight?" Anita asked after a few days of Emma and Precious moving back and forth between the two wagons.

"I'll have to ask mama," Precious said.

"All right, sweetheart, you do that," Anita replied with

a smile. She knew exactly what Norma would say, because she had already discussed it with her.

After the first night, the two girls moved back and forth between the wagons, every other night.

FORT LARAMIE – WEDNESDAY, JUNE 8TH, 1859

Fort Laramie was on the south side of the Platte River and the trail of the wagon train was on the north side. However, a ferry was available, so Cody took the wagons across the river so they could take advantage of the fort. Here, the travelers saw actual buildings for the first time in several weeks. Once all the wagons were across, Matt suggested that he and Cody should pay a courtesy call upon the commanding officer.

"Sounds like a good idea," Cody said.

Cody told Jared and Ellen where they were going.

"Are we going to be able to visit the post?" Ellen asked.

"Oh, better than that," Matt said.

"What do you mean, better that that?"

"You'll see," Matt replied, mysteriously.

"HELLO, SERGEANT MAJOR COBB," Matt said, greeting the impressive looking gentleman who was sitting at his desk in the post headquarters.

"Hello, Matt," Sergeant Major Cobb replied. "Bringing another train through, are you?"

"Yes, this is the wagon master, Captain McNair."

"Captain?"

"I once commanded a merchant ship," Cody replied.

"We'd like to see Major Lynde. Is he in?"

Cobb shook his head. "He's not the post commandant

no more. We've got a new one since you was through here last. Lieutenant Colonel John Munroe."

"All right then, we'd like to see him if he'll see us."

"Oh, I know he will. He likes to keep track of the folks coming through. Wait here, I'll tell him you want to see him."

Sergeant Cobb went through a door, then reappeared a moment later.

"The colonel will see you now," he said.

Colonel Munroe was about five feet eight inches tall with a slightly protruding stomach. He had dark hair and a full dark beard. He stuck his hand across the desk, offering a handshake.

"The Sergeant Major tells me you're a ship's captain?"

"I was," Cody said. "I left the sea a while back but somehow the title has stuck."

"I understand what you're saying, Captain. Long after I leave the army, I'm sure I'll still be called Colonel. Where did your train originate?"

"St. Louis."

"Ah, St. Louis. It's a wonderful town. I was at Jefferson Barracks for a while before I came out here."

The three men discussed the business at hand for the next several moments.

"Have you lost anyone to cholera?" Colonel Munroe asked.

"We've lost nine, six adults and three children."

"How long has it been since the most recent?"

"Three weeks."

"Nobody has it now, do they?"

"No, sir."

Munroe smiled. "Good, good. There'll be no restrictions placed on you, and your people are free to visit the sutler store, or any other place they wish to go."

"Thank you, Colonel, that's very good of you."

"Colonel, are you aware of any Indian problems?" Matt asked.

"There is some activity, but not for several weeks now. A couple of months ago, one of our patrols found a burned wagon and three bodies, two men and a woman. All three had been scalped. We have no idea who the people were, and no idea why they were alone. They were either abandoned for some reason, or they may have decided to make the trip by themselves, but if they did that was damn foolish of them."

"I wonder what put the Shoshone on the war path. They've been friendly with all the trains, certainly to me, and the ones I've brought through," Matt said.

"Well, from what we've been able to find out, it's not the main tribe that's causing all the mischief. It's a smaller group, led by a warrior named Hunting Bear."

"Hunting Bear, yeah, I know that son of a bitch," Matt said. "He's been a troublemaker from the beginning."

"But it's not only the Indians you have to worry about. There have been some wagon trains attacked by a group of whites, all of 'em wearing hoods. According to the women and children who have survived, the leader wears a red hood."

"Yes, I was warned about that group," Matt said. "Does anyone have any idea who it is?"

"One of the survivors heard one of them calling the leader Dace."

"Dace?"

"Does that name mean anything to you?"

Matt shook his head. "Not really, though I did hear the name mentioned when I was told about the outlaws. They said the one in the red hood used to be a wagon guide, but I never ran across him."

"That's quite understandable; there are so many trains on the trail now. In the meantime," Colonel Munroe added in a more upbeat tone, "I want you to have a pleasant stay with us and take advantage of whatever we have to offer."

"Thanks, Colonel, we'll do that," Cody replied.

WHEN MATT and Cody returned to the train, they were met by Ellen.

"Papa, how long are we going to be here?"

"We'll be here for a few days," Cody said. "I want to give the animals time to rest and there are some wagons that Lon wants to work on."

"Oh. Well, I suppose a little rest is good," Ellen said, "and, I suppose we can visit the post."

"Do you remember I told you that it might be a little better than that?" Matt asked.

"I remember you telling me, but you didn't tell me what you meant."

"How about if we have a dance?" Matt asked.

"A dance?"

"Yes. You know it's where they play music and men and women sort of move around together."

Ellen laughed. "I know what a dance is, silly. I just hadn't thought of having one in the middle of a trip halfway across the country."

"I think a dance would be a good idea. It gives people a chance to relax." Matt looked at Ellen. "That is, if you'll agree to let me be your escort. Otherwise, I think it's not that good of an idea."

"I'll do that, but only if you'll do something for me," Ellen said.

"Oh? And what's that?"

161

"I want you to suggest to Frank Wiley that he ask Rosie Sullivan."

"Why doesn't she ask him?"

"Matt!" Ellen said sharply. "Young women don't ask young men—young men ask young women."

Matt started laughing. "All right, I'll tell him to ask her."

"No, don't put it that way," Ellen said. "Just suggest that he ask her, so he'll think it's his own idea when he does."

Matt shook his head. "I'll see what I can do."

"What will we do for music?" Cody asked.

"That won't be a problem," Matt said. "There are always soldiers who play the fiddle, the guitar, the accordion, even a caller. We can pay 'em a few dollars and they'll be glad to provide the music for us. Oh, and if it's all right with you, we should let the soldiers come as well. In fact, if we're going to have it at Old Bedlam, then it would be rude not to allow the soldiers to participate."

"Old Bedlam?" Cody asked.

"Did you see that big building right in the center of the post?" Matt asked.

"It would be hard to miss it."

"Well, that's Old Bedlam. The sutler store is there, the officers are quartered there, the officers' club is there, and there's a community room that's large enough to hold dances. Every train I've guided through has taken advantage of the opportunity."

"So what you're saying is, I won't be the first woman you've taken to the ball," Ellen teased.

"No, but you'll be the prettiest."

Ellen laughed out loud. "You're the biggest liar I've ever met, but don't stop now. Yes, I would love to have you escort me to the dance."

WITH THE DOOLEY TRAIN

The Dooley train had stopped for the night along the North Platte River a little over fifty miles beyond Fort Laramie. Because there were only six wagons in the Dooley Company, they had community meals instead of each family preparing their own. The meals were larger, but because they all worked together, there was actually less work than if they had individual meals.

"You know what, I'm just as glad that Ledbetter and the others went back," Jennie Lou Culpepper said, as she lifted the lid on the Dutch oven.

"Why?" Agnes Burns asked.

"Well, look at us. We're just the right number to be able to eat together and visit. Why, it's become like a big family dinner," Jennie Lou said.

"That's true," Agnes said. "If there were any more of us, we wouldn't be able to share like this, and besides that, we're getting to know each so well that I just know we'll be friends for life."

"I see what you mean," Marilou Simmons said. "It will help us get over the sadness of having left so many friends and family behind."

The ladies began discussing what lay before them. Four of the families would be farmers, Marilou's husband planned on opening a store.

"And what about you, Nonnie? I know your brother will want you to be his nurse," Jennie Lou said. "You two work so well together."

"Actually, I have other plans," Nonnie Hughes replied.

"What sort of plans?"

"Just plans," Nonnie said, mysteriously.

"Ha, I know what your plans are. You're going to find

163

some good-looking man and get married again," Jennie Mathers said.

"You never can tell." Nonnie smiled as she stirred the stewed peaches.

FROM THE RIDGELINE, the Hood Raiders could see the wagons. Dace was surprised to see that there were only six. He had never seen a train with fewer than fifteen wagons, but here they were, right in front of him—six wagons.

There wouldn't be that much money with such a small train, but it would be easy to take. Dace smiled. And who knows? There might be a rich man on this small train.

He went back to where his men were camped. Emile Potter and Lenny Richards were playing split which was a game where they would throw a knife beside the other's foot, and the foot would have to be moved out to touch the knife. The game continued until one of them could no longer make the split. The knife couldn't be any farther from the foot than three inches, otherwise the thrower would miss his turn.

Potter threw the knife and Richards stretched out to meet it. By now, Richards was getting a little unsteady on his feet.

"Ha!" Potter said with a challenging laugh. "You know what? About two more throws, and you're goin' to fall right on your ass."

"Come on, Potter, I got ten dollars bet on you," Lewis said.

"Boys, I got us another train," Dace said, interrupting the game.

"How many wagons?" Potter asked.

"There's only six, so it'll be real easy."

"Six?" Richards said. "Hell, that ain't even hardly worth it, is it?"

"Look at it this way," Dace said. "All of them will have some money. They're everyone of them comin' west with all the money they got in the world. It's for sure that each one of 'em has close to four or five hundred dollars, and some of 'em may have more than that."

"They's only six wagons though," Potter said.

"Well look, even if they don't have much money at all, there'll be at least a thousand dollars and probably a lot more. We're bound to get a hundred dollars apiece," Dace said. "And gettin' it would be as easy as pickin' it up from the ground. If you saw a hundred dollars lyin' on the ground in front of you, would you pick it up?"

"Well, yeah," Potter replied.

Dace smiled. "Then, let's go pick it up."

THE NEXT MORNING, Dooley walked among the wagons.

"Ladies, I want us to start out a little earlier than usual. I'd like to get us closer to Laramie Peak today if we can, because the next day may be one of our hardest days yet."

"How many miles do you think that will be?" Gordon Parker asked.

"I'm thinking maybe twenty miles," Dooley said. "The animals had good water last night, and they are well rested."

"Will we stop for dinner?" Jennie Mathers asked.

"Probably not, so you need to make sure you've got plenty of water, and you might want to gather up some fuel for your fires, because more than likely, we'll stop around sunset or later."

Nonnie climbed down from the wagon and took a bucket. "I'll get us some water, Gordon."

"I'll do that, Aunt Nonnie," Fred offered.

"No, you need to gather up some buffalo chips. I'll take care of the water."

"All right, if you don't think it's too heavy for you to carry," Fred said.

"Young man, I carried you everywhere you went until you were four years old, I don't think a bucket of water is going to be too much."

"Huh, uh, you didn't carry me 'til I was four," Fred protested.

"Well, it sure seemed like I did. Now, you just scat. You heard Mr. Dooley say he wanted to get an early start."

"All right," Fred agreed.

Although they were still following the North Platte River, at this point the wagon trail was a good hundred yards away from the river. Nonnie didn't mind the walk and she found the river relaxing.

She thought about Andrew. If he were still alive, would he have come on this trip? She liked to think that he would. One of the things that had attracted her to him was his willingness to try new things.

Andrew had been dead for three years now. During those three years there had been a few men who let it be known that they were interested in her, but she had never returned that interest.

"Oh, Andrew," she said, quietly, "when will the hurt ever stop?"

Nonnie had just dipped the bucket in the water when she heard the first shot. At first, she thought it might be one of the men hunting, but immediately following that first shot, there were more coming one on top of the other.

Nonnie dropped the bucket and started running back toward the wagons, when she saw several men on horseback, all dressed as white men. To her absolute shock, they were firing at any person they saw.

Then, Nonnie realized how foolish it was for her to be running toward the men who were doing the shooting. She started to run back toward the river but thought that someone might see her. It would be better she decided, if she would just lie down among the scrub willow and stay as much out of sight as she could.

The intense shooting continued for another couple of minutes then it stopped, except for a few isolated shots. At first the single shots confused her. Then she realized, with horror, that the men on horseback were riding up and down the line of wagons, shooting people wherever they found them.

"That's it, Dace. There ain't no one left alive," she heard someone call out.

"All right, let's go through the wagons, get the money, then let's get out of here."

NONNIE LAY motionless watching as the men climbed through all the wagons. Their search took no more than fifteen minutes, and then they remounted and rode away at a gallop.

Nonnie remained where she was until she couldn't see or hear the raiders. Then she ran to the wagons, but even before she got there, she could see that at least one or two oxen were down from each of the wagons.

The first place she went was to her own wagon. When she got there, she saw Gordon and Fred lying lifeless. She continued to hurry to the other wagons and at each one, she saw that every man, woman, and child—all nineteen of them—were dead.

She wept over the carnage that she was seeing—the loss of her brother and nephew and the others who had become such good friends. Then, when the crying was over, she began to mull over her situation. At first, she attempted to free enough oxen to hitch to a wagon. Her thinking was that she could go back to Fort Laramie, but she found it impossible to move a wagon away from the dead animals.

28

FORT LARAMIE

"PA, I'M GOING TO ASK EMMA AND PRECIOUS IF THEY'D like to go with me," Jared said after he learned of the plans for the dance. "I think it might cheer Emma up a little, and she and Precious have been spending so much time together that I'm sure she would want Precious to go as well."

"I think that would be a fine idea," Cody said.

NEWS of the dance spread rapidly throughout the wagon train company, and soon the air was filled with a sense of excitement. For the moment, the melancholy of losing so many to cholera was set aside, and even Emma was able to smile at the prospect, especially when she learned that she and Precious would be going to the dance as well.

"I don't want to cause trouble," Lon said. "So me 'n Norma will stay in the wagon."

"Lon, when you were aboard ship did you ever feel like you weren't welcomed?" Cody asked.

"Well, no sir, I never felt nothin' like that, but that's 'cause I was a member of the crew."

"Exactly," Cody said, "and, you are as much a member of this wagon train company as you were a member of the crew of the *Sea Sprite.* By now, everyone has accepted you—hell, you've helped so many people that most are glad you're with us. So, I don't expect there will be any trouble."

"No, sir, there's not ever'one that's accepted me."

Cody smiled. "All right, Laycock and Pugh might have a problem with it, but they are assholes, and assholes don't count."

Lon laughed out loud. "All right, Cap'n, as long as assholes don't count, me 'n Norma 'n Precious will be there."

"Except Precious and Emma will be with Jared," Cody said.

Lon laughed again. "Yes, sir, I expect that's true."

THE MEN and women of the wagon train brought out their finest apparel for the dance. Matt and Frank Wiley walked together to the McNair wagon where Ellen and Rosie, both dressed in their best, stood waiting for them.

"I'm sorry," Matt said, by way of greeting, "but my friend and I are here to escort Ellen McNair and Rosie Sullivan to the dance. Would either of you ladies know where we might find them?"

Ellen laughed and playfully hit Matt on the shoulder.

"And just who do you think we are?"

"I recognize that voice," Matt said. "Frank, I swear, I

believe these two beautiful young women are the ones we have come for."

"Now you're just being silly," Rosie said.

Matt, Ellen, Frank and Rosie joined with the others in the walk from the parked wagons onto the Fort Laramie compound. They were watched by the soldiers of the post, from those who were on fatigue duty, to those who were wearing their dress uniforms in preparation for the dance.

Emma and Precious were walking with Lon and Norma. They came under particular observation from many of the soldiers, and some of the soldiers called out to them.

"What are you coloreds doin' here?"

"We ain't got no black folks here. They ain't welcome."

"Precious," Emma said, frightened by the hostile shouts and cat-calls. "Why are they mad at us?"

"They're not mad at you, Emma. They are mad at me, 'n' mama 'n' daddy."

"Why? What did Mister Lon do to them?"

"I didn' do nothin' to 'em chile," Lon said, having overheard the conversation between Emma and Precious. "That's just the way some folks is about people like us."

"People like us? What kind of people are we?" Precious asked. "We're good people, aren't we? Captain McNair likes us. And Mr. Matt, Mr. Jared, Mr. Tim and Miz Anita—they all like us."

"We *are* good people, 'n' you just remember that," Lon said.

"Mr. Laycock doesn't like us, but that's all right because I don't like him," Precious said.

Emma laughed. "I don't like him either."

. . .

ONE OF THE soldiers watching the people of the wagon train streaming across the post grounds was Private Jay Mullens. The arrival of another wagon train meant different things to different soldiers. Some, realizing there would be a dance, looked forward to the arrival of the women, even if they were married and their stay was only temporary. Others lamented the increased work-load of having so many people, livestock, and wagons arriving.

"Oh, look at this," Ellen said as they stepped into the community room of Old Bedlam. "It's been decorated so beautifully."

"Yes," Matt said. "The officers' wives do this every time a wagon train passes through. The truth is they are so isolated out here that they really enjoy these visits."

The band consisted of two fiddles, a bass fiddler, and an accordion. In addition, there was a dance caller. Matt had raised two hundred fifty dollars from among the members of the train, and that was enough for fifty dollars apiece for each of the musicians and the caller. That was more than two months' pay for each of them.

"Lon," Matt said, "when we form squares, Frank and I would appreciate it if you and Norma would join our square. Jared will be in the square too, and he'll dance with Emma and Precious."

"I thank you, Mr. Logan," Lon replied with a big smile. "Norma 'n' I would appreciate it. And I know that Precious and Emma will, because that's all they've been talkin' about."

"Ladies and gents!" the caller shouted. "Form your squares!"

Matt took Ellen by the arm and led her out onto the

floor. Frank and Rosie followed, then Lon and Norma, and Jared, Emma and Precious."

There was room enough for half-a-dozen squares to be formed, and those who weren't part of one, stood around the edge joining in the excitement.

The music started and the caller began his chants calling loudly and keeping time with the music by stomping his right foot.

> *Crack that whip, jerk the line,*
> *Let's start dancing and have a good time.*
> *Do si do don't you know,*
> *You can't catch a rabbit till it comes a snow.*
> *Dog in the corner gnawin' on a bone,*
> *Meet your girl, promenade 'er home.*
> *Down in the barnyard swinging on a gate,*
> *Swing your honey and don't be late.*

The festivities lasted until midnight, and though there were a few quietly spoken objections to Lon and his family being present, there were no overt incidents. When the dance ended, a lot of tired, but happy travelers returned to their wagons.

IT HAD BEEN six days since the wagon train had been attacked, and Nonnie Hughes was all alone. She wasn't concerned for her survival. There was plenty of food remaining, so she was in no danger of starving to death, but she had to force herself to eat, doing so only because she knew that she had to.

Nonnie was aware that this was a well-traveled route, and she knew that eventually there would be another train. Back at Fort Laramie, they were told that the trains were no more than a week apart, so all she had to do was wait.

She hadn't been able to bury anyone, but out of respect, she had covered all the bodies with a blanket.

Many of the oxen had been killed in the attack, and those still alive were in harness with those that were dead. Because of the dead oxen still in traces, the live ones weren't able to move, and now several of the oxen, frightened and hungry, were calling out.

Nonnie had faithfully carried a bucket of water to each of the surviving animals at least once a day. Having watered the last oxen, she sat with her back against the front wheel of her wagon, with her arms wrapped around her pulled up knees. She could do nothing more but wait.

29

MATT WAS ALMOST TWO MILES AHEAD OF THE TRAIN WHEN he heard the bellowing of oxen. Moving toward the sound, he came upon the six wagons located just off the main trail. At first, he thought that they were stopped, and he wondered why such a small train would be stopping in mid-morning. Then, as he got closer, he was surprised to see that there was at least one dead animal in the traces of every wagon. Then he saw several blankets spread out haphazardly on the ground, and he was confused as to why they would be there.

Apparently, whatever this was, it had happened during a meal, because there were kettles, frying pans, and Dutch ovens on grates over now-dead fires.

Matt dismounted, and ground tethered his horse. Pulling his pistol, he walked, cautiously, toward the wagons. When he got closer, from the smell and the flies, he surmised that the blankets were covering dead bodies and that was puzzling. If everyone was dead, who had covered the bodies?

He began checking them, one at a time. The first two

he checked were men, the third was a little boy who looked to be no more than nine or ten.

"They're all dead," a woman's voice said. "Nineteen of them, all but me," she added, her voice choking with the comment.

Startled by the voice, Matt whirled around to see a woman standing there.

"When did this happen?" Matt asked.

"Six days ago."

"Indians?" Matt asked, putting his pistol away.

The woman shook her head. "No. They were white men."

"White men did this?"

"Yes. They came riding toward us, and no one suspected anything. Then, when they got right on top of us, they began shooting. They shot everyone—men, women, children."

"How did you escape?"

The woman let out a sob.

"I had gone to the river for water, and when I saw the riders coming, I was afraid." She hesitated but then she continued. "I hid in the willows, and I did nothing to help them." She started sobbing uncontrollably.

"What could you have done to help?" Matt asked, moving toward the woman. "Had you let yourself be known, you would only have been killed, too, but now you are helping them by telling what happened. What's your name, ma'am?"

"Hughes. Nonnie Hughes. My brother's name was Gordon Parker. And my nephew was Fred. Fred was . . ." again she let out a sob. "Fred was only fourteen."

"Mrs. Hughes, you need to come with me," Matt said.

"No," she said, resolutely. "I'm not leaving here until

my brother and my nephew are buried. And all the rest. They were my friends."

"I'm with a wagon train that's only about two miles back. When we get here, we'll bury everyone."

"Do you promise?"

"I promise."

JARED WAS RIDING BACK along the line of wagons, checking to see if anyone had any problems. Cody, who had made the same check half an hour previous, was now riding alongside his wagon talking with Ellen.

"Yes, ma'am, your mama would have been right here with us. She always was one for adventure. Why, when we left Virginia, she thought nothing about coming to Missouri, even though she'd never been there."

"She would have, I agree. She was . . ." Ellen paused in mid-sentence. "Papa, here comes Matt, and there's someone riding double with him. I think it's a woman."

"What in the world?" Cody replied, the tone of his voice reflecting his curiosity.

Cody rode out to meet them. Ellen was right—the person riding with Matt was a woman. As he made a closer perusal, he saw that she appeared to be in her late thirties, or early forties.

"Cody, this is Mrs. Hughes," Matt said. "She's the only survivor from an attack on her wagon train. And get this. They were white men."

"White? I wonder if it was Hood Raiders."

"Hood Raiders? Yes, they were all wearing black hoods, except for one. He was wearing a red hood," the woman said, speaking for the first time.

"Did you hear anyone say anything?" Matt asked.

"When they were leaving, I heard someone call out

the word face or something like that. Then he said 'you told us it would be like picking up hundred-dollar bills'. And then they all laughed."

"Damn, it was Dace," Cody said. Then, quickly, "Excuse the language, ma'am. I apologize."

"No apology needed," Nonnie said.

"Matt, let's get her back to the train. She can ride on my wagon with Ellen."

"You said you would bury them," Nonnie said.

"Yes, ma'am, I did say that," Matt replied, "and we will. Cody, there are nineteen bodies ahead. I promised Mrs. Hughes we would bury them."

"And so we shall," Cody replied.

IT TOOK MORE than an hour for the men to dig the graves where the families were laid to rest together. Then Reverend Owen said their names as he offered prayers for each of the nineteen people.

"Captain McNair, they do call you Captain McNair, I believe," Nonnie said.

"Yes, ma'am."

"I think there are enough live animals to pull my wagon. I wonder if it would be all right to put together a team, so I could join my wagon with your train."

"Excellent suggestion," Cody said. "We'll put together a team for your wagon, then bring the remaining animals with us. There's no sense in leaving them here to die, and it would be good to have a few extra oxen with us as spares."

"JARED, I'm going to ride alongside Mrs. Hughes' wagon for a while," Cody said when they returned to the train.

"She's been through a lot, and now she's thrown in with a bunch of strangers."

Jared smiled. "And she's a good-looking woman, too."

"Jared," Cody said sharply.

"I didn't mean anything by it, Pa," Jared said holding up both hands, palms out, but the smile didn't leave his face.

"You're right, she is a handsome woman," Cody replied, returning his son's smile.

Cody rode back along the string of wagons, exchanging greetings with those who were driving, and those who were walking. Nonnie Hughes' wagon was next to the very last one, followed by Harm and Gretchen Schultz.

"Mrs. Hughes, how are you getting along?" Cody asked.

"Other than the fact that my entire world has just come apart, I suppose you could say I'm doing all right."

"I'm so sorry about your brother and your nephew. Please forgive me for being so casual about it," Cody replied.

"No," Nonnie said with a dismissive wave of her hand. "I'm the one who needs forgiveness. You were being considerate of my situation, and I was inconsiderate with my answer. I'm sorry."

"You have nothing to be sorry for, ma'am."

"Nonnie."

"I beg your pardon?"

"If I'm going to be a part of your wagon train, I would like to fit in. Please, call me Nonnie."

"Nonnie it is," Cody replied. "And I'm Cody. The reason I came back here, was to invite you to have dinner this evening with me and my children. It'll keep you from having to eat alone, and it will give us the opportunity to get to know you better."

"I will be pleased to join you," Nonnie replied, "and I thank you for your kindness."

Cody touched the brim of his hat, then dropped on back to the trailing wagon.

"Everything going all right with you, Harm?"

"Ja, alles gut."

"What about the lady in front of us, Captain?" Gretchen asked. "How terrible things must be for her."

"She's been through a terrible ordeal, but she seems to be a strong woman. I have a feeling she'll get through this just fine."

"Do you think it would be all right if I rode with her for a while? She may want to talk to someone," Gretchen asked.

"Ich weis nicht, wirst du Englisch sprechen?" Cody asked, with a smile.

Gretchen laughed. *"Ja*, I will speak English."

"Then I think she would appreciate the company."

As Cody rode back to the front of the train, Emma called out to him as he passed the Murray wagon.

"Captain McNair, look. Me 'n Precious are riding with Miz Murray."

Emma had stood on the seat to wave at him.

"I see that, darlin', but you need to sit down so you don't fall," Cody called back to her.

Emma sat down, quickly. "All right," she said.

Cody was pleased with the way Lon and Norma, and Tim and Anita were taking care of Emma. He knew that the eventual plan was for Emma to wind up with the Murrays, and it was good to see that Emma seemed to be responding well.

"How was your meeting with Mrs. Hughes?" Jared asked when Cody returned to the front of the train.

"I asked her to eat with us tonight and she accepted."

"Wow, you just met her, and you've already asked her out to supper. You work fast, Pa."

"I haven't asked her out to supper."

"Didn't you say you asked her to eat, and she accepted?"

"Yes, but that's not asking her out. Asking her out would be if I took her to some restaurant or something."

"You know of any restaurants around here?" Jared asked with a taunting smile.

"No."

"You asked her to eat with you, but the only restaurant around, under the circumstances, is what Ellen fixes for us. So what is that, if it isn't a date?"

"It's a . . . date," Cody said with a surrendering laugh.

INDIAN VILLAGE

Darcy was taken by still another warrior. She bore the attack in silence and couldn't help but consider such attacks as a rape against her soul as well as against her body. When finally, she was returned to the tipi of Spirit Woman, she lay on her pallet and cried, quietly. Again, Spirit Woman gave her the prophylactic potion which thus far, had prevented her from getting pregnant. She prayed that it would continue to work.

She had seen her mother, father, and brother murdered before her very eyes. Why hadn't they killed her as well? She prayed that she would die, but she couldn't take her own life.

. . .

181

THE NEXT MORNING Darcy went down to the creek to get water when Hunting Bear came to her. There was another Indian with him.

"This is Swift Eagle," Hunting Bear said. "Today, you be his woman."

Was there no end to the degradation? When Darcy started to cry, Hunting Bear slapped her, hard.

"Do not cry," Hunting Bear ordered as he raised his hand again.

Darcy couldn't stop the tears from sliding down her cheeks, but she was able to keep her sobs silent.

"Come," Swift Eagle said. "You work."

Work? Yes, no matter what it might be, work was preferable to the other use made of her. And after she began the tasks Swift Eagle had assigned her, she found the work itself to be therapeutic. It allowed her to think about something other than her plight.

30

DARCY LAY IN THE DARK, LISTENING TO THE SNORES OF Spirit Woman. She was determined to try to escape tonight. She had planned it many times, and over the last few days, she had put together an escape kit. There were a few slices of cooked buffalo and deer, even some rabbit meat, along with some arrowroot and pine nuts. She figured it was sustenance enough for three days.

But where would she go? When her family's wagon had been attacked, it had been almost a month since they had last gone through any kind of settlement.

Based upon the average number of miles they covered in a day, that would mean she would have to travel many miles to get back to civilization. And all that without food, except for what she was taking with her and what she might be able to gather from the wild.

On the other hand, if she could make it back to the trail the wagon train had been following, there would be a good chance that another train would come along, and she could be rescued by them.

But where would they take her?

She knew that her family had been going to Oregon, though just where in Oregon, she wasn't sure. She had no relatives where they were going and had left no relatives back in Paducah, Kentucky. She was, quite literally, all alone in the world, except ironically, for Spirit Woman.

Darcy knew that Spirit Woman had been given the task of guarding her because she could speak some English, but Spirit Woman had taken on that task with compassion. Darcy was concerned that if she succeeded in escaping, Spirit Woman would be held responsible. Darcy didn't want anything bad to happen to the woman who had not only been guarding her but had, to the extent that she could, protected her. But she couldn't allow herself to think about that. She was determined to escape, and if she died in the attempt, so be it.

She had no idea what time it was, but she knew it was late. It was routine for several of the men to stay awake well into the night, but it had been a long time since she had heard anyone talking.

Getting up quietly so as not to awaken Spirit Woman, Darcy retrieved the escape kit which she had wrapped in a piece of deerskin that she had hidden away. Then, she slipped through the slit in the tipi and started toward the edge of the village where the horses were kept. She had little experience with horses, though after she was captured, she had been brought here by horse. However, she was riding with Red Hawk, who when they reached the village, claimed his prize by taking her virginity.

She had seen Red Hawk's horse several times since then and knew she would be able to recognize it. She had the idea that because she had been on the horse before, the horse might recognize her and be more receptive to her.

It was hard to find the exact horse in the dark, as it was one of several dark shadows, but she was quite certain she had found him. And here, she encountered the first problem.

There was no saddle, so there were no stirrups. There was nothing to climb up on to help her mount the horse, and she knew she could not leap upon the horse's back as the Indians did. Disappointed that she would not be able to escape on horseback, she set out on foot.

Her escape attempt ended the next day, when Red Hawk and four others tracked her down.

When she was taken back to the village, she was put under the charge of Buffalo Horn Woman, a woman who had shown her contempt for her.

"Where is Spirit Woman?" Darcy asked.

"Spirit Woman no more," Hunting Bear said. "You run from Spirit Woman. Now you with Buffalo Horn Woman."

Darcy looked toward Buffalo Horn Woman.

"Spirit Woman is old, weak woman. I, strong woman. You work."

What did Hunting Bear mean when he said "Spirit Woman no more"? God in heaven, had she been killed? If her old Indian guardian had been killed, it would be her fault.

Darcy prayed that she was still alive. She was the only one in the entire village who had ever shown her any tenderness or compassion.

Later that same day, Darcy saw Spirit Woman and was thankful for that, but when she tried to speak to her, Spirit Woman turned her back and walked away.

Darcy felt her heart sink. Spirit Woman had been her only link with humanity and now that link was gone.

What would she do now? How could she survive this ordeal?

WITH THE MCNAIR COMPANY

Cody called for a one-day halt to rest the animals and to take a break from the trail. Matt, Jared, and Frank Wiley went hunting and brought back three elk. The two halves of one of the elks were now suspended over the open fires, and the aroma of the cooking meat permeated the circle of wagons. Several of the women had made desserts so that the halt turned into a large picnic.

DALE GUTHRIE PLAYED the guitar and Rosie, who had a beautiful voice, sang for the group.

After the meal and the music, the children organized a game of hide and seek. Drew Guthrie, who was sixteen and the oldest of the group of children, volunteered to be "it" for the game. Emma and Precious were the two youngest of the children, so they chose to hide together.

"There, behind that bush by the creek," Emma said, pointing. "Drew won't see us if we hide there."

"Yes," Precious said. "This is the best hiding place of them all. He won't find us."

It wasn't only the children who drifted away from the encircled wagons. Ellen and Matt, Rosie and Frank left as well.

"You know what, Pa? It looks to me like Matt and my little sister seem to be hitting it off," Jared said.

"Matt's a good man," Cody said. "Ellen could do worse."

. . .

"Precious, you stay here," Emma said, shortly after they took up their position behind the creek-side juniper shrub. "I'm going to see where Drew is."

"I'm scared to be by myself," Precious said.

"I won't be gone long. I just want to see where Drew is, so if he's close, we can move to another hiding place and he can't find us. You stay hidden, here."

"All right, I'll stay right here," Precious said, "but come back real quick."

There was absolutely no privacy on the train, so when Matt, Ellen, Frank and Rosie had walked some distance from the train, they separated. Frank and Rosie went about a hundred yards farther west so that each couple was able to enjoy some isolation.

"Frank and Rosie seem to be getting along quite well, don't you think?" Ellen asked.

"What about us?" Matt replied. "Are we getting along quite well?"

Ellen smiled, then leaned toward Matt and kissed him on the lips. Matt was surprised by her unexpected boldness.

"Does that answer your question?"

"Uh, yeah," Matt said. "I would say that it does."

They kissed again, and this time the kiss deepened until the point that they forced themselves to separate before it got out of hand.

Hunting Bear and three of his warriors were out hunting when they smelled the aroma of cooking meat. Hoping that it might be the campfire of a solitary traveler, they followed the scent.

"It is the white man's wagons," Hunting Bear said. "Too many men."

As they turned to leave, they saw a movement behind a bush near the creek. When they approached, they saw that it was a small girl, and that she was out of sight from the wagons.

"A black, white girl," Lone Coyote said.

"Never see a black, white girl," Red Hawk said as he moved closer.

"A black white girl will be good medicine. We take," Hunting Bear said.

Lone Coyote and Red Hawk dismounted, then crept up on the little girl. She was looking away and didn't see them until Red Hawk grabbed her. He covered her mouth with his hand so she couldn't cry out. She began kicking hard trying to get away, but he was holding her too tight.

Lone Coyote mounted his horse and Red Hawk passed the child up to him.

Emma was just returning to the bush where she had left Precious, when she saw the Indians grab her, then ride away with her.

Emma started to scream in protest, but reason overcame panic, and she bit on her hand to keep from crying out.

"SHE'S GONE! Precious is gone! Indians took her!" Emma shouted, running back toward the wagons.

"What's Emma yelling about?" Cody asked.

"I don't know, but I'll find out," Jared said. He started toward her. "Emma, what's wrong?"

"Oh, Mr. Jared, Precious is gone, and it's my fault!" Emma yelled.

"Gone? Gone where? And why do you say it's your fault?"

"We were hiding, and I left her behind the bush so I could see where Drew was. She said she was scared, but I left her anyway. And when I came back, I saw them. Indians were riding off and they had Precious."

Cody and Lon had both come up in time to hear Emma tell the others about the Indians.

By now, Emma was crying. "Oh, Mr. Baker, it's my fault, it's all my fault. I left her behind the bush and the Indians got her." Emma ran to Lon and wrapped her arms around his leg.

"Hush, child," Lon said gently. "It wasn't your fault."

"Jared, go find Matt," Cody said.

"Where's Precious? Oh, where is my sweet Precious?" Norma called out, running out to join them. By now nearly a dozen members of the train had arrived in time to hear Emma explain again about leaving Precious behind a shrub, then returning in time to see Indians taking her away.

"What are we goin' to do, Cap'n?" Chub Collins asked.

"There's no question," Cody said. "We're going to get her back."

By then Jared returned with Matt and Ellen, and Frank and Rosie.

"It must be Hunting Bear," Matt said. "It has to be."

"Do you know where he might have taken her?" Cody asked.

"I have a pretty good idea where he might be, but, Cody, he's not going to just give her up."

"Then we'll damn well just take her," Jared said.

"What does that mean when you say you're goin' to

have to take her?" Laycock asked. "You mean get into a battle with the Indians? A shootin' battle?"

"I'm afraid so," Matt said.

"Well, do you think that's smart? I mean, if you leave her with 'em, maybe the Indians will be satisfied and won't come after us. If you grab her, don't you think they'll go on the warpath?"

"Laycock, are you suggesting we just leave that little girl with the Indians?" Cody asked, the expression of his voice indicating his anger with Laycock for even suggesting such a thing.

"I'm just sayin' that one little colored girl is not worth puttin' the whole wagon train in dang . . ."

That was as far as Laycock got, before he was laid out by a round-house right from Lon. Laycock lay flat on his back, unconscious.

"Pugh, when he comes to, it might be a good idea to keep him out of the way," Matt said.

"I'll be goin' with you, Matt," Lon said.

"You're going to need some more volunteers, aren't you?" Tim asked.

"Yes, we will."

"Then I'll be your first volunteer."

"I know I ain't been all that friendly with ever'one, but I volunteer too," Raymond Pugh said.

"What will Laycock think of that?" Matt asked.

"Frankly, Mr. Logan, I don't give a damn what he thinks."

Matt smiled. "In that case, Mr. Pugh, you're welcome to join us."

"Matt, if we can get a couple of people to keep an eye on the cattle, me 'n' my brother, 'n' Chub 'n' Deacon will come with you," Frank said.

"I'll keep watch over the cattle," David Sullivan offered.

"I'll help you, Mr. Sullivan," Drew offered.

Craig Patterson, Clay Ditmore, Joe Atwood, and Luke Taylor also volunteered, bringing the little rescue force to twelve men.

Before leaving, Matt made certain that all twelve men were armed with the Collier Flintlock revolver which would give them a total of seventy-eight rounds they could fire without reloading. In addition, each man carried a double-barrel shotgun which gave them an additional twenty-four rounds.

"The shotgun is a lot better than a rifle at close range," Matt said. "We'll use them first, then if we have to, we'll go to the pistols."

The volunteers collected the guns they would need, a couple of them having to borrow the weapons, then they gathered with their horses, alongside Cody's wagon.

"Gentlemen, charge your weapons," Matt ordered, and the men all saw to their cap and ball pistols and the shotguns.

The wives of the militia force gave frightened, tearful kisses to the men. Then the men mounted and looked to Matt for orders.

"Let's go," Matt said, waving them on.

"Oh, Papa, I'm so afraid for Matt and Jared," Ellen said.

Cody couldn't help but notice that she said Matt's name before she said her brother's name. He put his arm around her and pulled her to his side as they watched the men ride away.

31

IN THE INDIAN ENCAMPMENT OF HUNTING BEAR

Darcy was doing forced labor for Buffalo Horn Woman when she saw Hunting Bear return. She saw something on the horse with Lone Coyote but for a moment, she didn't know what it was. Then she saw that it was a child, and not just any child—it was a young, black girl.

Several of the Indians began running toward the returning braves all shouting in their excitement.

"A black, white girl," Hunting Bear said proudly as he pointed to Precious.

Several Indians gathered around as Lone Coyote lowered Precious to the ground. They all started stroking her skin and touching her hair.

"Never before see a black, white girl," Mean to His Horses said.

"She will be good medicine," Hunting Bear told the others as he beat himself on the chest.

. . .

PRECIOUS WAS TERRIFIED and her were eyes opened wide. She couldn't understand anything that was being said, but she was sure they were talking about her. She wanted her mama and daddy.

She saw one of the Indian women coming toward her.

"Honey, what is your name?" the woman asked.

"Precious." Her voice was barely above a whisper.

"Don't be afraid. I was taken by the Indians just like you."

"Will they kill me?" Precious asked.

"No, they won't hurt you. They think you are good medicine," Darcy said, speaking as soothingly as she could.

"Medicine? I'm not medicine."

"That means they think you will bring them good luck. They won't hurt you."

"I want my mama and daddy."

"I know you do, sweetheart. I can't give you your mama and daddy, but I can be your special friend. And you can be my special friend, too."

"What is your name?"

"My name is Darcy."

"Miss Darcy, will they ever let me go?"

"I don't know, but now we have each other," Darcy said as she embraced the child.

MATT HAD LEARNED tracking from Jim Bridger, and he was good at it. He was able to pick up the tracks of unshod horses in a wide expanse of grass-free soil. Then, after leaving the bare ground he could see the crushed and broken grass stems.

"I'm pretty sure I know where they are," Matt said to

Jared. "They have to be on Middle Fork of the Pao Agie River. It's the only good water around here."

The men continued ahead, spreading out in two columns, as they followed Matt. After about a half-hour's ride, Matt held up his hand to stop them.

"Jared, keep everybody here," Matt said. "I'm going to have a look at what's ahead."

Matt dismounted, pulled a telescope from his saddle-bag, then moved on foot until he reached a mesa. Climbing to the top, he saw a small village of about twenty or more tipis, exactly where he thought they would be, scattered alongside the middle fork of the river.

Putting the telescope to his eye, he got a closer look, then felt a charge of excitement when he saw her. Precious was standing out in the open. An Indian woman was standing beside her, holding her hand.

Matt slithered back down from the mesa, then hurried back to the others.

"I saw her!" he said.

"Is she all right?" Lon asked, anxiously.

"She looks fine, Mr. Baker. Apparently, some Indian woman is looking after her. She's holding Precious' hand, and Precious doesn't seem to be fighting her."

"What do we do now, Matt?" Jared asked.

"We're going in after her. Be careful where you shoot, we don't want to hit Precious or the woman who's with her. Actually, we don't want to shoot any of the women or children."

"How are we going to avoid that?"

"More than likely, when the shooting starts, the women will all run into the tipis, and I expect that's where Precious will go, so don't shoot into any tipi."

After a brief discussion, it was decided that they

would storm into the village on horseback, hoping to catch the Indians off guard.

"Have your shotguns ready and fire only at what you can see," Matt ordered.

THE INDIANS AND DARCY, too, were taken by complete surprise when a large body of men came charging in on galloping horses, firing shotguns at point blank range.

"Precious, come with me!" Darcy shouted pulling the little girl with her. It wasn't by chance that she ran into Spirit Woman's tipi.

"Down on the ground," Darcy ordered, and she and Precious joined Spirit Woman who was already lying down.

Outside the gunfire continued, accompanied by shouts of anger and screams of terror. The shooting was fast and furious, but it ended within no more than a minute.

"Is it over?" Precious asked in a frightened voice.

"I don't know," Darcy said. "Let's wait a while and see what happens."

"Precious!" a voice shouted.

"That's my daddy!" Precious said and getting up, she ran outside before Darcy could stop her. "Daddy, I'm here!"

When Darcy heard the happy greeting, she left the tipi as well. She saw the bloody bodies of nearly a dozen Indians, including Hunting Bear, Lone Coyote, Red Hawk, and Swift Eagle.

"Daddy, this is my friend," Precious said, when she saw Darcy emerge from the tipi.

"Do you speak English? I want to thank you for

looking after my little girl," Lon said.

"I'm not an Indian," Darcy said.

Darcy's pronouncement caught the attention of Matt and Jared.

"What are you doing here?" Jared asked.

"I was captured by the Indians when my family was killed," Darcy said.

Spirit Woman came, hesitantly, from the tipi and looked on with fear reflected in her face. She spoke to Darcy so quietly, that no one else could hear.

Darcy replied in the same *soto voce*.

"What did she say?" Matt asked.

"She wanted to know if you were going to hurt them. I told her no, that you were good people."

"She need not worry," Matt said. "Now that we have rescued the little girl we have come for, we'll be leaving."

"Please," Darcy said. "Take me with you as well."

"We won't leave you here. You can ride with me," Jared said.

"Return to your people, live well," Spirit Woman called out to Darcy as she left. This time Spirit Woman spoke loudly enough that all could hear.

"Thank you, Spirit Woman, for being my friend," Darcy called back to her.

On the return ride to the wagon train encampment, Darcy told Jared how she came to be with the Indians.

"Do you remember that wagon Colonel Munroe told us about?" Jared said to his father, after they returned to the train with Precious and Darcy. "The one where an entire family had been killed and scalped by Indians?"

"Yes, I remember."

"This is Darcy Clinton. That was her family."

Darcy then told Cody and the others how their wagon had been expelled from the Pollard wagon train because her younger brother had contracted cholera.

"And that is exactly why we won't leave any of our people behind," Cody said.

AT THE BEGINNING of the western expedition of the McNair train, some of the members of the train had been a little put-off by having a black family traveling with them. However, as the trek west continued, Lon's mechanical skills and willingness to help had won almost everyone over. And now, everyone expressed their happiness over the safe return of Precious.

Cody wasn't surprised when Anita Murray and Jane Guthrie came to him with the suggestion that they have a large, communal supper that evening to celebrate.

Since Precious had rejoined the train, Emma hadn't let her out of her sight.

"I'm not going to leave you, ever again," Emma said. "It was my fault that the Indians got you."

"Oh, Emma, it wasn't your fault," Darcy said. "If you had been with her, Hunting Bear would have taken both of you. I know, because I lived with them. And if they had taken both of you, who would been there to tell the others what happened?"

"How long were you with the Indians?" David Sullivan asked.

"I don't know, really. I had no way of keeping time while I was with them. But I'm sure it was for at least two months, maybe even longer."

"Any decent white woman would have done the right thing," Laycock said.

"And just what is the right thing, Laycock?" Jared

challenged.

"Uh, nothin'," Laycock said in a hesitant voice. He rubbed his chin, remembering the punch he had received from Lon Baker.

"I was just commentin', is all."

"Yeah, well you just keep comments like that to yourself," Jared said.

"Darcy, you can ride with us," Ellen said.

"I hate to impose," Darcy said.

Jared laughed. "We found you all alone, in the middle of the desert, so to speak. We certainly can't leave you here. If we did, how would you survive? Besides, we've asked you to join us, and if we ask, it isn't an imposition."

Darcy smiled. "Well, I have to admit that I'm glad someone found me. Anyone."

"Oh, so the fact that I'm brave, handsome, and loveable doesn't matter, just as long as I was someone," Jared said.

"Oh, no, I'm glad you're handsome and, uh," Darcy paused in mid-sentence.

"Jared, stop that!" Ellen said, hitting him on the shoulder. "Pay no attention to my brother," she added. "I swear, sometimes he can be such a child."

Darcy, realizing that she was being teased, laughed. "I'm sorry if I appear to be a bit addled. The last several weeks have been . . . trying."

"Oh, no, Darcy, please, you have nothing to apologize for," Jared said. "I was just teasing, and I shouldn't have done that. You've been through a lot, and only someone with courage and determination could have survived it. Please forgive me for being so . . . ," he stopped, looking for the word.

Ellen supplied it.

"For being such an insensitive lout."

Jared laughed. "What she said."

"You are forgiven my, how did you put it? Handsome, brave, lovable . . . shall I add hero?"

"Now it's your turn to tease, and I confess, I deserve it. But, like my sister said, we want you to ride with us."

"At least until we get to some place where you can arrange to go back home, if you want to," Ellen added.

"I have no place to go back to," Darcy said. "All the family I had was killed by the Indians so I may as well go on to Oregon. That's where my father had planned to take us."

"What will you do when you get there?" Ellen asked.

"I had planned to teach. And it's just as well for me to teach in Oregon as to teach in Kentucky, since I don't have any family in either place. In the meantime, we were on the trail for two months before we were attacked, so I know what chores have to be done, and I promise to do anything I can to help."

AT SUPPER THAT EVENING, Precious and Emma came to the McNair wagon, bringing a pie with them.

"Miss Darcy, this is for you, for taking care of my sister," Emma said.

"Your sister?" Darcy replied.

"Like you, Emma lost her whole family, but in her case, it was cholera. The Bakers took her in. I know it might seem a little odd but . . ."

"It isn't odd at all," Darcy said. "Apparently, the Bakers are like the McNairs. They are a family that reaches out to those in need."

. . .

OVER THE NEXT two weeks of travel Darcy began to be more comfortable with the people of the wagon train, and they with her. She and Ellen and Rosie became friends quickly. In addition, despite the differences in ages, she began to regard Precious and Emma as her little sisters.

For mile after stupefying mile, and day after numbing day, the oxen pulled the wagons through what Matt identified as the Sand Hill plains. It was flat and feature-less sand, except for occasional sagebrush and hills on the horizon.

There was barely enough water and vegetation to support the cattle and oxen. And the only fuel available to them was buffalo chips, which they gathered then stored in hammocks that were suspended from beneath the wagons.

Gradually, Darcy's feelings about Jared began to grow from one of gratitude, to one of attraction. He had teased her about him being handsome, but Darcy realized that he was handsome. He was also a person of some promi-nence within the train, because she learned early on, that he was the sheriff, or the head of the train constabularies.

"You like Matt, don't you?" Darcy asked Ellen once while she was riding in the wagon with Ellen.

"What makes you say that?"

Darcy chuckled. "It's easy to see that you like him. I can tell by the way you look at him."

"Is it that obvious?"

"No more obvious than the way he looks at you."

"Or the way you and my brother look at each other?" Ellen added.

Darcy chuckled again. "There might be something to that," she admitted.

A few days later, the train stopped a little earlier than usual so they could take advantage of available water. The water was Poison Creek, which despite its unflattering name, was a source of potable water.

32

THAT EVENING ELLEN AND MATT, ROSIE AND FRANK, AND Darcy and Jared took their supper on a quilt, spread out on the banks of the creek.

"How much longer before we get out of this sand?" Frank asked. "I've driven herds of cattle before, and I've never found any of 'em who could eat sand. What little vegetation we can find, is barely enough to keep 'em alive. We've got to get to some grass, or these critters are goin' to be nothin' but skin and bones."

"We'll be into some good graze within another week," Matt said. He pointed to one of the hills, far to the west that was standing separate from the others.

"That's Independence Rock."

"Why is it called that?"

"For a very important reason," Matt said. "If you're not there by the Fourth of July, you're left with only two choices. You either find some place where you can camp out for the better part of a year, or you turn around and go back home."

"Why is that?"

"Because if you aren't there by the Fourth of July, you won't make it to the mountain pass before snow closes it for the winter."

"Closes it? You mean we can't get through a little snow?" Frank asked.

"We might be able to. Then again, we might wind up like the Donner Party."

"Don't know as I've ever heard of that."

"The Donner party was a group of travelers who broke away from the rest of the wagon train because someone told them there was a shorter route. But it wasn't shorter, and because of that, they didn't reach the pass through the mountains until much later. Then, they got caught when a heavy snowfall blocked all the passes so that they couldn't move. They were trapped, and within three weeks, they ran out of food with absolutely no way of replenishing their food supply. One by one, they began dying of starvation."

"Oh, how horrible," Rosie said.

Matt shook his head. "You haven't heard the worst of it."

"What could be worse than starving to death?" Darcy asked.

"To keep from starving to death, the living ate the dead."

"Oh, Lord in Heaven!" Ellen gasped. "That's awful!"

"I know it's awful, but they felt they had no choice," Matt explained. "Of the eighty-nine who started through the pass, only forty-five survived."

HARM CHECKED his hops and was gratified by what he saw.

"The rootstocks seemed to have survived," he said. "None of them look withered."

"Ja, but we nearly didn't survive, you watered those rootstocks when we barely had enough to drink."

"Liebchen, without the hops, how will we survive when we get to Oregon?" as he sprinkled the fresh supply of water from the Poison River onto the sawdust filled boxes.

After finishing with the hops, Harm sat down beside Gretchen and leaned back against the wagon wheel.

Harm had learned the art of brewing from his father. It had been his intention to stay in Germany and operate his father's brewery, but his plans changed as a result of the Schleswig War. The war, which lasted from 1848 to 1851, ended when the Prussians had to withdraw their forces and resulted in a Danish victory.

Harm had participated in that war. It had been a costly experience for him. When the Danes had rained cannon fire down upon the town of Schleswig, Harm lost his mother, father, and the family business. In addition, he had sustained a leg wound which still bothered him.

It was something that he wanted to forget, but the death and destruction of that war still haunted him.

Harm had remained quiet for a long time, until Gretchen reached over to lay her hand on his leg.

"You're thinking of the war, aren't you?"

Harm nodded but made no audible reply.

"It will pass, Harm. You are in a new world now; you are in America, with a woman who loves you."

Du bist eine gute Frau, Gretchen. Du bist es, der mir ein neues Leben geschenkt hat.

"I'm glad you think I am a good woman who has

given you a new life. But in this country, you must speak English."

"*Ja, ich spreche Englisch.*"

Gretchen laughed. "You're impossible," she said.

"Hops," Harm said.

"Hops?"

"I must have a steady supply of hops if I am to make beer," Harm said.

"I thought that was the reason why you are taking such good care of these rootstock," Gretchen said. "If not, why are you coddling them so much?"

"It takes much work to raise hops."

"Maybe you can persuade someone to grow them for you."

"They would have to take a chance the first year," Harm said. "I would not be able to pay until the beer was brewed."

"Yes, but then a crop of hops would pay better than almost any other crop, wouldn't it?"

"Yes," Harm said. "If a person is willing to take the chance, he can make a lot of money."

Gretchen laughed.

"Why do you laugh?"

"Take a chance, Harm? Everyone on this train is taking a chance, aren't they?"

Harm laughed as well. "*Ja, jeder nimmt eine Chance wahr.*"

"English, Harm."

"Yes, everyone is taking a chance."

"Then I think you will have no problem finding someone who is willing to grow hops and wait for the money."

INDEPENDENCE ROCK – JULY 2, 1859

Cody and Matt were riding together, about a quarter of a mile ahead of the wagon column. Just ahead of them was an oval-shaped rise of granite rock. From this distance, it looked like a turtle shell.

"There it is—Independence Rock," Matt said, pointing to the rise ahead of them. "And by my calculation, today is Friday, the twenty-sixth of June. We have a week and a day until the Fourth of July, and that's plenty of time."

"Plenty of time for what?" Cody asked.

"Plenty of time to take a short break. You're in charge of this train, so it's your decision to make. But if you'd like a few days to rest the animals, make any repairs on the wagons, and just to rest, when we reach Independence Rock, it would be a good time to do that."

"Yes, Matt, thank you," Cody said. "I think that's an excellent idea. It might give us an opportunity to get in some hunting and restock our larder with meat, too."

Matt nodded his head. "This would be the place to do that. There's just about every kind of game you can think of here: buffalo, elk, deer, sage hen, rabbit. I think everyone would welcome a little variety."

"I'll go back and pass the word," Cody said.

They rode back together, and Cody held up his hand to stop the wagon that Ellen and Darcy were driving. Because they were first in line, it had the effect of stopping the whole train. Then he rode alongside the long line of wagons, making the announcement that he wanted to hold a meeting.

. . .

HALF AN HOUR LATER, more than eighty men, women, and children were gathered alongside Cody's wagon.

"What is it, Cody, what's going on?" Dale Guthrie asked.

"Folks, that rock you see just in front of us, is Independence Rock, and we'll be there by mid-afternoon. Matt tells me that if you reach this rock by the Fourth of July, you're in good position to make it through the pass before it's closed by the winter snows. Well, sir, we've got eight days before Independence Day, so I intend to hold us up here for most of that time. That'll give you and your animals time to rest. And, Lon?"

"Yes, sir, Cap'n?"

"Why don't you check in with everyone and see if anyone wants their wagon repaired, or even just checked over? Folks, you can have your wagons looked at for a dollar. Any work that has to be done, well, that'll be between you and Mr. Baker."

"Do we put the wagons in a circle?" someone asked.

"Yes. I certainly don't anticipate any Indian trouble while we're here, but if we keep our wagons in a tight circle, it'll just be easier for us to keep our animals together."

"All right, let's get to Independence Rock and circle the wagons!" Jared called out to the others.

After the circle was formed, half a dozen hunting teams went out, two men to a team. Jared and Matt went out together.

"This will, more than likely, be my last time to bring a wagon train through," Matt said.

"I don't blame you. This is the only trip I've made and it's exhausting. I can't imagine ever doing this again, but this is what? Your third?"

"My fourth by myself—Danny and I brought two through, together."

"Danny, your brother," Jared said.

Matt laughed. "Same as my brother. He's the closest to real family that I've ever had."

"If you leave the trail, what are you going to do?"

"I'm going to buy some land in the Willamette Valley, then settle down and farm it."

Jared nodded his head. "I feel like we've become friends during this trip, and it will be good to have you close enough that we can keep the friendship going."

"If things work out like I hope, we'd be more than friends," Matt said.

"Well now, how is it that we could be more than friends?" Jared asked, with a big smile.

"You'll have to ask your sister that."

"It seems to me like you're the one who'll have to do that."

Matt laughed. "I reckon you've got that right. I'll . . ." Matt paused in mid-comment. "Look, just through that draw."

Jared looked in the direction Matt had pointed. There, he saw a stand of about ten or twelve buffalo.

"Damn, just one of those could about feed the whole train," Jared said.

"Two of them would feed the train, and give your family and me," he added, "enough meat to last for a month. First, we'll take the one in the lead, then we'll get the one just behind it."

"If we both shoot at the same buffalo, won't the others run away?" Jared asked.

"No, if you take down the leader, there won't be anyone to tell the others to run."

Jared laughed. "You're not serious."

"Yes, I am. Buffalo are that way. That's how the buff hunters have been able to kill so many. That's why they call them a stand."

"All right, let's do it."

Matt and Jared aimed at the lead buffalo, and when they had their sight picture established, Matt counted down from three.

"Three, two, one," he said, slowly.

Both rifles fired at the same time, and two puffs of dust erupted from the impact of the bullets, then the lead buffalo went down.

The same procedure worked with the second buffalo, and only then did the others move away, more from a sense of confusion than panic.

IT WAS mid-afternoon before they had the two animals skinned and butchered. Then, putting the cut pieces of meat onto the two skins, they attached the skins to the horses, and pulled their treasure back to the circle of wagons.

MOST OF THE other hunter teams had had fruitful outings as well, as deer and elk had been brought back.

With open-fire roasted buffalo meat providing the central fare, every other wagon contributed something, from baked bread to beans and vegetables, to sweets and pies for the community dinner that was to be that evening.

"Harm, you know what would have made this dinner *sehr gut?*"

"*Ja, mein bier.*"

"How soon do you think we'll be able to drink some of that beer, Hans?" Craig Patterson asked.

"All I'll need will be some barley, some yeast, and of course, my hops."

"What are hops?" Joe Atwood asked.

"They are plants that grow a special kind of flower. And from that flower, beer gets its flavor."

"And where do you get these hops?" Tim Murray asked.

"Ah—I have the rootstocks," Harm said. "But it takes much work to grow hops."

"Then it seems to me like we need to help you grow some hops," Tim Murray said.

"*Ja*, that would be *gut*," Harm said.

33

DARCY FELT SAFE WITH THIS WAGON TRAIN. MORE THAN safe, she felt welcome, and she was so appreciative that she couldn't help but feel a little guilt, as well.

Darcy's youngest brother had died with cholera, her mother, father, and other brother had been killed, and yet she was here among good people, about to take part in a gala celebration. Somehow it didn't seem right, but she couldn't turn her back on it.

"Darcy, would you like to help me make some graham buns?" Ellen asked. "I've been saving my graham flour for just such an occasion."

"I would love to help," Darcy said.

As Darcy lowered the table off the back of the wagon, Ellen took out the ingredients and utensils they would need for making the dough. Jared and Matt were in a conversation nearby, and one of them must have said something funny, because now, both men were laughing. The sound caused Darcy to look toward the two men.

She was feeling a strong attraction to Jared. He was nice looking, and she was certainly grateful that he had rescued her. But Darcy hoped, and she certainly believed, that the attraction was based upon something stronger than mere gratitude.

"I can't tell you how grateful I am that your family has taken me in," Darcy said, as she helped Ellen knead the dough.

"We are enjoying having you with us," Ellen said. She smiled. "And who knows, you might be a part of our family someday."

"What . . . what do you mean?" Darcy asked.

"Darcy, are you really trying to tell me that you have no idea that my brother is attracted to you?"

"I, I've been . . ." Darcy said her face coloring as she quickly looked away.

Ellen laughed. "Ha. I knew it! You're attracted to him, too."

"I might be, but I don't know what to do about it."

"That's easy. You don't have to do anything, it'll happen, just as it is happening with Matt and me."

"Is happening, or has happened?"

"Let's just say that it is a thing in progress."

"I . . . I can't hope for such a thing," Darcy said.

"What do you mean, of course you can. I know my brother, and I know that he's interested in you."

"But you don't understand," Darcy said.

"What is it I don't understand?"

Darcy didn't answer immediately. Instead, tears began flowing down her cheeks.

"Darcy, what is it? What's wrong?"

"I'm no good for him," Darcy said. "The Indians, they . . ." she paused in mid-sentence. "They used me."

"They *used* you?" Ellen said as if not comprehending what Darcy was saying.

"Yes, I am no longer innocent."

Then, it came to Ellen what Darcy meant.

Ellen reached out to put her hand on Darcy's arm. "Darcy, of course you are still innocent, that was none of your doing," she said. "Believe me, that's not something Jared would even begin to consider, other than to feel compassion for what you had to go through. I know it will be hard for you to do, but please just put that thought out of your mind."

"You're a good woman, Ellen. I've never had a friend quite like you."

Ellen smiled. "Like I said, Darcy, who knows, someday we may well be sisters."

WHILE ELLEN, Darcy, and the other women cooked, the men tended to the meat and to their wagons, and the children played, Cody took it upon himself, to seek out Nonnie's wagon. He saw her conversing with Harm and Gretchen Schultz.

"*Hauptmann* McNair," Harm said by way of greeting. "It is good of you to visit with us."

Cody smiled. "I like to keep up with everyone. Mrs. Hughes, how are you getting along?"

"I'm doing well, thank you."

"I wonder if I could convince you to be my guest for supper, tonight."

"I thought this was supposed to be a communal supper."

"It is, but I would like for you to join my family and me."

213

"Oh, you've done so much for me as it is, I wouldn't want to put you out."

"Believe me, you wouldn't be putting us out. And I would welcome your company."

Nonnie smiled. He had thought, all along, that she was attractive, but the smile made her beautiful.

"All right then, I would be happy to join you."

"I'll call for you at six o'clock," Cody said.

"Oh, that won't be necessary. I can find my way to your wagon."

"You don't understand," Cody said, with a broad smile. "I *want* to call for you."

NONNIE WATCHED Cody walk away until he disappeared around the circle of wagons. She wondered about him, and more specifically how she felt about him.

She had been so specific in telling her brother how she had no interest in forming any relationship with another man. But now she was beginning to have second thoughts about that, because she was attracted to Cody. But the question she had to ask herself was whether what she felt for Cody was genuine interest, or merely a sense of gratitude for being rescued and accepted by him.

THE SUPPER that evening was the most gala event to have happened since the wagon train had formed back in St. Louis, more enjoyable even than their time at Fort Laramie. There, it had been a joint celebration between soldiers stationed at the fort and members of the McNair company. Tonight, the setting was more inti-mate—more like one big family, as it involved only those who had become so close while traveling with the train.

Emma, Precious, and a dozen other children enjoyed each other's company, regardless of their age, and Precious was just as welcome as any other child.

Alonzo Baker had already won over most of the travelers. Wagons that might have been left abandoned on the side of the trail, were able to stay with the train because of Lon's ability to repair just about anything.

Now, many of those who had had no previous experience with Lon, hired him to examine their wagons for the second half, and the more challenging part of their journey.

Even Peter Laycock and Pugh made use of Lon's services.

Nonnie wasn't sure how she would fit in as she had so recently joined the train.

Cody had invited her to sit next to him, and he was very solicitous of her, engaging her in conversation and fetching things for her.

Nonnie was enjoying the intimacy, so much so that she experienced a feeling of guilt, as if she were cheating on Andrew.

Andrew W. Hughes had been a doctor, working with her brother, when he contracted pneumonia and died.

Andrew, this is just innocent conversation, she thought. *You know that I will always love you.*

CODY FOUND himself enjoying Nonnie's company much more than he thought he would. There had been nobody but Lucinda for him, though there had been women who had managed to let him know that they would welcome his interest.

This is foolish, he thought. Here he was, sitting with, and enjoying the company of a warm and beautiful woman, but thinking of his late wife. He knew that Nonnie was a widow, and he couldn't help but wonder if she was thinking of her late husband now.

"When you think about it, being on a wagon train is sort of like being in a town that's moving. And like a town, you can meet your neighbors," Ellen said.

"Ellen, what are you talking about?" Jared asked.

"Well, think about it. You, papa and I started out on this trip, not knowing anyone. Now we know a lot of people, and we've made particular friends with some of them, Matt, Darcy, and papa's new friend, Mrs. Hughes."

"Ellen, if I'm going to be a part of this town's neighbors you're talking about, I'd like it if you would call me Nonnie."

"Then Nonnie it will be," Ellen said with a smile.

"And here's something else interesting about it," she said. "Two of our neighbors weren't even with us when we left St. Louis."

As soon as Ellen spoke, she saw Nonnie and Darcy's reaction to her words, and she regretted saying it.

"Oh," Ellen said, reaching out to lay her hand on Darcy's. "I wasn't thinking, I'm sorry my words brought up unpleasant memories for either of you."

"No need to apologize. What happened to us is in our past, and it will be in our past forever. We're going to have to embrace the future," Nonnie said.

"Yes," Darcy agreed.

Emma and Precious came running up to them. "Captain McNair, Miz Norma wants to know can she 'n' Mr. Lon come over 'n' join up with you?" Emma asked.

"Of course, they can," Cody replied.

The two little girls ran away, disappearing into the

darkness that lay beyond the golden bubble of light from the fire. A moment later they returned with Lon and Norma.

"Lon, you can join us on one condition," Cody said. "You have to sing a song for us."

A broad smile spread across Lon's face. "Yes, sir," he said. "Yes, sir, I can do that."

Lon began to sing a song entitled *The Poor Old Slave*. His deep voice, the melody and lyrics reached into the very souls of all who were sitting around the campfire.

> *The poor old slave has gone to rest,*
> *We know that he is free.*
> *Disturb him not but let him rest,*
> *'Way down in Tennessee.*

When Lon and Norma started back to their wagon, later that evening, Cody went with them.

"Cap'n, we thank you for lettin' us join up with your family tonight."

"You didn't just join with my family, Lon, you and Norma *are* family."

"Yes, sir, I know we been together so long it seems like family," Lon said.

"No," Cody said. He was quiet for a moment. "It doesn't just seem like you are family. You *are* family. You're my brother-in-law, Alonzo."

"Cap'n, I don't know what it is that you're sayin'."

"Norma knows, don't you, Norma," Cody said.

"Yes, sir, I know. I didn't know that you knew."

"Norma what are you talkin' about?" Lon asked.

"I'm talking about Lucinda, Lon," Norma answered. "She was more than my childhood friend. She was my blood sister."

"Your sister? Miz Lucinda was your sister?"

"Haven't you ever wondered why I'm so fair?"

"No, I've know'd lots of folks that are," Lon said.

"The reason I am light toned is 'cause my mama was a slave girl, but my papa and Lucinda's papa be the same man. Lucinda was my sister."

"How come you never told me?"

"Lucinda make me swear I'd never tell nobody, but I reckon it'll be all right to tell now."

"So, Lon," Cody said, "you are my brother-in-law, Norma is my sister-in-law, and Precious is my niece."

"All this time we were on the ship together, you don't say nothin' 'bout this," Lon said, his voice almost an accusation.

"I didn't know it until about a month before Lucinda died," Cody replied. "And now that she's gone, I see no reason to keep it a secret any longer. Especially since we are going west together."

A big smile spread across Lon's face. "Lawd, that's good to hear. But don't worry, I won't never tell no one."

"Why not? I'm going to tell Jared and Ellen so that they know you and Norma are their uncle and aunt and Precious is their cousin."

"I expects that's somethin' Precious will like to hear."

"What about Jared and Ellen?" Norma asked. "Aren't you worried 'bout what they may think?"

"I'll be telling them as soon as I get back to the wagon. I expect they'll be happy about it, too."

THAT NIGHT, as Norma lay on her blankets under the wagon, she thought back to the conversation she and Lucinda had had, so many years before. Lucinda's mother had died when Lucinda was twelve years old.

Lucinda's father died when she was nineteen. The farm was sold, though there was a stipulation in Tom Monroe's will, that the slave, Norma, who was eighteen, would become the personal property of Lucinda.

When all the paperwork for the farm was completed, Lucinda sat down with Norma. The two girls had been playmates for as long as either of them could remember.

"Norma, you know what this paper is?" Lucinda asked, holding up a sheet of paper.

"No, ma'am, I don't," Norma said.

"Ma'am?" Lucinda laughed. "Norma, you have never called me ma'am."

"Yes, ma'am, I know but we were only little girls then. It ain't like that now. Now you own me."

Lucinda shook her head. "No, that's just it. I don't own you, Norma. That's what this paper says. This is your manumission paper, and that means you are a free woman."

"Lawd, Miss Lucinda, do you mean that?" Norma asked, happily.

"Yes, I do mean that. And I have some other news for you as well, but if I tell you, you must swear to me that you'll never tell anyone else."

"I won't tell."

Lucinda smiled, then reached out and took both of Norma's hands into her own.

"Norma, do you know who your papa was?"

"No, ma'am, my mama died without never tellin' me who it was."

"Your papa and my papa were the same man. Norma, you're my half-sister," Lucinda said, as with a big smile, she wrapped her arms around Norma and pulled her to her in an embrace.

. . .

Lucinda had asked Norma never to tell and she hadn't. She would have gone to her grave with the secret of who her father was, if it hadn't been for Cody McNair. He was the one who had told, so Norma had been true to her vow.

34

"JARED, I WONDER IF YOU AND DARCY WOULD LIKE TO come with Ellen and me. I have something I'd like to show you," Matt said the next morning after the community dinner.

"What is it?" Jared asked.

Matt smiled and shook his head. "No, if I tell you what it is, it won't be a surprise."

"All right, sure, I'd like to go. But I don't know about Darcy."

"And tell me, Jared McNair, just why do you think Darcy wouldn't want to come with us?" Ellen asked in a sharp-edged voice.

"Here now," Matt said, laughing. "Don't you go picking on my friend like that."

"I'm just suggesting that if he is a gentleman, he'll ask her," Ellen said.

"Where is she?"

"She's over at Uncle Lon's wagon, visiting with Precious and Emma. I think she has taken them on as her first students."

"I can see her doing that," Matt said. Ellen referring to Lon as Uncle Lon didn't surprise Matt because he had heard the story.

"So, go ask her," Ellen said.

"What if she says no?"

Ellen sighed. "I can't believe I have a brother as dense as you are. Will you just ask her, for crying out loud?"

When Jared stepped over to Lon's wagon, he saw that Darcy was watching Precious and Emma playing the game of graces. The game was played with two wooden throwing rings decorated with ribbons and four catching wands. The players held a wand in each hand. Emma would place the rings over each wand in her hands and then toss the rings, one at a time, to Precious, who would try to catch them on her wands.

Emma tossed one of the rings and Precious caught it.

"That's good, Precious," Darcy said, clapping her hands. "Now, you toss the rings back to Emma."

"It won't do any good. Emma won't be able to catch it," Jared said, making his presence known.

"Oh yeah? You just watch me, Mr. Jared," Emma said. "Come on, Precious, toss one to me."

Precious tossed the ring, Emma caught it on her wand, and all four of them applauded.

"Have you come to see Mr. Baker?" Darcy asked. "I think he stepped over to Mr. Taylor's wagon."

"No, I came to see you. Matt has something he wants to show you and my sister . . . and me, too."

"What is it?"

"He won't tell. He says it's a surprise."

Darcy smiled. "Well, then, I suppose we'll have to go with him to find out what it is."

"Matt said we're going to need a bite to eat, before this day's over so I've packed us some biscuits and some sliced buffalo," Ellen said when Jared and Darcy returned to the McNair wagon.

"Well, then we're ready to go," Matt said.

"Are you going to tell us where we're going?" Jared asked.

"Sure, I can tell you now," Matt said. "We're going to climb to the top of Independence Rock."

"Ha, I thought you might have something like that in mind," Jared said. "I'll bet you have a pretty good view from up there."

"You do," Matt said. "Among other things," he added mysteriously.

"Other things? What other things?" Ellen asked.

"You'll see when we get there."

They rode horses about three miles from the circle of wagons. As they approached Independence Rock, Matt pointed out Devil's Gate through which the Sweetwater River passed. But it was the rock itself that he wanted them to see.

They ground-staked their horses at the foot of the rock.

"How big is this thing?" Jared asked as he looked up.

"Somebody measured it once and they say it's about 130 feet high, 1,900 feet long, and 850 feet wide," Matt said.

"Wow," Jared said. "I knew it was big."

"Do we want to eat our biscuits here, or on top of the rock?" Matt asked.

"Oh, let's climb to the top and eat there," Ellen said.

"All right, let's go."

The climb wasn't difficult, and within fifteen minutes they were standing on top.

"Oh, what a beautiful view!" Darcy said, as the four of

them took in the panoramic view of the valley below. "Thank you for bringing us up here."

"I'm glad you're enjoying the view, but there's something else I want you to see."

"Yes, you've been hinting at something special. Whatever it is, I'm ready for it."

"Let's eat first. We'll have to go back down to see them."

"Them?" Jared asked.

"Yeah, them."

During their picnic, they spoke of their plans for what they would do once they reached Oregon.

"Pa and I plan to buy adjacent properties. We can only buy three hundred acres apiece, but put together will be six hundred acres," Jared said. "What about you, Matt? You said this might be the last time you take a train through."

"I'm planning on getting about three hundred acres as well," Matt said. "Maybe we can be neighbors."

"I'd like that," Jared said. "Pa could help you put in a crop, because I'll bet you've never been a farmer."

Matt laughed. "You don't know that. The sisters at the orphanage put in a big garden, and I've hoed many a row."

"But that's vegetables. I mean a real crop."

"Silly," Ellen said, "you don't think people need to eat. I'll bet someday Oregon will grow all kinds of crops if the land's as good as everybody says."

"I suppose so," Matt said.

When they got to the base of Independence Rock, Matt showed them what he had brought them to see. The rock was covered with names.

"Names? They're everywhere, but who are they and why are they here?" Jared asked.

"These are the names of travelers who have come through here before."

"Is your name here?" Ellen asked.

"No."

"Why not? You've been here, haven't you?"

"I've always thought that since I was a guide, and not one of the settlers, that my name didn't belong here."

"But now that you plan to buy land, you need to add your name," Ellen said.

Matt smiled. "I intend for us all to put our names here," he said.

"Our names?"

Matt walked over to his horse and removed a hammer and chisel from the saddlebags.

"And I'm going to do it in a way that our names will be here two hundred years from now."

Before they went back, there were four new names chiseled into the side of the rock:

MATT LOGAN– ELLEN McNAIR
JARED McNAIR – DARCY CLINTON

It was late afternoon when they returned, and they shared with the others, about the names. The next day several more from the group visited Independence Rock to add their own name to the many hundreds of names that were already there.

On the Fourth of July, boards were taken from some of the wagons and used to make long tables. Dried buffalo, antelope, sage hens and rabbit provided the meat, while every wagon contributed whatever they could. Reverend Owen read the Declaration of Independence, then led a prayer of thanks for having brought them this far and asking His blessing for their future.

With Dale Guthrie playing the guitar, Lon Baker sang, *My Country 'Tis of Thee*, and *Amazing Grace*. Rosie Sullivan sang *Santa Lucia*.

When it grew dark, Cody had a surprise for everyone.

"We used these on-board ships for signaling," he said, "but I think they would be appropriate to use on this Independence Day."

Cody had four rockets which he sent streaking into the air to the delight of every member of the wagon train.

WHEN NONNIE WENT to bed that night she thought of the short time since she had joined with this train. At first, she had considered it only a matter of expediency. . . everyone in the train she had started with, was now dead, including her brother and her nephew.

By all rights, she should be melancholy, but she couldn't be. Though it defied all odds, she felt at home here, perhaps even more than she had felt when she was part of the train with her brother and nephew.

She also felt a growing attraction for Cody McNair.

Was it wrong for her to feel like this?

THE DESCENT DOWN Bear Mountain was quite steep and filled with sharp, pumpkin–sized rocks. It was hard enough to walk through, but it was exceptionally difficult to pull a wagon through.

Every trail guide was well aware of the difficulty of passage, and all explained to the wagons in their charge, that they would have to proceed at a snail's pace to keep from damaging the wagon wheels.

Arnie Boyd had taken three previous trains down the Bear Mountain descent and after cautioning all twenty-seven wagons in the train being captained by Marvin Long, they started down the mountain.

DUDLEY DACE WAS WELL aware of the difficulty the wagons would have in coming down Bear Mountain. He was just behind a slight rise as he watched the wagons start down the mountainside. When the last wagon was committed, he turned to look at the men who were waiting behind him and smiled. Then he pulled the red hood down over his head.

That was the signal for the others to do the same.

"Let's go," he said.

Arnie Boyd saw the approaching riders, noticing them first with a sense of curiosity. Then, when they were close enough to see that they were all wearing hoods, he knew who and what they were.

He started back up along the struggling wagons to sound the alert.

"It's the Hood Raiders, the Hood Raiders!" he shouted. "Get your guns!"

Most of the men of the wagon train didn't have their rifles at hand, and for those who did have them close by, most weren't even loaded.

Dace and the Hood Raiders shot the oxen in the lead wagon which had the effect of bringing the train to a halt. They made short work of the Boyd wagon train, killing all the men within the first few moments, and shooting any of the women who attempted to resist them when they robbed the wagons.

Then leaving behind forty bodies and wailing women and children, they rode off with their loot. When they gathered to count it later, it came to six thousand, five hundred dollars.

One more raid, Dace thought. One more and I'll have enough money to start a new life somewhere back east.

Back with the McNair train, it was one day's travel from Independence Rock to Devil's Gate, which was a narrow pass through the Antelope Range. Here, they were on the Sweetwater River, which was a welcome break from the alkali desert they had been on for the previous seven days.

Everyone took advantage of the cool water filling the water barrels, canteens, and water pouches. The women, happily, began washing clothes then, taking turns to preserve modesty, began bathing in the river.

While families were gathered around the individual campfires that night, Ellen, Darcy, and Rosie, took a walk away from the wagon camping ground along with Matt, Jared, and Frank. The river was a ribbon of black and silver, its gentle waves reflecting the light of the full moon.

"Jared, why don't you and Darcy go up river for a little way, and do some scouting. See if there's anything up there that we need to know about," Matt suggested. "Frank, you and Rosie can go downstream for, oh fifty yards or so, and do the same thing. Have a good look around and see if there's anything we should know about down river. If you don't see anything, just sit there for an hour or two and listen. Ellen and I will wait here for you until you come back."

"Sounds like a good idea," Jared said. "Come on, Darcy, you can help me look."

Matt and Ellen waited on the side of the river until Jared and Darcy, and Frank and Rosie disappeared into the darkness.

Ellen laughed, quietly. "Beautifully done," she said.

"What?" Matt asked, innocently.

"Yeah, what?" Ellen replied, with another soft laugh. "Do you have a plan as to how we should spend the time while we wait on them?"

Now it was Matt's time to chuckle. "I have an idea," he said, pulling her face to his.

After the kiss Ellen smiled. "Do you think the others are spending time the same way?"

"Nah," Matt said. "I'm sure they're just skipping rocks across the river."

Ellen laughed. "Would you rather be doing that?"

"Not unless we get bored," Matt replied.

"I'll try and keep you from getting bored," Ellen said.

THEY GOT UNDERWAY AGAIN the next morning. From Devil's Gate the trail started to rise gradually at first, then steeper and steeper still, until they reached South Pass. Here, the teams could no longer pull the wagons.

"You've been through here before," Cody said to Matt. "What do we do now?"

"Disconnect the teams from yours and Lon's wagons," Matt said. "We'll take the teams to the top of the pass, then using both teams, we'll connect them to your wagon by rope and pull it up. After we have your wagon at the top, we'll do the same thing to Lon's wagon. After we have both yours and Lon's wagons up, we'll disconnect the teams from the next two wagons and do the same thing with them, then the next two wagons following, and so on until we have every wagon up. It'll take us the whole day, but by the end of the day we'll be over the pass."

The last two wagons to make the climb to the summit

of South Pass were those belonging to Nonnie Hughes and Harm Schultz. Having worked hard at getting the wagons to the top of the pass, the noon meal had been cold biscuits and bacon or ham, whatever had been left over from breakfast. But once every wagon had negotiated the summit, dozens of cooking fires were lit as supper was prepared.

"You know where we are?" Matt asked over supper.

"You said this was South Pass," Jared said.

"Yes, but it's more than that. This is what they call the continental divide."

"What's that?" Ellen asked.

"So far, all the water we have passed flows east. From here on, all the water will flow west, toward the Pacific Ocean."

"I have another way to put it," Jared said. He pointed to the east. "Behind us is our past—homes, childhood, and memories." He pointed west. "Before us is the future —new lives, new friends, and ambition."

On the morning of the fourth day after coming through South Pass, Matt approached Jared just after breakfast.

"Fort Bridger is about five miles ahead of us. I'm going to ride on ahead and report that we have a wagon train on the way. We'll be able to rejoin the train before noon. Would you like to come with me?"

"Yes," Jared replied. "Yes, I think I'd like that."

"Cody, after breakfast, just keep the train moving. Like I told Jared, we'll rejoin you before noon."

On the way to the fort, Matt and Jared entered into conversation.

"Fort Bridger has an interesting history. It was built by my friend Jim Bridger to be used as a trading fort. He put in a blacksmith shop to support the wagon trains going west," Matt said.

"But now it belongs to the army, doesn't it?" Jared asked.

"Yes. It's a stockade post now with a ten-foot-high

wall," Matt said, "and I think the commander, Colonel Albert Sidney Johnston, should be a general."

"Why do you say that?"

"Because of all that he has done. He was in the Blackhawk War, he fought for Texas Independence, and he settled the Mormon dispute," Matt said.

"You talk as if you hold him in high regard," Jared replied.

"The highest regard," Matt said.

After a ride of less than an hour, they reached Fort Bridger.

"I'm Matt Logan and this is Jared McNair," Matt told the guard at the gate. "We're bringing a wagon train through, and we'd like to meet with Colonel Johnston, if we may."

"Colonel Johnston?"

"Yes, the commandant of the post."

"Oh, sir, that would be Colonel Edward Canby."

"Canby? What happened to Colonel Johnston?"

"He's commanding a post down around Salt Lake City. He's keepin' the Mormons in place, don't you know," the gate guard said with a little chuckle.

"Well, in that case, we'd like to meet with Colonel Canby."

"Yes, sir, go on up to the post headquarters building. The sergeant major will take care of you," the gate sentry said.

There were two infantry companies and one cavalry troop at the post, and as Matt and Jared rode across the parade grounds, one of the units was involved in dismounted drill. They could hear the drill sergeant's commands.

"Hut two, three, four, hut two, three, four, to the rear, march—to the rear, march!"

Once inside the headquarters building, they were ushered in to see Colonel Canby.

"Any cholera outbreaks?"

"Yes," Matt said, "but it's been more than a month since the last case."

"Well, bring 'em on in, we'll make our services available for you."

"Thank you, sir," Matt said.

"Oh, by the way, I feel I should warn you," Colonel Canby said.

"About what?"

"Have you ever heard of a group of outlaws that call themselves the Hood Raiders?"

"That's the group led by Dace?" Matt asked.

"Yes, do you know Dace?"

"No, I don't know him."

"The reason I asked, is folks say he once guided wagon trains over the trail," Colonel Canby said.

"Yes, I've heard that, but he must have operated out of St. Joseph, or perhaps up in Council Bluffs. I've never met him, and from what I hear about him, I'm just as glad that I haven't."

"Well, the reason I brought him up is, he and his band of outlaws recently attacked a wagon train at Bear Mountain. Killed all the men but stranded fourteen women and three children on the trail."

"What happened to the survivors?"

"One of our scouting patrols found them trying to walk back to the fort, so they brought them here. They weren't here more than a week when another train came through and those women joined up and went on west."

"I'd say that was a brave bunch of women," Jared said.

"I guess, but what choice did they have?" the colonel asked. "I think these Hood Raiders are working Bear

Mountain pretty hard, so I'd suggest you keep your eyes open."

"Thank you, we will," Matt said.

THE WAGON TRAIN spent two days at Fort Bridger giving the ox teams and the horses a rest, as well as the people. Also, here they were able to replenish supplies of flour, sugar, coffee, bacon, and beans. The cattle found good graze just outside the post.

Not long after leaving Fort Bridger, they came to a place known as "Parting of the Ways". Here, the wagon trail they had been following formed a "Y", and both trails were clearly marked by the wheel ruts of the many wagons which had preceded them.

The Southern trail continued straight to California. The other trail angled north and would take them to Oregon.

"Folks," Matt said, "here is where a decision has to be made."

He pointed toward the southern trail. "If any of you have decided to go to California, this is the trail for you. This trail," he said, pointing to the northern trail, "will take you to Oregon."

"Which way are you going, Matt?" Sullivan asked.

"I was paid to take this train to Oregon and that's where I'm going, with or without the wagons."

"Cody, what are you going to do?" Sullivan asked.

"I set out for Oregon and that's where I'm going," Cody said.

"Me too," Guthrie said.

"Hell, there ain't no question in my mind," Atwood said. "I'm goin' to Oregon."

Morris tried to convince a few people to go to California with him, but when he was unsuccessful, he reluctantly agreed to go on to Oregon with the others.

"All right," Matt said, "now comes the hard part so listen to me and listen well. We are about to cross sixty miles of desert. That means we need to fill every keg, bag, canteen, and any other receptacle that will hold water. It's going to be the hardest five days we've had so far."

"Can the animals go five days without water?" Cody asked.

"It's going to be hard on them, but this isn't my first time through here, and most of them make it."

"Most of them?" Laycock asked.

"That's what I said. Most of them."

"That means some of them died," Laycock challenged.

"Unfortunately, that's true."

"We paid you good money to get us to Oregon, and now you're about to take us through a desert where, by your own admission, many of the animals, if not some of us, will die."

"There is no other way, Mr. Laycock," Matt said, patiently. "If you want to go to Oregon, we have to cross sixty miles of desert. If you don't want to cross this desert, you won't be going to Oregon."

Laycock didn't respond to Matt's comment, so Matt continued his address to the others.

"For the next sixty miles we'll rest during the day and travel at night. By traveling at night, we can avoid the heat of the desert, and that will keep us from getting so thirsty. It will also be easier on the animals."

"We need to go as far as we can on the first night. That's when the teams will be the freshest, but as they get more tired, we won't be able to cover as much distance with them."

"How long will it take us to cross this desert?" Cody asked.

"If all goes well, we should be across in five days," Matt said. "It'll take an extra day because we won't be able to go as far each day as we normally do."

After filling every container they had with water, they rested for the rest of the day, trying to sleep in the shade of the wagons. Finally, after supper that evening and just as the sun was going down, they started their trip across the desert.

"Nonnie, if you are up to walking, I'll walk with you and handle your team," Cody said.

"Why thank you Cody. That would be very nice of you." Nonnie gave Cody what could best be described as a welcoming smile.

Everyone who could, walked, thus reducing the weight of the wagons and the labor of the oxen. The teams were driven by someone walking alongside, sometimes guiding them by holding onto their harness.

At midnight the train stopped for lunch. Nonnie had a more than ample supply of food, having taken what she could from the wagons of the ill-fated Dooley Train.

"Cody, you will take your midnight meal with me," Nonnie said. It was more of a statement, than a request.

"Yes, I'd love to."

"And, if you don't mind, I will invite Harm and Gretchen to eat with us. They have been so nice to me since I joined the train."

"Of course, by all means."

A few minutes later, as Nonnie and Gretchen prepared the meal, Cody and Harm visited.

"What crop will you grow?" Harm asked.

"I'm not sure—wheat, oats, corn, alfalfa. I haven't

given it too much thought." Cody laughed. "The only thing I know for sure I won't be growing is tobacco."

"Hops."

"What?"

"It is hops you should grow."

Cody shook his head. "I don't think I know about hops."

"It's a plant that I use to make beer. If you grow hops, I will sell you rootstocks you will need to plant your field, then I buy your crop. Then when hops are ready, I make beer."

"What about wheat, oats, corn and alfalfa?" Cody asked.

"You can still grow other crops, but ten acres you should make hops. From one acre you can make three hundred dollars."

"Ten acres? I'll plant a hundred acres."

"Enough roots I do not have for one hundred acres, but ten acres will make many roots and you can grow more the next year."

"I have an idea," Cody proposed. "Suppose I come in with you, I will supply the hops, and I'll pay half the cost of getting a brewery built. And we will supply saloons all over Oregon and California."

A big smile spread across Schultz's face. "*Hauptman,* you would do this?"

"Yes," Cody replied, matching Harm's smile. "And if we are going to be business partners, I am Cody, not captain."

"*Ja, Cody, wir werden Partner und Freunde sein.*"

Cody stuck out his hand. "Indeed," he said as he and Harm shook hands. "We will not only be partners—we will be friends."

"*Gut,* then some water you will give me so I can keep

the plants wet? I will not need too much, but I think going across the desert it take more."

"Sure, if we're partners, I'll give you some water. We wouldn't want to lose the hops."

"Nonnie says she will give some water too, so I think we will not lose hops."

"Cody, Harm killed a rabbit yesterday," Nonnie said. "Gretchen has been marinading it for six hours and has made *hassenpfeffer*."

"That sounds great," Cody said.

After a break of no more than an hour, the wagon train resumed its western trek.

THEY MADE twenty miles that first night and after resting all day, made another fifteen miles on the second night.

There was near disaster on the third night when the wagon belonging to Luke Taylor got the right wheels up on a rise, causing it to tip over. Fortunately, Alice Taylor, who was walking beside the wagon, was able to get out of the way.

The crashing sound alerted the wagons closest to the Taylor wagon, and shouts were passed up and down the line telling what had happened.

Matt, Cody and Jared hurried back to the scene of the upset wagon, joining half-a-dozen more who were already there.

"Was anyone hurt?" Cody asked, anxiously.

"No, Alice was walking alongside 'n' she got out the way," Luke said. "I was walking with the team, so I warn't never in no danger from it."

"Lon, take a look at it. See if it can still be pulled if we get it set back up on its wheels," Cody said.

"How we goin' to get that thing back up, heavy as it is?" Laycock asked.

"Yeah, if you ask me, we should just leave it here," Pugh added.

"We'll unload it, get it set up, then load it again," Cody said.

"I thought we was in a hurry to get acrost this desert," Laycock said. "Hell, why don't we just leave it?"

"Laycock, do you understand the purpose of a wagon train?" Cody asked.

"Yeah, it's to get somewhere."

"Together," Cody said pointedly. "It is to go together and to provide mutual protection and help when it's needed. Right now, it's Mr. Taylor who needs help, and we will help him."

After unloading the wagon, it took eight men to get it set back on its wheels. An examination of the wagon showed that the doubletree was broken, but there was a spare in the hoodlum wagon, and Lon got it replaced rather quickly.

The wagon train got underway again, but it only made five miles that night.

"I'm goin' on ahead," Laycock said the next morning.

"I'd advise against it," Matt cautioned. "Your team hasn't had any water to speak of for three days. If you work them in the hot sun, they may collapse on you."

"They're goin' to collapse anyway if I don't get them to water. And hangin' around here, ain't gettin' 'em no water."

"Do what you think you have to do," Matt said.

"I'll be waitin' for you at the river," Laycock said, as he moved his team around the wagons and continued on ahead.

When the rest of the company caught up with

Laycock that night, he had progressed only five more miles, and was now sitting with two oxen dead in their traces.

"Now what are we going to do?" Jared asked.

"I've got an idea, Cap'n," Lon said.

"What's that?"

"Remember when we found Miz Nonnie? Besides her team, we took seven more oxen. We could use two of 'em for Mr. Laycock's wagon."

"Yes!" Cody said. "Yes, of course we can."

Laycock stood by as Lon and Frank brought up two more oxen. The dead animals were pulled aside, and the new ones put in their place.

"Mr. Baker?" Laycock said, in a conciliatory tone of voice. "I . . . thank you. I may have been wrong about you."

Lon smiled and stuck out his hand. "Mr. Laycock, it's a good man who will admit when he was wrong. And you're a good man."

Laycock, surprised by how readily his apology had been accepted, smiled and gladly took Lon's hand. "You'll get no more trouble from me."

They advanced fifteen miles by sunrise, when Matt announced that they were within five miles of the river.

"I know we've gone all night," he said. "But it would be my recommendation that we continue on for another couple of hours. By then we'll be at the river, and we can lay up for the rest of the day and spend the night, so that we'll be back on our regular schedule. And," he added with a smile, "while we are resting, we will be resting with plenty of water."

"I say we go on," Atwood said.

There was no one who disagreed with him.

36

SNAKE RIVER – JULY 12TH, 1859

THE SNAKE RIVER WAS A MAJOR DISAPPOINTMENT TO THE travelers. The trail was basalt-encrusted barren ground with sharp broken rock that injured hooves of the animals and feet of the walkers. Instead of lush grass for the live-stock, there was gray-green sagebrush.

And though they were parallel with the river, there were few places where they could actually get water because for miles at a time, the river flowed between high walls of black basalt and all a thirsty man or animal could do was look down at the water, sometimes a hundred feet or more below.

During the several days of following the river there were, however, occasions where there was access to cool drinking water, graze for the cattle and oxen, and trees for shade. At the most generous of these places, Matt said that if they wanted to, they could stop here for up to three days without getting behind on their trip. As wagon master, it was Cody's decision to make and believing that both animals and travelers needed rest and replenishment, he decided they would stay.

The company had not been in better spirits since departing St. Louis, and instead of individual meals, they combined their food and once again came together for a festive gathering.

The universal joy was somewhat abated on the third day, when Emma developed a very high fever and complained of a bad headache. Then, instead of fever, she would have chills. She was staying with Tim and Anita at the time and Tim reported her illness to Cody.

"Oh, Lord," Cody said. "Is it cholera?"

"No, it isn't cholera," Nonnie said as she put a wet cloth on the child's head.

"How do you know it isn't cholera?"

"It isn't presenting itself as cholera. With the high fever and headache then alternating with chills, it sounds as if it may be mountain sickness."

"What's mountain sickness?" Cody asked. "Is it bad?"

"Yes, it can be very bad," Nonnie said. "I won't lie to you. It isn't necessarily a fatal outcome, but. . ." She left the sentence uncompleted.

"How is it that you know about this?"

"My husband and my brother were both doctors, and I often worked with them. We had two cases of mountain sickness in our wagon train and one of them passed."

A pall was cast over the entire company as they realized that the little girl who ran up and down the wagons, laughing, and greeting everyone could die.

But two days later, all seemed better. Emma was her old self again playing with Precious.

"I guess we didn't need to worry," Cody said. "Emma seems to be over whatever it was she had."

Nonnie shook her head. "If I'm right and it is the mountain sickness, it will recur."

And true to Nonnie's prediction, a few days later the sickness returned.

"I had hoped that maybe it wasn't the mountain sickness, but now I know that it is," Nonnie said. "This is exactly how the disease behaves. A person will be very sick with fever, chills, and a headache, then after a few days they feel fine and think all is well. But the sickness comes back."

"Is it contagious?" Cody asked.

"No, that's the good thing about it. It's very dangerous, but it isn't contagious."

"What can we do?" Tim Murray asked. "Can it be treated?"

"Symptomatically only, we can't address the cause, because we don't know the cause. Basically, all we can do is cool her when she has the fever, and warm her when she has chills. Whether or not she lives or dies, will depend on the good Lord and whether or not her constitution is strong enough to fight it off. She is young and healthy, so I think she has a better than even chance of surviving," Nonnie said. "If you don't mind, I would like to move her to my wagon. That way I can keep an eye on her."

"I want to come too," Precious said. She had been closely following the conversation of the adults.

"No, child. I know how much you 'n' Emma love each other, but I'll not be wantin' you to catch this from her," Norma said.

"There's no danger of her catching this from Emma because it doesn't seem to be contagious," Nonnie said. "If you would allow Precious to stay with Emma, it would help me to have her. She can put a wet cloth on her head when Emma needs it and put more quilts on her when she is having chills."

"Please, Mama?"

Norma reached down to put her arm around Precious and pulled her daughter to her.

"All right, if Miz Nonnie says she needs you, then you can stay with Emma."

"Oh, thank you, Mama!"

"Nonnie, I'm going to drive your wagon," Cody said.

"You don't have to do that, Cody," Nonnie said as she lowered her head.

"I know I don't have to, but I want to. You need to attend to Emma."

Nonnie sighed. "That will be a big help."

For the next three weeks as Emma would suffer a high fever and then chills, interspaced with periods of feeling all right, every member of the wagon train kept up with her condition.

When her time of feeling fine extended beyond a week, Nonnie declared her to be past the danger point. She was welcomed back to the Murray wagon with open arms. When the train stopped for the night, Norma Baker invited Emma, Tim and Anita, Cody, and Nonnie to have supper with them.

"Some people was sayin' you might die, but I knew you wasn't goin' to," Precious said. "Miz Nonnie took real good care of you."

"That's true," Anita said. She smiled at Precious. "But Miss Nonnie told me that having you there with Emma helped a lot, too."

"It did, having Precious there was a good thing," Nonnie said.

"Precious is my friend," Emma said as she reached out to take her hand.

THREE ISLAND CROSSING – JULY 18TH, 1859

After a little over a week of following the Snake River, the train came to a spot known as Three Island Crossing. It was easy enough to see why the ford was so named, because at this point there were three islands lined up almost as steppingstones across the river.

"This is a difficult place to ford, but it isn't impossible. We'll go from island to island," Matt said. "It will take some time to get us all across, so who wants to go first?"

"I'll go first," Jared said, snapping the reins to move the team forward.

When he got down to the edge of the water, the oxen stopped, hesitant to go into the water. Matt rode up to the near leader ox, grabbed the halter, and pulled him into the water.

It was about a hundred yards to the first island, then seventy-five to the second. With a short distance to the third island, the team pulled the wagon up onto the bank.

During the crossing, the water rose ten inches up on some of the wagon beds. Jared drove half-a-dozen of the wagons himself, the owners expressing some doubt if they could make the crossing.

Cody drove Nonnie's wagon across.

It took most of the day to get all the wagons across the river, and once all had made the crossing, Cody called a much-needed halt so that man and beast could recover from the ordeal of the crossing

*FAREWELL BEND, OREGON – AUGUST
12TH, 1859*

At Farewell Bend, the train left the Snake River and
there were few who regretted it. However, there was
little improvement in conditions. For the next several
days a cloud of thick, almost asphyxiating dust, hung
over the wagons. Cody hit upon the idea of rotating the
wagons every hour, with the last wagon moving up to
the front of the line, to be number two. Then, one hour
later it would become number three as the last wagon
moved in front of it. In that way they had periodic relief
from the choking dust.

When it was time for Nonnie's wagon to move
forward, Cody dropped back alongside.

"Do you mind if I join you?" he asked.

"No, I don't mind at all," Nonnie replied.

Nonnie stopped the wagon long enough for Cody to
tie off his horse, then he climbed up into the wagon and
took the reins.

"It's a little more difficult for the wagon to move up
alongside the actual trail, so maybe I'd better drive."

"Thank you," Nonnie said as, with a smile, she
handed him the reins.

Emma and Precious were walking alongside the
train, but far enough off the trail to avoid most of the
dust.

"Miz Nonnie, hello!" Emma called.

"Hello, dear, how are you feeling?"

"Good," Emma said, a broad smile crossing her face.

"That's wonderful," Nonnie replied.

When they got alongside the number two wagon,
which at the moment was the Guthrie wagon, Dale

stopped to allow Cody to position Nonnie's wagon in front of him.

"All right, here you go," Cody said as he jumped down. "It should be a lot more comfortable up here."

"Cody, thank you," Nonnie said.

"Ah, I didn't do much, just drove your wagon up to the front of the line."

"I don't mean just for that. I mean everything."

Cody smiled. "Nonnie, having you join our train has been a real blessing. And with your nursing, you've certainly earned your place."

SNAKE RIVER MOUNTAINS – SEPTEMBER 3RD, 1859

The Snake River Mountains proved to be one of the most difficult obstacles they had encountered thus far. It took them all day to climb to the top and in order to do that, as they had done at the Continental Divide, they had to double up the teams and use ropes to pull each wagon up inch by slow, agonizing inch.

When they stopped for the night, Nonnie invited Cody to eat with her. Because they were in the mountains, the wagons were not formed in a circle.

As she set the rolled out noodle dough, she thought about what she was doing. Was she being too forward in asking him to have supper with her, just the two of them?

He had been rather open in expressing his interest in her. But was it a genuine interest, or was he just being nice to her because of how they had found her?

No, she was sure that her interest in him was genuine, and she knew that what she was feeling for him was something beyond gratitude for being rescued. Not

since Andrew died, had she even considered a relationship with another man, but Cody McNair had changed
all that. She knew that she felt as strongly for Cody as
she had ever felt for Andrew.

But how did he feel about her? It was time for her to
find out. If there was nothing there, she could put a
check on her own feelings and prevent any heartbreak
from an unrequited investment.

Before time for him to come, she changed from the
drab, shapeless dress she had been wearing, into a calico
print dress that was cut so as to show her womanly
curves. This would be the first time she had worn the
dress since she had left home. She had given it some
thought, knowing that he might think she was trying to
send a message.

She smiled as she finished dressing. She *was* sending a
message.

37

BY NECESSITY, THE WAGONS WERE SPREAD OUT, AND AS Cody walked down the line, he exchanged greetings with the others. Even Laycock was more personable since Cody had arranged for him to have a couple of the spare oxen.

Cody saw Nonnie before she saw him, and he stopped and took in a quick, short breath that was almost a gasp. He had thought all along, that Nonnie was an attractive woman. But the woman standing beside her wagon now, was beautiful.

He saw, also, that she had dressed for the occasion, and for a moment he felt ashamed that he hadn't shown her the same consideration. He stopped for a moment, then steeling himself, continued on to her wagon.

Nonnie greeted him with a smile. "Hello," she said.

"You are beautiful," Cody said, then he put his hand to his mouth. Had he overstepped?

Her smile broadened, telling him that his comment had not been unwelcomed.

During the supper of elk and noodles, they shared

249

some of their past. Cody told Nonnie about his experience as a ship's captain. He paused for a moment trying to decide whether it was appropriate now, to tell her about Lucinda. He decided that it was.

"I want to tell you a little about Lucinda Monroe, my late wife. Her father owned a plantation near Denbigh, Virginia, and I met her when I visited him with the owner of the *Sea Sprite*. We had gone because the ship's owner was going to try and convince Mr. Monroe to invest in another ship. Lucinda was there, a pretty . . ." Cody paused for a moment, then took a sharp breath before he continued, "a pretty, feisty young woman who appeared to be fascinated by the idea of her father investing in a sailing ship. She came along with her father when he came to look at the ship, and after my next two voyages, I saw her again. When I saw her after my third voyage, we got married."

"Then, when I left the sea and came back to Missouri, Lucinda came with me without hesitation. We were married for twenty-two years, then . . ." Again, Cody paused, obviously having trouble with the next statement. "Then, she got sick, and she didn't get well.

"If Lucinda were still alive, she would have been the most enthusiastic traveler on this whole train. I wish you would have known her. I know the two of you would have been great friends."

"I'm sure that we would have been."

"What about you, Nonnie? What about your husband?"

"I met Andrew when I was nineteen and he and my brother were students at East Tennessee College. They both became doctors, and shared an office, and I became their nurse. Then, three years ago Andrew died of winter fever."

"Winter fever," Cody said. "That's what they said my Lucinda had."

"Winter fever is a very dangerous condition. More people die from pneumonia than anything else."

"What did you call it?"

"Pneumonia. That's the medical term for winter fever."

"So, both your husband and your brother were doctors, and you were their nurse. No wonder you were able to cure Emma," Cody said.

Nonnie chuckled. "Technically I didn't cure her, I gave her no nostrums. I just treated her symptoms until she recovered on her own."

"Well, you certainly won the gratitude of Tim and Anita Murray as well as Lon and Norma Baker, and to be truthful, the whole train. Everybody loves little Emma."

"Yes, I know that the child is an orphan. I'm glad there are people who are willing to give her the love she needs."

"You're not disturbed that one of those families who love her is colored?"

"No, why should I be?"

Cody smiled and took Nonnie's hand. "Why should you be, indeed. I'm glad to hear that, because I think now would be a good time to tell you that Norma is my sister-in-law."

"Your sister-in-law? You mean Lucinda . . ."

Cody interrupted her in mid-sentence. "Lucinda and Norma shared the same father."

"Oh, I see, so your friendship with Mr. Baker is deeper than just having sailed together."

"I don't think our friendship could have been any deeper than it is. But not even Lon knew of our family relationship until I told him a short time ago. Norma knew, but she had made a vow to Lucinda never to tell anyone, so she hadn't even told her husband."

"How did Mr. Baker take the news? I mean, was he upset that she hadn't told him?"

Cody smiled. "No, he understood. And you know, I think he was pleased that she hadn't said a word. She had kept her promise."

Cody and Nonnie visited far into the night, sharing stories of their past as they watched the golden bits of ash from the fire lifted by the rising heat wave until they blended with the stars.

"Oh, damn," Cody suddenly said as he jumped up. "I wonder what time it is. I'd better be going, because we'll have to get underway as early as possible tomorrow. Matt says it will be a hard day, but not as bad as today."

Nonnie smiled as she stood as well. "It has been a pleasant evening."

Cody looked at Nonnie and for a moment, she thought he was going to kiss her. She waited for it and was disappointed when it didn't come.

"I, uh, have really enjoyed it, too." He smiled. "If you don't mind, maybe we can share more suppers."

"I would like that," Nonnie said.

As CODY LAY on his blanket beneath his wagon that night, he thought about the evening he had spent with Nonnie Hughes. Not since Lucinda's death, had he felt such a connection with another woman. He wished he had kissed her—he should have because he was pretty sure she wouldn't have turned him away.

He would not pass up the opportunity if it presented itself again, and he was determined to make certain that the opportunity would present itself.

THE DESCENT from the Snake River Mountains was on a rough, uneven road, requiring the utmost skill and attention from the drivers to keep the oxen under control. Jared drove the McNair wagon, though by now, Ellen, having driven over fifteen hundred miles, would have been up to the task.

Cody rode alongside the wagons, checking with each driver to see if anyone needed help. No one seemed to need any assistance, not even Nonnie. However, since she was alone with this wagon, Cody offered to take the reins, and Nonnie, as much for the company as the need, welcomed the offer. She stopped the wagon to let him tie off his horse, then climb up onto the seat. There was enough separation between Nonnie's wagon, and the wagon behind her, that Cody was easily able to put it into motion again without the trailing wagon having to stop.

"Cody, just when do you plan to kiss me? Or are you ever going to kiss me?" Nonnie asked.

"What?" Cody replied, surprised by the question.

"Am I misreading this, Cody? I was under the impression that you . . . that is, that we might actually feel . . ."

That was as far as Nonnie got before Cody put his hand behind her head and pulled her to him for a deep kiss that lasted for several seconds.

"Is this what you were talking about?" Cody asked.

"It's a start," Nonnie replied with a happy smile.

"Nonnie, I don't know how this is possible. I had so much love for Lucinda that I didn't think I would ever have room to love someone else. And even now, I still love Lucinda. Does that bother you?"

"No, it doesn't bother me at all. Anyone who is

capable of that much love for a woman, is the man I want to be with."

EMILE POTTER, one of the Hood Raiders, had gone down trail to scout for the next train of wagons to come along. When he saw the wagons, he came back to report on them.

"I counted thirty-seven wagons in this here train," Potter said. "How much money do you reckon that is?"

"With that many wagons, there should be at least a thousand dollars for each of us," Dace said.

"A thousand dollars, huh? A thousand dollars here, a thousand dollars there, pretty soon that builds up into real money."

"Yeah, well, you just do what I tell you to do, and you'll all be rich," Dace said.

"All right, what's our plan?" Potter asked.

"Same as before. We're going to kill all the men in the train, 'n' any of the women that gets in the way of our doin' business."

"Hey, if some of the women's good-lookin', could we maybe have us a little fun with 'em?" Bates asked.

"We've never done that before, and we're not goin' to start now. Anyway, why bother with 'em? With a thousand dollars you can have all the whores you want," Dace said. "Best thing to do is to hit the wagon, kill the men, take the money and leave as quick as we can get everythin' done."

"Yeah, come to think of it, that's right," Bates said. "We can get all the whores we want."

Dace walked away from the others and stood alone, looking in the direction from which the wagon train would be coming.

What had become of him? He had killed and here he was giving orders to kill again. He had started out to be an honest trail guide except for a little pilfering here and there. Then he got caught, had to kill someone, and had been killing ever since. And the thing is the killing had gotten easier and easier.

MATT LOGAN WAS AT LEAST a mile in front of the train when he saw several men moving around. It appeared that they were trying to find positions to be able to watch the approach of the train without being observed.

That alone would be disturbing enough, but then he saw some of them putting on hoods, and he instantly knew who they were.

These men were the Hood Raiders, and there was no doubt in Matt's mind that Dudley Dace was setting up an ambush. And considering what had happened when the raiders had attacked previous trains, he knew that the ambush Dace was planning, would be bloody.

Turning, Matt rode back to rejoin the train, breaking into a gallop when he knew he was far enough away from Dace and the others, not to be seen.

JARED WAS RIDING alongside his father when they saw Matt coming back toward them at a gallop.

"I wonder what the big hurry is," Jared said.

"Whatever it is, it isn't good," Cody said. "Let's ride out to meet him. I think it might be better to hear what he has to say without alarming the others."

The two of them urged their horses into a rapid trot, meeting Matt about two hundred yards ahead of the train.

"What's up, Matt?" Cody asked.

"We've got trouble, Captain," Matt replied.

Cody nodded. "I figured as much, seeing the way you were riding. Indians?"

"No, the Hood Raiders."

"Do you think they plan to attack the train?" Cody asked.

"I would bet on it."

"That's not good," Cody said. "We could lose a lot of people."

"Yeah, if we let him attack us. On the other hand, we could attack him," Matt said.

"What do you have in mind?" Cody asked.

"I know where they are, so we can attack them before they attack us. Jared, I'll need you and your deputies. Better get all of them."

"All right."

"Wait a minute, I have an idea," Cody said. "What if we hold the train back, and when they come to attack us, we ambush them?"

Matt smiled. "Yes, that's a good idea."

"But, Pa, if they see the train has stopped, won't they get suspicious?" Jared asked.

"I'll talk to Lon," Cody said. "We can have a 'breakdown' that will cause us to have to stop, without making this Dace and his Hood Raiders suspicious."

"Yes," Matt said. "That's as good an idea as your first one was."

The three men returned to the train, then Cody summoned Lon.

"Yes, sir?"

"Lon, we have reason to believe that the Hood Raiders are waiting ahead to attack us. I'm going to stop the train while Matt, Jared, and our deputies deal with it.

But I'll need an excuse for stopping it, so I want you to find some repair to make that will delay us for a while."

"Mr. Sullivan asked me to check one of his wheels. I'll jack the wagon up and pull the wheel off. I can take as long as you need me to take."

"Pa, we should let Mr. Sullivan in on what's happening," Jared said.

"Yes, you're right," Cody said. "Come along, Lon, we'll talk to him now."

Rosie was walking alongside her father when Cody and Lon approached him.

"David, I wonder if you'd step back here and have a word with Lon and me," Cody said.

"Sure thing, Cap'n," David Sullivan replied.

When they were separated enough where they could talk without being overheard, Cody told about the outlaws who were lying in wait for them.

"We need to stop the train without arousing any suspicion," Cody said, "so we want to pull your wheel."

"All right," Sullivan agreed.

With need for the "repair" established, Cody halted the train informing the others that they would be delayed until Lon could change a wheel for David Sullivan.

"I, uh, hesitate to tell you this, but I feel it must be said," Cody said.

He paused for a moment before he continued. "We have reason to believe that our train may be attacked by the Hood Raiders."

"Oh, my!" Millie Patterson said.

"Shouldn't we get the wagons in a circle?" Dale Guthrie asked.

"No," Cody replied. "We need to give every impression that we don't suspect anything. We want to draw them to us, because Matt and Jared and a few others are going to go out and set up an ambush."

"My brother and I will be going with you, Jared," Frank said.

"Cody, I have a suggestion," Nonnie said.

"What is it?"

"What if everyone who doesn't go along with Matt and Jared would come back to my wagon? We could put out some pots, start a couple of fires, and it would look as if we're preparing a meal. That would get all of us out of the line of fire, except for Mr. Baker of course, who would have to work on Mr. Sullivan's wagon."

"That's an excellent idea," Matt said.

"I'd better stay with Lon," David Sullivan said. "That way it will look like everything is normal."

"I'll be there as well," Cody said. He glanced over at Matt and Jared. "All right, boys, it's all up to you, now."

As Matt, Jared, and the others rode out, Cody asked Tim to stay with him and Lon and Dave.

"I would like for the four of us to be ready for any of them that might get through."

"All right," Tim agreed.

38

Potter saw that the wagons had stopped, and then a wheel was being pulled from one of them. Because of that, he realized that the stop would be longer than just a moment too.

"Damn!" he said under his breath. He thought about waiting until they were underway again, then realized that Dace would start wondering what was keeping him, so he started back to report.

"The sons of bitches have stopped," Potter said reporting to Dace.

"Stopped? Did they give any indication that they know we're here?" Dace asked.

Potter shook his head. "Nah, I don't think so. They've pulled a wheel offen one o' the wagons. I don't reckon they would'a done that iffen they had 'a know'd we was here. I expect they've all stopped so as to get that took care of. It's just that much longer 'til we can get to 'em though."

"Not necessarily," Dace said. "I've been on enough wagon trains to know how they work. When they're on the trail, nearly everyone is alert and lookin' for trouble. But when they're stopped like this, the men are all putterin' with their wagons, the women are gossipin', and the kids are runnin' around all over. This will be the best time to hit 'em. We'll get mounted and ride through them shootin'. Aim for the men. Hell, we'll have most of them down before any of them can even get to a gun."

"Yeah," Lewis said, "let's do it."

MATT, Jared, Frank and Gus Wiley, Chub Collins, Clay Ditmore, Joe Atwood, and Luke Taylor moved to take up an ambush position about five-hundred yards ahead of the train

Matt, Frank, Gus, and Clay were waiting on one side of the trail while Jared, Chub, Joe, and Luke were on the other side.

They heard the horses approaching before they saw them, then cresting the hill about fifty yards ahead of them, they saw a group of ten mounted men, all wearing hoods, and all with guns drawn. Their leader was wearing a red hood and the outlaws were approaching the wagons at a gallop.

Matt waited until they were within pistol range, then he fired, picking the red hood as his target. Red Hood went down, then the others in the ambush team started shooting.

"It's a trap!" Potter shouted. Those were his last words as he went down as well.

Shooting was fast and furious for about thirty seconds, then all the outlaws who had been caught by complete surprise, were down.

Now, with guns drawn, Matt, Jared and the others approached the downed men, cautiously. By design, Matt went directly to where the man in the red hood lay.

Red Hood was still alive, though it was obvious that he was in his last moments. When he tried to take his hood off, Matt reached down for it.

"Dace, you son of a bitch, I want your last sight on earth to be of the man who killed you," he said, and he pulled the hood off.

When Matt saw the man's face, he gasped.

"Danny!" He literally shouted the word. "Danny, you're Dudley Dace?"

Danny snorted what could have been a painful chuckle. "Yeah, Dudley. That's a pretty high falutin' name, don't you think?"

"Why?"

"Because when I got through here and went back East, I didn't want anyone to know who I was."

"No, I mean why?" Matt repeated, his pain reflected in his voice. "What happened to you?"

"Matt, do you remember Sister Naomi Louise?" Danny asked, in a strained voice.

"Of course I remember her."

"Do you remember when she taught us this, from the Bible? *We should not be like Cain, who was of the evil one and murdered his brother. And why did he murder him? Because his own deeds were evil and his brother's righteous.*

"I should have listened to her, Matt. She told me the story of Cain, killin' his brother. And here, I wanted to kill you . . . but you have killed . . ." Danny interrupted his sentence, then after a couple of gasps said . . . "me." Danny spoke the last word with his dying breath, and Matt watched the life leave his still-opened eyes.

Jared came over to stand beside Matt. "You knew this guy?"

"He was my brother," Matt said in a choked voice.

"Your brother?" Jared asked in surprise.

"He wasn't born, my brother, but Sister Naomi Louise made him my brother. I would never have thought that Danny would turn out like this."

"I'm sorry it had to end this way for you," Jared said, putting his hand on his friend's shoulder.

"Yeah, well, it could have been worse," Matt said. "It could have been some, or all of us lying here."

WHEN THE TRAIN stopped that night, Matt had the wagons form into a circle, then he walked down to the edge of the river and stood there, looking out over the water, thinking about the man who had once been his closest friend.

Over the last couple of years, he and Danny had seen one another only occasionally when their paths crossed. The last time had been in Kansas City, a couple of years ago, when the two friends had stood back-to-back to fight off a group of men who had come after Danny.

Matt found out later, that Danny had been cheating at cards, and that was why he was attacked.

"What the hell were you cheating for? We damn near got our ass whipped," Matt said.

Danny laughed. "Well hell, Matt, it's the only way I knew I could win."

The memory faded.

"Danny," Matt said aloud, but speaking only to the river. "I wish I had left you in the orphanage."

. . .

It was almost a week after the aborted Hood Raider attack on the wagon train, and while there was a jubilant air among all the other members of the train, Matt had not been able to escape his melancholy.

"Matt, I wish there was something I could say or do, that would make you feel better," Ellen said.

"There's nothing you can do, because you aren't the one who killed him. I did. I killed the only brother I ever had."

"You had no choice. It was either him or you. You didn't know who he was, and besides, he wasn't your real brother."

"Ellen, if Danny wasn't my real brother, then nothing about me is real."

Ellen took Matt's hand in her own and looked into his eyes.

"Oh, Matt, please forgive me," she said. "I had no right to say such a thing. Of course, he was your brother if you thought of him as such. I have no right to infringe upon your pain."

Matt put his other hand on top of Ellen's and held her hand between his. He looked at her with a sad smile.

"And I have no right to subject you to what I'm going through right now. I'm a big boy, and I'll get over this."

BLUE MOUNTAINS

Nonnie and Darcy were talking about their personal histories and their plans for the future.

"I may have to make a choice," Darcy said.

"What sort of choice?"

"I came out here with my family with all intentions of being a schoolteacher."

"And you've changed your mind?"

"No, and that's just it. I would still like to be a school-teacher, but none of the schools I've ever known, have allowed their teachers to be married."

"And you want to marry Jared," Nonnie said. It was a statement, not a question.

"Yes. That is, if he asks me."

Nonnie chuckled. "Oh, he's going to ask you, I've no doubt about that."

"And that's my dilemma. Yes, to marriage? Or yes to the career I studied for?"

"I'm somewhat in the same dilemma," Nonnie replied. "It has been my intention to open a boarding house but. . ."

"If Captain McNair asks you," Darcy said, completing Nonnie's sentence.

"Yes."

Darcy laughed.

"What is it?"

"Ellen is in the same boat. She confided to me that she would marry Matt if he asked her, and if he would give up guiding wagon trains."

DARCY LEFT NONNIE and took her place beside Ellen. The two took turns driving the wagon which, fortunately for them, was always the lead wagon. Because of that, they never had to deal with the constant cloud of dust that was raised by the wheels of the other wagons.

When the path turned uphill, the wagons began their climb out of the trees and up through wildflowers and sage to the ridge where forested slopes dropped steeply into the next drainage.

Because the wagons tipped easily on side hills, they

drove them straight up or down slopes. The resulting ride could be a long, rough roll over the mountains.

"Will we ever get through these mountains?" Darcy asked Ellen. "First up a long hill, then down a long ridge, then up another long ridge and down a steep hill, and then onto the next ridge."

Matt and Jared, who had been riding about a hundred yards ahead of the train, came back alongside the wagon then.

"All right, ladies, hold up here. We're going to need some help going up this next one," Matt said.

Matt and Jared then rode back to the second wagon, which belonged to Lon.

"Mr. Baker, we're going to need to borrow your team for a bit," Matt said.

As Jared and Lon disconnected the team from Lon's wagon, Matt rode alongside the train, talking to the others.

"We're going to have to double up the teams again here, like we did before," he said. "So, every second wagon, move your team to the wagon in front. Once we get those up, we'll bring the teams back down for you."

It took all day to climb to the top of the pass and once there, they camped for the night. This time Nonnie ate with Cody and his family, to include Matt and Darcy.

LATER THAT SAME NIGHT, Jared led Darcy a short distance away from the circle of wagons.

"Just look at the stars," Darcy said. "Aren't they beautiful?"

"They're all right."

"All right? They're just all right?" Darcy said, a little disappointed with Jared's response.

"Yeah. Just all right. You see, right now I'm looking at something so beautiful that everything else pales in comparison."

Darcy looked back at Jared and saw that he was staring at her with a smile on his face.

"You . . . you're going to make me blush," she said.

"Will you marry me?"

Jared's question was asked without any preliminary or build up. It was asked in the same tone of voice he would have used if he had asked her to hand him a bucket.

"I . . . uh, Jared . . . are you sure about this?"

"I'm sorry, did I ask too soon? Or maybe you just don't feel the same . . ."

"Wait, before you say anything else," Darcy said. "Jared, you know that I was with the Indians for several weeks."

Jared smiled. "Of course, I know. You haven't forgotten that I was the handsome hero who rescued you, have you?"

Darcy chuckled slightly, then she continued with her declaration.

"While I was with the Indians, they . . . uh," she paused and took a deep breath.

"Darcy, are you trying to tell me that you're pregnant? If you are, I don't care. We'll raise the baby as if it's our own."

"You mean you would do that? You would raise my baby as if it were yours?"

"I love you, Darcy, and yes, I would do that. And it wouldn't be *your* baby, it would be *our* baby."

Darcy laughed in relief. "Yes, I'll marry you, and no, I'm not pregnant."

Jared pulled her to him and kissed her, holding his lips to hers for a long time.

"Let's go tell the others," Jared said, excitedly.

Hand in hand, the two hurried back to the circle of wagons, specifically to the McNair wagon.

"Darcy and I have an announcement to make," Jared said.

Family and friends sitting around the campfire looked over toward them expectantly, their eyes shining gold in the firelight.

"When are you getting married?" Cody asked, even before Jared could make the announcement.

"As soon as we get to where we're going."

Jared's announcement was met with applause and shouts of congratulations.

39

THE DALLES

WHEN THEY REACHED THE DALLES, IT HAD LONG BEEN considered the end of the Oregon Trail. The banks of the Columbia River were steep, and immigrants had to portage their belongings around the rocky trail, and then set out on rafts to run the rapids of the Columbia.

But an enterprising gentleman named Sam Barlow had devised a plan to bypass the Columbia River altogether. He built a road from The Dalles to the Willamette Valley, going around the main obstacle which was Mount Hood. Barlow was granted permission to charge five dollars a wagon and ten cents a head for any livestock that would use his road. Because of that, many chose to stay in the vicinity of The Dalles.

After resting a few days, Joe Atwood came to Cody's wagon.

"Cap'n McNair, I've been talkin' with some of the other folks, and well, just to come right out 'n' tell you, me 'n' Dave Sullivan 'n' our cows are goin' to stay here. I just don't think I can pay the toll to take 'em on the Barlow Road."

"I can understand that, Joe."

"Hank 'n' the other cowboys will be stayin' too. The way I see it, this looks like good cattle land, 'n' I don't see as how we could do any better by goin' on any farther. And with the army at Fort Dalles, why I think this place'll be as safe as anyplace we can find."

Cody nodded his head. "All right, if that's what you want. I want to say that it's been a pleasure knowing you and having you as a member of the train."

"Yes, sir, well, we couldn't have had us any better of a wagon master," Atwood said, extending his hand. "We're goin' to slaughter one of the beeves and have a big celebration, if that's all right with you."

Cody smiled. "When have I ever objected to some good eating?"

THE STEER WAS CUT in halves, spitted, and cooked over an open fire. The aroma of cooking meat permeated the entire train and it put everyone in a good mood.

When they gathered for the dinner, several other travelers announced to Cody that they, too would be remaining at the Dalles.

The dinner provided a poignant separation for Ellen and Rosie who had become close friends during the long trek westward.

"But you've got Darcy as a friend now," Rosie said.

"Oh, you're still my friend," Ellen said. "Just because we'll be in two different places, we're both in Oregon. And," she added with a smile, "I understand that Frank will be staying here as well."

Rosie's smile grew even larger. "Yes," she said, "he

asked me to marry him. I haven't told Papa yet, but I said yes."

"Oh, good for you!" Ellen said as the two embraced.

Two DAYS LATER, the rest of the wagons met to discuss the remainder of their journey. Matt gave them the choice of floating down the river on rafts or taking the Barlow Road ending in Oregon City. From The Dalles to Oregon City would be a distance of about one-hundred-fifty miles. At the time, there was talk of a gold strike near the mouth of the Colville River on the Columbia, and many travelers chose to stay behind. A few of those who were farmers recognized the potential to raise grain near the river, while others were determined to try their hands at finding gold.

In the end, only eleven of all the wagons that had started out in St. Louis, continued on to Oregon City. Those who were still a part of the train were Cody, Jared and Ellen, and their wagon, followed by the wagons of Lon, Norma, and Precious, then Tim and Anita Murray, whose wagon now included Emma, Peter Laycock and Raymond Pugh, Clay and Edna Ditmore, Luke and Alice Taylor, Craig and Millie Patterson, the Reverend E.D. Owen, and his wife Suzanne, Dale Guthrie, his wife, Jane, and their sixteen year-old son, Drew, Nonnie Hughes, who was now sharing her wagon with Darcy Clinton, and Harm and Gretchen Schultz, whose wagon was carrying the containers of hops rootstock.

Harm had managed to keep the rootstock viable for the entire trip westward, by keeping them packed in sawdust, and frequently sprinkling them with water.

. . .

"MISS 'NITA, can I come up on the wagon and ride with you? I'm getting tired of walking," Emma said.

"Of course, you can, sweetheart," Anita replied. She halted the team so Emma could climb up onto the seat, using the wheel spokes.

"Emma, Tim and I have wanted to talk to you about something," Anita said.

"I know what it is," Emma said.

"Oh, you do? And just what do you think that would be?" Anita asked.

"You want me to come live with you."

Anita was surprised by Emma's response.

"Well, yes, that's exactly what we want to talk about. How did you know?"

"Mr. Baker told me. He said that he couldn't adopt me but you wanted to, and that would make you and Mr. Tim my mama and daddy."

"The parents who birthed you will always be your mother and father, and I would never want you to forget them. But we want you to come be our little girl now. That is, if you would be willing to."

"Could I call you mama and daddy?"

"Of course, you can, sweetheart, we would love that," Anita said as her eyes filled with tears.

"And can Precious still be my best friend?"

"For as long as you want her to be."

"Then, yes, I want to come live with you and daddy. Why are you crying? Don't you want me to come live with you?"

"I'm crying because I'm happy, darling." Anita put her arm around Emma and pulled the child to her. "And I want you to be my little girl more than anything in the world."

271

ALTHOUGH THE FINAL part of the trek from St. Louis took less than three weeks, the trail on to Oregon City was as treacherous as any they had already crossed, the only difference being that the vegetation was overgrown. In some places it required that some of the younger men cut brush to get the wagons through. The good thing was there was an ample supply of water, because there were endless waterways. The bad thing was that the Tygh, Rock, Gate, Barlow and Camp Creeks, had to be crossed, and the meandering Sandy River had to be crossed several times before reaching the Clackamas River, and many of the crossings were hazardous. Also, in some places the mountains were as steep as any they had crossed thus far.

FINALLY, five months and ten days after they left St. Louis, the remaining wagons of the McNair Wagon Train, reached Oregon City. Although arriving wagon trains were nothing new to the citizens of Oregon City, many of whom themselves had arrived by wagon, both sides of the road were lined with a significant number of Oregon City's almost 700 residents to welcome the arrival.

Oregon City was located on the east side of the Willamette River. It had long been a trading location for Indian tribes that had roamed the area, but it was the Hudson Bay Company that had established it as a trading post. Its location below the Willamette Falls made it extremely valuable for steamboats bringing produce from the lower valley.

Oregon City was built on three tiers and Matt held up the train on the upper terrace.

"Cody, it might be a good idea for you to go check in

with the authorities," Matt said. "The sheriff likes to keep a census of all the immigrants."

"I'll go with you," Lon Baker said. "I want to get a few supplies before we move on down the valley."

Matt lowered his head. "Uh, Lon, it might be a good idea for you to stay with the train."

"All right," Lon said. "I can do my shoppin' later."

CODY WENT DIRECTLY to the clerk's office that was in the log building serving as a courthouse. Here, he turned in a list of all the people on the train.

"Welcome to Oregon City," John Bidwell said. "I suppose you'll be staying here for a while."

"No," Cody said, "it's our intention to go on down the river and find us a place to settle."

Bidwell cocked his head. "You don't know much about Oregon, do you?"

"What do you mean? We've been told the Willamette Valley is some of the richest farmland in the country and it's my understanding that the state of Oregon is encouraging immigrants to settle."

"All that is true, sir. Of course, the Donation Law has expired, so you'll be expected to buy your land, now."

Cody was beginning to get impatient with the clerk. "Yes, we know, and that had been our intention. Why did you suggest we would want to stay in Oregon City and not move on to our final destination?"

Bidwell smiled. "Rain. If you're planning on living in your wagons or putting up tents, you might want to wait until spring before you move on farther south. The roads will be impassable with the mud and the steamships won't be doing many runs when the water gets high. Most folks coming in so late, usually spend the rainy season with us, and then move on in the spring."

"And where would we spend the winter if we decide to take you up on this idea?"

Bidwell handed Cody a copy of the local newspaper. "There's going to be an auction of town lots soon. Other folks like you buy a lot to spend the winter, then they move off without paying their taxes. You'll see the list of lots available and the taxes that are due on them."

Cody took the paper and found the article. "I appreciate the information, Mr. Bidwell. We'll see you at the auction."

40

WHEN CODY RETURNED TO THE TRAIN, HE CALLED A meeting, then told the others that it might be a good idea for them to remain here until spring, explaining about the rain.

"Where will we live?" Anita asked.

Cody told about lots that were available. "We can live in our wagons, but," he added with a smile, "there is also a house close to the lots that's available that I plan to buy so that all the ladies will be able to use it for preparing the meals. That way, we can all eat together."

"That's a good idea," Tim said. "That is, if you don't mind everyone tromping around in your house three times a day."

Cody chuckled. "Tromp all you like, I won't mind at all."

"I've got an idea," Clay Ditmore said. "Suppose that we all go together to buy the lots?"

"All right," Cody said. "We'll get those lots first, then we'll buy the property down in the Willamette Valley that we came out here for."

275

After the meeting broke up, Matt came over to join Cody and Jared.

"That's a good idea about buying the lots, it'll take care of any question as to where we stay while we're here," Matt said.

"Yes, I was thinking the same thing." Cody smiled. "You said 'we'. Does that mean you're still planning on staying here, rather than bringing in another train?"

"Whether or not I stay here depends on something," Matt replied.

"Oh? And just what would that be?"

"I want your permission to ask Ellen to marry me."

Jared laughed. "Pop, you owe me five dollars. I told you it wouldn't be just Darcy and me."

"As you can see, Matt, your question isn't a surprise to us, and of course you have my permission. I'm sure it won't be a surprise to Ellen either."

Matt smiled. "I don't reckon it will be, seeing as I've already asked her, and she's already said yes."

"You know what would be a good idea? After we are all settled in here, we could all go into town together to get the marriage licenses," Jared said.

AFTER COLLECTING THE MONEY, Cody went to the courthouse to purchase the lots in the name of the St. Louis Western Trek Company. He also made a personal purchase of the house. Lon, Laycock, Pugh and Ditmore went with him.

"Is he a part of the St. Louis Western Trek Company?" Bidwell asked, indicating Lon.

"Yes, of course he is," Cody replied.

"I'm afraid that blacks are not authorized to own land in Oregon."

"Mr. Baker is a free man," Cody said.

"That makes no difference, blacks aren't authorized to own land in Oregon, so he can't be a part of the company that makes this purchase."

"That's not a problem," Cody said. "Lon, the company will rent you your share of the lots for one dollar."

Bidwell shook his head. "That won't work either," he said. "The black exclusion law of 1844 was put into the constitution when we became a state, earlier this year. That means no blacks are allowed to be residents of the state of Oregon."

"Tell me, just how is it that you plan to get rid of Mr. Baker?" Peter Laycock asked.

"The sheriff will order him to leave," Bidwell said.

"Is that a fact? Well, let me tell you somethin', Mr. Bidwell. If the sheriff plans on forcin' Mr. Baker out of the state, he had better come with a passel of deputies to back 'im up. Because he's goin' to have to come through about ten or fifteen of us, to get to Mr. Baker. And we will be armed."

"This is really none of your concern, sir," Bidwell said.

"That's where you're wrong, Bidwell. Mr. Baker is one of us. And if you come after one of us, you are goin' to have to come after all of us."

"Mr. McNair, I understand that you are the captain of this train," Bidwell said.

"I am."

"Well, can't you do something about this?"

"Yes, I can do something. I'll be standing alongside Mr. Baker, along with Mr. Laycock, and every other man of this train."

Bidwell drummed his fingers on the counter for a few minutes, then sighed. "Well, I know for a fact that despite the law, there are already a few dozen blacks living in the state. So I can't see as it would be a problem for another one."

"Not another *one*," Lon said.

"I beg your pardon?"

"Another three," Lon said. "Me, my wife, and our daughter."

"Another three," Bidwell agreed.

GENERALLY, when the men went to town to take care of business, the women would stay behind, camping in the wagons just as they had done during the trek west. Those wagons would be their homes until they were able to move south, find their land, and build their houses.

The exceptions were Ellen and Darcy, who went into town with Matt and Jared. They went first to the courthouse where they got marriage licenses, then to a restaurant overlooking the Willamette River.

"Matt, Darcy and I have been talking," Ellen said.

"Oh, oh," Jared teased. "Matt, I need to warn you, when my sister starts a sentence like that, that means she's already made up her mind about something, and you won't be able to change it."

"What have you and Darcy been talking about?" Matt asked.

"We think we would like to have a double wedding. I mean, it seems only right, since we are going to be in-laws," Ellen said.

"I have no problem with that," Matt replied. "Do you, Jared?"

"No, it's like I told you, when my sister starts a sentence like that, it means she has a really good idea."

Ellen laughed. "See what you're going to have to put up with, Darcy?"

NONNIE WAS DECORATING the wedding cake when Cody went into the kitchen to speak to her.

"You know this wedding they've got planned is going to involve everyone in the train."

"Yes."

"I was thinking, in order not to detract from the festivities, it might be a good idea for you and me to go into town and get married rather quietly."

Nonnie gasped. "Cody, are you asking me to marry you?"

Cody chuckled. "Yeah, I guess I should have done that first, huh? So, will you?"

Nonnie laughed. "How could I possibly turn down such a romantic proposal?"

A LOOK AT TRAIL OF VENGEANCE:
THE CROCKETS BOOK ONE

BY ROBERT VAUGHAN

A five-star masterpiece from best-selling author Robert Vaughan.

Will Crockett and his brother Gid go from card players to bar owners when the winning poker pot includes the deed to a Belle Springs saloon. But Belle Springs is run by a crooked sheriff who is determined to get his special "sheriff's tax."

AVAILABLE NOW!

ABOUT THE AUTHOR

Robert Vaughan sold his first book when he was 19. That was 57 years and nearly 500 books ago. He wrote the novelization for the miniseries *Andersonville*. Vaughan wrote, produced, and appeared in the History Channel documentary *Vietnam Homecoming*. His books have hit the NYT bestseller list seven times. He has won the Spur Award, the PORGIE Award (Best Paperback Original), the Western Fictioneers Lifetime Achievement Award, received the Readwest President's Award for Excellence in Western Fiction, is a member of the American Writers Hall of Fame and is a Pulitzer Prize nominee. Vaughn is also a retired army officer, helicopter pilot with three tours in Vietnam. And received the Distinguished Flying Cross, the Purple Heart, The Bronze Star with three oak leaf clusters, the Air Medal for valor with 35 oak leaf clusters, the Army Commendation Medal, the Meritorious Service Medal, and the Vietnamese Cross of Gallantry.

CPSIA information can be obtained
at www.ICGtesting.com
Printed in the USA
LVHW040717221221
706908LV00008B/364

9 781639 774104